MY HEART UNDERWATER

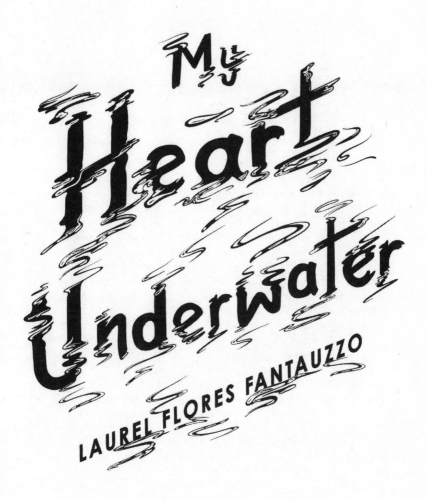

My Heart Underwater

LAUREL FLORES FANTAUZZO

Quill Tree Books
An Imprint of HarperCollinsPublishers

Library of Congress Cataloging-in-Publication Data
Names: Fantauzzo, Laurel Flores, author.
Title: My heart underwater / Laurel Flores Fantauzzo.
Description: First edition. | New York, NY : HarperTeen, [2020] | Audience: Ages
    14 up. | Audience: Grades 10-12. | Summary: Reeling from her father's coma
    and kissing a female teacher, seventeen-year-old Corazon suddenly finds herself
    in the Philippines with a half-brother she had never met.
Identifiers: LCCN 2020008867 | ISBN 978-0-06-297228-6 (hardcover)
Subjects: CYAC: Brothers and sisters—Fiction. | Filipino Americans—Fiction.
    | High schools—Fiction. | Schools—Fiction. | Lesbians—Fiction. |
    Philippines—Fiction.
Classification: LCC PZ7.1.F362 My 2020 | DDC [Fic]—dc23
LC record available at https://lccn.loc.gov/2020008867

Typography by David Curtis
20 21 22 23 24   PC/LSCH   10 9 8 7 6 5 4 3 2 1

First Edition

For my wife, Katherine,
whose love changed the course of my history

MY HEART UNDERWATER

PART ONE

SOUTHERN CALIFORNIA

THURSDAY, FEBRUARY 5, 2009
FEAST OF SAINT AGATHA

The Virgin Mary is giving me the stink eye again. I can feel her watching me as I cross through the courtyard to AP European History. Her open stone hands struggle to make a wagging finger. She wants to chisel a message into me, I know: *Don't think about her! Don't you dare! Fight your thoughts! Fight your body! Think of me at your age! Think of how brave and willing I was! Think of the heaviness I bore under my skin! You're not being asked to carry something as huge as the destiny of the Christ child, are you? No! Think of your family duty, like I thought of mine!*

I think of you, Mary. I think of my family.

But I also think of Ms. Holden.

I never knew what the word "crush" actually meant—thought it was a stupid, unrealistic word, actually, until January this year, on her first day of school as our long-term substitute, and she wrote her name on the classroom whiteboard for the first time.

When I saw Ms. Holden's hands, the hands mysteriously scarred, the hint of a long, black tree tattoo peeking out toward her wrists, her limbs so imperfectly beautiful and strong, I was sure she could heal broken bones, hold any falling building upright, squeeze all the wrongness out of my life. The feeling suddenly stomped all over my chest, and then I understood. Crush.

Now, a month later, I try to look at just the floor, because I really can't handle looking at her.

In my peripheral vision, I sense Ms. Holden nod at me as I take my seat, surrounded by other girls dressed in green plaid skirts and white blouses. I begin my private daily project: trying to be in the world with everyone else, concerned with the numbers and letters spelling out my future, not just obsessing over my crush.

When Melissa and Rika get their quizzes back and wilt, I prepare for my own wilting. They're headed for famous, one-name schools gathered under the league of a regal-sounding plant, while I have no idea where I'm headed. I've never been remarkable; I can't even keep my homework organized, and there's nothing special about my story that would make an admissions counselor sit up straight and say, "Aha! I choose her!"

Not like Ms. Holden, former Saint Agatha valedictorian. Ms. Holden, semiprofessional surfer, fluent in German, just for fun. Ms. Holden, who finished her undergraduate courses a year early, finished her PhD coursework at age twenty-two, earned every fellowship under the sun, and now writes her dissertation in between teaching a class for her high school alma mater and surfing every day.

Not that I'm keeping track.

She drops my quiz onto my desk.

"You've got a good memory, Tagubio," she says. "Wish I could borrow it."

I stare at the paper.

There is a happy face. There is a 100 percent. A percentage I've never seen during my three years in high school.

The score sweeps away my caution. I look up.

She's got black-rimmed glasses and sun-and-saltwater-mussed blond hair trimmed short, and messy, rough bangs swept to the left side of her forehead. Her dark eyes dance at me. She's a head taller than me, and as she smiles, I instantly memorize all the random tiny gaps in her teeth.

The want springs up before I can tamp it down. I want to put my mouth on the small mole just below her bottom lip.

I've never wanted to put my mouth on another person before.

I don't know where all this want came from.

"I was going to grade the quiz on a curve, since a lot of you seemed to have trouble with it," Ms. Holden says to the class, blessedly turning away from me. "But one of you messed it up by getting all the questions right."

The other girls frown at Melissa and Rika, who frown back at them with equally baffled, blemish-free faces. Ms. Holden winks at me over the quiet commotion. I stare down at my desk again, trying to hide whatever's happening behind my face, and Ms. Holden begins the rest of her lesson.

"So! Osnabrück. What is it?"

The class quiets. Now everyone seems shy and sleepy. Someone coughs. I stare at the sheen of my fake-laminate desk.

"Is Osnabrück the name of my cat?" Ms. Holden asks, leaning one arm against her podium. "Is it a bodily function?"

There are some laughs. I smile, hoping my smile seems as shy and neutral as the class laughing.

"Hmm. This is fun. Okay. If someone can come up and write a short summary of what occurred at Osnabrück in 1648—there, I gave it away, it's a place—I will raise that person's entire grade by five percent."

The class buzzes. I think of the minimum required grade point average for entering a University of California campus.

"But if no one knows the answer, I'll have to pop you another quiz," Ms. Holden says.

Melissa and Rika jab their hands into the air.

Melissa says, "Ms. Holden, we don't think this is very fair, since almost the whole class was at my house studying for the SAT. We're sorry we didn't get to the reading."

I feel anger grip my insides. Then it falls away. I'm unsurprised no one invited me.

"Huh," Ms. Holden says. "What kinda snacks do your parents provide for your study sessions, Grayson?"

Melissa pauses, confused. "Um, my mom isn't in charge of cooking, Maria is. She gave us turkey lettuce wraps. Why?"

Melissa doesn't specify who Maria is. She expects everyone to know Maria is her maid. My middle name is Maria. I hold back a tired sigh.

"Maybe if you bring me some of Maria's turkey lettuce wraps, you can bribe me into not giving you a pop quiz," Ms. Holden says. "Anyone else?"

I stifle a laugh. Melissa's eyes flare toward me, then she looks around for everyone to agree how messed up this is. The other girls nod and glance at each other.

Ms. Holden looks toward me again. I think, Mary! Mom! Dad! Sin! Quiz! I feel my eyes moving fast, flashing these random words to warn me away from wrongdoing, and I force my gaze down again.

"C'mere, Tagubio," Ms. Holden says.

Oh god.

I rise. Then I trip a little on my backpack strap. Some girls snicker. A smile dances across Ms. Holden's mouth. I want to see her teeth. What is wrong with me?!

I take the whiteboard marker. I think of my parents; my mom in front of a computer terminal, my dad in someone's yard. I could bring them the quiz, and the victory of a higher grade, all at once. I could hide, with my grades, the bigger truth: how I'm failing them in this moment, with the crush I can't control.

"Um," I say.

"Ja?" Ms. Holden says, and more girls laugh.

I remember a heading on one of our readings. "Peace of Westphalia and the Making of a New Europe." I write the first three words.

"Which was about?" Ms. Holden says.

"Independence," I say, since most of history seems to be about that anyway.

"You're feeding her answers!" Melissa cries.

"You're full of turkey," Ms. Holden replies without looking at Melissa, and the class laughs, shocked.

I look at Ms. Holden's mischievous eyes, her serious mouth. I want her to keep looking at me. I don't even care anymore that the rest of the class is looking at me too.

Is this what opens the door in my brain? Is Ms. Holden's attention the thing that crowds out my terror and brings the answer rushing forward?

I remember key words in a yellow box in our textbook, a grand, grave painting of dozens of longhaired European men.

"Sovereignty! Osnabrück is where the second treaty was signed. The first treaty was at Münster. These treaties ended the Thirty Years' War. The treaty at Osnabrück started a new political order in Europe. The Peace of Westphalia. Westphalian sovereignty!"

"Sehr gut!" Ms. Holden says, pumping her fist. "From a B to an A minus."

But now I can't stop. "The Thirty Years' War began with the Defenestration of Prague. The Protestants threw the Catholics out the window to signify their defiance to the people in power. But no one died, which, I mean, is good; it was more symbolic—"

"Rocking that knowledge and memory," Ms. Holden says, and nods at me, a nod that means I should sit down. Some of my classmates clap a little. So I sit. I feel like I've been running; I wish I could bend at the waist and breathe hard. I feel magical for a moment, capable of any victory. I hardly hear Rika's and Melissa's muttering.

Ms. Holden grins at me again, stands behind her podium, and rests her hands on its surface.

Her hands. All my desire comes back. My own hands sweat. I sit on them.

Later, Mary gazes down at me, interrupting my walk home.

I heard that students in the past used to put underwear on her head, so the faculty moved her higher and threatened students with expulsion if anyone did it again.

I wonder what she would look like with a bra on her head. I wonder if Ms. Holden put a bra on Mary's head when she was a student here.

I wonder about Ms. Holden in just a bra.

I press my palms against my eyes.

When I look up, some teachers walking by give me warm nods. They like when students contemplate the Mary statue.

WORK

I unlock the front door to our townhome. I do it quietly, not knowing who's here yet. I sidestep one of the open cardboard boxes always partly blocking the entryway, halfway filled with corned beef and clearance clothes from Ross.

I tug off my sneakers and slip my feet into flip-flops. My mom sits at our old wood table, penciling and erasing in a dollar-store Sudoku book. She hasn't changed out of her slacks and button-down shirt yet. I wonder if something annoying happened at work; she usually plays Sudoku to relax. Numbers calm her. One of the many ways my mom and I are super different.

A classical music station is set low on our old FM radio.

Behind her, on the kitchen counter, is a wooden statue of Jesus's head, his suffering eyes looking heavenward, toward magnet memorial photographs of my parents' moms. His head is a mess of thorns, but his neck bears the necklace of fresh white flowers my dad places there every week.

I can hear my dad too, upstairs in their bedroom. He's speaking Tagalog, and tinny voices respond through his laptop speaker.

Near Jesus are piles of my parents' bills and work invoices. My mom sorts them out every day, noting purchases on budget spreadsheets on our secondhand laptop, since, being a coder (I don't think I'll ever understand exactly what my mom does, her superbrain is an eternal mystery to me), she's the only one in our thousand-square-foot radius who excels at Excel.

Besides the portion of my crazy-high tuition not covered by scholarships, our food, and some money they send back home, there aren't too many other purchases to record. Sometimes they'll buy a ninety-nine-cent DVD from the drugstore discount bins—ridiculous action movies and sci-fi that makes my dad giggle his high-pitched giggle. Buying an old DVD every few weeks is still cheaper than a subscription.

At night I always think about how I can shove that 3.2 grade point average closer to the golden 4.0. It's the least I could do for all my parents' crappy workdays and budgeting on my behalf. But there always seems to be something. That hard unit in chemistry, angle degrees, sentence mapping, the back of Ms. Holden's neck.

I'm steeped in shame. I'm sure that somewhere, there's a better version of the daughter my parents could have had—a violinist/aspiring scientist/freelance model like my cousin Bea, maybe—and then my mom glances up.

"Oh, why are you standing there? Come here. Gutom ka ba?" I think she's going to go into the fridge to feed me something, but she looks back down at the grid and sets her pencil to it again, seeing another pattern.

"Ma, I thought I should show you," I say.

She looks up over the rims of her reading glasses, suspicion wrinkling her forehead. In early elementary school, I'd bring home notes about when I wouldn't stop crying over being left out, or when I stomped on boys' toes and made them cry. I haven't brought home much since high school started. Now I hand her the quiz.

"One hundred!" She stands, startling me. "Come, we'll go to In-N-Out. Tara na."

"I just wanted to show you! You don't have to take me out!" Though I know she loves In-N-Out and uses any small celebration as an excuse to go.

"You'll get that milkshake, the weird one you like, with all three flavors."

"Dad's busy talking to—"

"Ay, never mind, he has to eat also. Rom!" she calls upstairs.

He doesn't answer, so we go upstairs. He's sitting at the desk in their bedroom, still in his work polo, covered in splashes of plaster and paint.

Usually Papa's wide brown face splits into a smile as soon as he sees us. But he looks serious and startled when we enter. His eyes dart from us to the screen and back to us, like he's balancing and about to fall if he doesn't watch out. My mom doesn't seem to notice. "Look, oh, your daughter got one hundred on a test!"

"It's just a quiz," I mumble, but finally my dad smiles. "Ay, ang galing naman!" His eyes jitter back toward the screen.

"Show your kuya Jun."

I see the dark-haired guy onscreen, pixelated, wearing glasses. Jun, the faraway half brother I've never met in person before. I've seen him about once a week onscreen, though, since I was a kid.

I'm a little annoyed that I have to talk to a screen, instead of just my parents, now, when my mom is having such a rare moment of pride in me.

I've always been a little annoyed at these moments. Living my life with my family, then being forced to share something with near-strangers my parents insist are close to me.

"Hi, Kuya Jun," I say.

There's a pause. Maybe there's a delay. But he's not smiling. Maybe he's annoyed too. "Hey, congrats," the pixelated face finally says. "Can I talk to our dad again?"

Now I'm fully annoyed. But I don't say anything.

"I'm just a few more minutes with your brother, anak," our dad says in his low voice. "A few more minutes?" Jun protests from thousands of miles away. "Talaga, Tay?" He sounds more than annoyed.

"Come," my mom says, and pulls me back downstairs, away from their conversation. Behind us, I hear the voice on the computer rise, and I wish my dad would just turn off the screen.

In our dad's rattling Tacoma, we pass the big, uniform tract developments my parents always mutter about in Tagalog. Some of them are abandoned, the building stopped months ago. We maneuver around SUVs and convertibles and pass strip malls and chain restaurants and gas stations. Then we come to In-N-Out and park near a BMW.

"We have a BMW also," my dad says, patting the hood of his rusty truck. "Bulacan Motor Works!" I think he's referring to somewhere in the Philippines. He giggles at his own joke.

We get in a busy line filled with firefighters and police officers, random road trippers, and parents with nannies and toddlers. When we get to the front, there's a girl with curly brown hair taking the orders, maybe a couple of years older than me. I don't think she's that cute, but I do notice a small gap in her front teeth, and that sets me off thinking about Ms. Holden again.

"Um," I mumble.

"What? Sorry, can you repeat?" the girl says.

My mom orders. "One cheeseburger, the animal fries, and the shake, what's the one?" She looks at me.

"Neapolitan," I manage to say.

"One burger also with extra lettuce, one cheeseburger, no lettuce, no tomato," my dad finishes, remembering my mom's order.

When we choose a table and get our food, sitting with my celebratory parents and feeling my want for Ms. Holden at the same time is too weird. It makes my throat close up.

"O, bakit? You're not hungry?" my mother says. To my parents, not eating a ready meal means I might as well have stepped on it, it's so insulting.

My dad gazes at me. His gaze is as strong as any saint's, any statue's, and I chomp my burger to avoid it.

"I thought of you today, anak," he says. "I was painting the wall in a house blue, hah? And the lady of the house, she came and start speaking Spanish to me. Very bad Spanish, only 'hola' and 'I like enchilada.' Tanga. I tell her, 'Ma'am, you can speak English to me, or Filipino.' And she give me a dirty look! Her little dog came in, a little white dog, so I had an 'accident.' I drop my paintbrush on the ass of the dog! Now she has a blue-and-white dog! I thought, maybe I'll add red, patriotic for the USA! I thought, if my FilAm daughter is here, she will be proud."

He laughs his high-pitched laugh. Some of the officers around look at him, a Filipino man giggling so silly. It makes me nervous, but I start to laugh too, thinking of my dad and the little painted dog and the frowning lady.

Ma tries to restrain her own smile. "Rom, you shouldn't paint dogs. You need the work. So many customers love their dogs."

My dad winks at me with both eyes, and then I realize the story isn't true. He just wanted to make me laugh. He has mean clients a lot, though. People who think he's dumber than he is, just because of the English he speaks. But he always gets the job done.

As if on cue, his Nokia buzzes. He checks a text. And another buzz, another text.

"Just your brother, texting again," he says. He smiles a little sadly this time. "Small misunderstanding."

The phone rings before I can ask what happened. I get triply annoyed at Kuya Jun. My dad looks at the number, frowns meaningfully at my mom, then answers. "Sir, good evening, sir."

"That client again," my mom sighs.

I relax a little. It's not Jun.

"The client with a blue dog?" I ask.

"No," my mom says. "A different one. A Filipino with a lot of demands."

Papa gets up from the table to talk outside, switching to Tagalog.

I watch my dad, standing in the sparse garden outside In-N-Out, wiping his forehead. He's been up since 4:30 a.m., trying to get as many jobs as he can. He catches me looking and smiles, masking his worry.

He returns. "Just one more thing at the Potrera Street house," he says.

"Rom!" my mom protests. "It's almost sundown. Where's your crew?"

He shrugs. "Okay lang, mahal, easy lang. May flashlight naman."

"It's the middle of your dinner—how can Manolo ask you at this hour—"

"Mom." I'm annoyed at her rising voice. "Tatay is strong, he doesn't even need glasses. He can work if he wants to."

"Oh, see?" My dad laughs again. "Your daughter believes in my work! Finish your food, take your time, I'll drop you at home after."

My mom wraps our half-eaten burgers to take home. She cuts her eyes at me. "We'll go now, Rommel," she says, "so you can work with the light."

In the truck my parents simmer. My dad turns on pop music. My mom turns it down. She looks at me in the rearview mirror.

"So, Corazon," she says. "You know what this quiz means?"

"Not necessarily," I say, though I have a feeling I know what she'll tell me.

"It means you do it once, you can do it again," she says. "Again and again, until succeeding is normal to you. Whatever happens to us, whatever happens in life, your education. Your work. That will protect you."

My dad nods. He reaches for my mom's hand. A truce. I watch the houses and trees speeding by. I don't think I can guarantee that rate of success; I don't think "normal" will ever apply to me. I feel like a failure already.

My dad parks on our street, turns around to me, and snaps his sandpaper fingers in front of my face, making me jump.

"Easy! Easy like that," he says. "You'll do it, anak. Kaya mo yan."

I smile, but my smile isn't real. All their faith in me. It scares me.

My dad walked barefoot through the streets when he was a kid in the Philippines, selling cigarettes and breath mints and newspapers to angry drivers stuck in traffic on their way to the business district. One time someone dumped a can of Coke over his head and laughed. Another time someone took his wooden box of stuff without paying.

Then one time someone peed on him from the high window of an SUV, but he only told that story once.

"Just watch out if ever you think it's raining," he said, cutting off any of my childish questions. "It's not always rain."

He smiled, but his smile folded into something hard and far away.

* * *

My dad drives away to work in the demanding client's yard.

I bargain with myself and with Mary again. I'll give my whole mind to my homework. I'll give up sleep, Facebook, staring into space, staring at Ms. Holden. No, no, no, no more Ms. Holden. She doesn't exist. My crush is fleeting. My GPA is forever.

Except I remember her smiling at me today, asking me about history, and all my resolve gets thrown out the window like a defenestrated Catholic official in 1419 Prague.

I run up the stairs to my desk. I spread my homework out.

This is what I know about her:

1. She graduated from my high school herself, class of 2003.
2. She surfs! I looked at her old Honda Civic one day and saw a longboard!
3. She has a tattoo of a black, jagged tree on her right arm. The only time she revealed it was when she absentmindedly rolled up her shirt sleeves on a warmer day. "The principal will fire me for corrupting you," she joked, realizing her mistake, and she rolled her sleeves back down, covering the tree forever.
4. Ms. Holden was living with her mom again in Thousand Oaks, finishing her European History dissertation at UCLA. She took over as a last-minute substitute because our first AP European History teacher, Mrs. Carmody, had to take a leave for mysterious "health reasons," aka she never seemed quite sober during our morning classes.
5. There is a black-and-white photo of Grace Holden from her

junior high-school year. The same year I'm in now. I was looking at the Saint Agatha's Facebook page, and there it was. I memorized it. In the photo she's standing at her open locker and her eyes are closed. Her books are scattered on the floor, and she's laughing. Her hair is in her face. She looks happy. She looks like she likes who she is.

So in my history notebook, I write this list:

1. *2003*
2. *SURFER!*
3. *Tree tattoo OMG*
4. *Knows Germannnnn*
5. *UCLA genius*
6. *Best photo ever, wish it were me almost*

And then I cross out everything.

1. ~~*2003*~~
2. ~~*SURFER!*~~
3. ~~*Tree tattoo OMG*~~
4. ~~*Knows Germannnnn*~~
5. ~~*UCLA genius*~~
6. ~~*Best photo ever, wish it were me almost*~~

I do this instead of reading about Martin Luther and European peace treaties in the 1600s.

I look at the cross-outs. Then I look again at item three. I start to draw.

It's an automatic thing my hand does sometimes, drawing.

I think of Ms. Holden's arm, and the shirt sleeves slipping closer to her elbows as she lectures and quizzes. I draw the branches of the tree, and I imagine the trunk beneath the sleeve. I draw the outline of her hand.

It doesn't look as lifelike, of course. It looks like a cartoon trying to be real. But I keep going. I draw the shape of a surfboard, and an outline of the letters UCLA.

I hear my mom turn on the radio. She arranges our leftovers on plates. The ghost of her sigh travels up to me. I know she's sitting alone.

I fight to climb back into the moment. To be the version of me that would make them happy.

I go downstairs. My mom is back at the table, playing Sudoku again. I reach under the couch. I pull out our old sungka board and a dusty pouch of shells.

"Sungka? So ready to lose to me again?" my mom teases.

"You said it's time for me to succeed always," I say. "Why not try now?"

She rolls her eyes, but I can see she's happy about my invitation to play. We haven't played sungka in months, since I started junior year. My dad always tells her to let me win, but she always repeats: "She has to earn her win."

I sit cross-legged at the coffee table. She sits on her knees. We clink the shells into the indentations of the wooden board and play

Rock-Paper-Scissors to decide who goes first. She does, scooping the shells and dropping them, one by one, across the board.

She tsks me when I gather seven shells into my hand. "You never have a strategy," she says.

"You're just trying to distract me," I say. Really, I don't care if I lose. I'm soothed by the feel of the old wood board, the tapping sound of the cowrie shells. My mom's shells start to run out soon; she's winning just like she predicted.

We finish my cold fries and our burgers. We share my Neapolitan milkshake.

The landline rings. I let it ring. If it's Kuya Jun, he can leave a message or just call Pa.

The ringing stops.

Then it rings again. My mom scolds me to get it. I pick it up; a dial tone.

When I sit back down at the coffee table, my mom's cell phone rings in her purse. She looks out the window, the reverie and strategy of our sungka game breaking. "So dark na," she says to herself.

She digs into her purse and misses that call too. The landline rings again. "Naku," my mom mutters, exasperated, and answers.

"Yes, this is she," she says, using the official voice she uses when she talks to the principal, or to her managers.

I look at the sungka board, trying to calculate as fast as my mom does, even though I know it's impossible.

She hangs up, exasperated.

"That client," she mutters.

Then my dad opens the door, limping and grinning. But there's pain in his grin; it keeps flashing from grin to wince. His left foot hits one of the cardboard boxes, and he gasps. We rush to greet him.

"It's okay, it's okay," he says. He sits in a chair, panting. "Just swollen, not broken. I can still move the joint, look, oh."

My mom tugs his left pant leg up. His ankle is shiny and swollen.

"Just a sprain," he says. "No break. Ice and then I'm okay."

"The client keeps calling to complain you're too slow," my mom mutters, "and here, now, you can't walk. You drove home like this?"

We act as Papa's crutches, helping him over to the couch. My mom takes out the frozen peas and carrots she uses for fried rice, and sets the bag on his ankle. "Aray!" Papa cries, then relaxes. "Grabe. I step off the sidewalk only. Mali."

"Just rest," my mom says.

I look through a stack of DVDs. I pick out one my aunt brought back from her last trip to Manila, a pirated version of *Gagamboy*. Filipino Spider-Man. The cheap insect costumes and the self-deprecating jokes always make my dad giggle.

He falls asleep on the couch during the scene when a cockroach lands on a lady character's face. My mom removes the thawed, mushy peas and carrots from his ankle, drapes a blanket over him, and turns off the movie.

I go back upstairs, tear the pages from my notebook, and toss them in the trash.

My dad's bedroom door slams, waking me up.

Not that I slept that well, after my homework for Morality class.

I wake enough to realize: He never slams doors. This is weird. I hear muffled Tagalog. The tinny voices through the computer speakers.

"Corazon Maria, shower and take your breakfast or I'll throw it!" my mom calls up to me.

I check the clock; it's too late for a shower. I throw on my uniform and splash water on my face. I linger near my dad's door. I hear him, but I can't make out the words, just the rhythm of his Tagalog.

Soon I'm sitting between my parents at our table. No one chats, so I just look at the plastic flower-patterned table cover. They both sip their Nescafé. My mom takes hers black. My dad adds spoonful after spoonful of sugar, his usual. But there's something heavy about how quiet he is now.

I pour hot water into my own mug, add a pile of powdered hot chocolate, and poke one of the lukewarm eggs my mom fried us. I squirt ketchup on the plate, scoop some rice next to it from the night before, and eat the red-yellow-white salty mix. No sausage or bacon today. Maybe my parents are rationing. I don't ask for any.

"Still cold this morning," my mom says, and shivers.

"We need heat," my dad says. "Sana umitin. We are creatures of the tropics, the islands."

"You guys are." I yawn. "Not me. I'm, like, just Californian. And it gets cold here."

My dad clatters his fork onto his plate. I jump, wondering what annoyed him so much. "What?" Is this one of his jokes?

"You think you're not part of us?" he asks. And then I know it's not a joke.

I can sense something under his anger: sadness, or fear. I glance at my mom for help, like I usually do in these rare moments of my dad's coldness, but she looks at her coffee.

"You are FilAm," he says in Tagalog, his low voice even lower. "Huwag mong kalimutan yan." Don't you forget. "When people here look at you, they see that. They see you come from us."

My mom lets the moment go on, but she looks my dad's way. Warning? Noticing?

"Okay," I say.

My dad limps up. He says his ankle is better, but it still seems to pain him, especially during cooler mornings. "Tara na." Let's go now. He leans over and kisses my mom on both cheeks. He goes out to his truck.

I pause for my mom to give me her blessing, a quick tracing of her thumb on my forehead. "You talk to your father," she says. "He's only stressed right now."

I don't know what to say, though, as I get into the front seat of the Tacoma. I don't know what to apologize for. I do feel different from my parents. I get hints of the country they came from, and my mom did teach me Tagalog.

It's weird. My dad was the one who worried I might speak bad English if I learned Tagalog. My mom told him it's good for kids to be bilingual. But now he's being gung-ho about me being Filipino.

I sit silent, feeling useless and confused.

I might be brown, and I can understand what they say, but I don't sound like my parents. So much of me is different. So much of me feels like it deserves a name different from the ones they use for themselves. There's so much of me they don't know.

I clench the handle of my backpack as my dad drives. We watch the damp, deep green lawns, the little kids at crosswalks, the oak trees towering. He rolls down his window. I know we both smell sea salt, but we don't say so to each other.

He pauses a couple of blocks from Saint Agatha's. He always says it's to avoid the traffic. But I think he doesn't want to embarrass me with his truck—its clattering lawn mower and paint cans and random lumber in the back.

The truck rumbles. I know this is my chance to say something that will dissolve the sudden tension at breakfast.

"Bless," he says. He makes a small cross on my head with

his thumb. He does it every morning, but it feels quicker today, like he's tracing quick evidence of his disappointment on the skin of my head.

"Ladies," Mrs. Scott says, tapping a small pile of worksheets on her lectern.

She's starting the class in a good mood. I feel my jaw tense.

"Today we'll talk about something that you daydream about a lot, I'm sure, this Saturday being Valentine's Day. Hope that always stays a happy holiday for you."

The class giggles. Mrs. Scott smiles. She has huge, curly, tel-evangelist '80s hair, blond dyed blonder, and stabby blue eyes. Every day she wears the inch-long wooden cross that also hangs from the necks of the convent sisters who own the school.

I look down at the cover of our Morality textbook, *Your Life in God's Love!* The words from the assignment last night splash across my mind like ugly paint. I was too scared to highlight them, but I read them over and over, memorizing them. *A distinction must be made between a tendency that can be innate and acts of homosexuality that are intrinsically disordered and contrary to Natural Law.*

I've seen Mrs. Scott's car in the parking lot. It's been a year since the election, but she still has the YES ON PROP 8 (PROTECT MARRIAGE!) sticker on her town car bumper. I see the two same-gender stick figures, crossed out, in the faculty parking lot very time I walk to school in the morning.

"How many of you have started going on dates?" Mrs. Scott the class.

The class laughs openly now. A few rows away from me, Rika lifts Melissa's hand. They share a secret grin with each other, probably thinking about the water polo players from Saint Dominic's.

"Okay, focus," Mrs. Scott says. "Another question. How many of you want to get married one day?"

Everyone raises a hand. I scan the classroom for anyone who wants to stay single forever. Or be a nun. Or be free! To date whoever, forever!

Everyone wants marriage. No one wants to be a crossed-out stick figure.

I raise both my hands, panicked, and then I put them both down. Melissa looks at me, looks at Rika, and they smirk.

"All right, of course!" Mrs. Scott says. "Ladies, marriage is one of the most joyful, stressful life transitions a person can endure. It's also one of the holiest. It's the foundation of a healthy society."

With that, Mrs. Scott tells us the story of her two marriages.

Her personal stories are a hallmark of her teaching style. So are the stories of other Saint Agatha's students too. Unnamed students who had premarital sex; students who came to class smelling like "Mary Jane dope"; "stupid" students who stayed with boyfriends who called them stupid. Students tease each other not to become a Scott story.

Mrs. Scott's story now is about her first marriage to a man who'd started his own company manufacturing smartphone accessories in some province in China. He'd gotten wealthy really fast, and he was everything Mrs. Scott had imagined in a husband. Taller than she was, also blond, athletic but not too muscle-head huge, and loved to cook. They had fireworks and two live bands at their wedding, which cost about eighteen thousand plastic smartphone cases.

But after just six months, Mrs. Scott used her husband's laptop and peeked at his browser history.

"I don't recommend snooping, ladies," she says, "but sometimes we sin against each other in relationships. My small sin discovered his greater sin."

He was addicted, she saw, "to a certain kind of obscene movie. Ladies, he just had hundreds of links to these movies. The obscenity. I can't even—" She shakes her head.

We all look at each other, united for a moment in imagining just what kind of "obscenity" this was. I see a deer and a blond boy on a random page of my Morality textbook. I close the book.

Mrs. Scott got a Church annulment, citing her husband's "lack of mental capacity."

Mrs. Scott's new husband is a plumber and an air conditioner repairman. He came into class on her birthday, bringing a whole cake and an armful of roses. He had dark hair and a mustache and seemed older than she was. He seemed solid, like the kind of white guy my dad would hang out with, or lend his tools to.

"All this is to say, ladies," she finishes, handing out worksheets, "I had a lot of assumptions about what marriage was supposed to mean, and who my future husband was going to be. I'm giving you this exercise so you can examine assumptions of your own."

MY PLAN FOR DATING AND
FUTURE MATRIMONY

Some of the reasons I date are:
In the future, I want to do the following with my husband:
I think matrimonial love is supposed to:
I'm most worried about my future husband finding out:
I'm most hopeful that marriage will:
I imagine my role as a wife to be:

After completing your answers, review them
with a classmate. Discuss:
What does this list tell others about you?
How would your parents read it?
How would a future husband read it?
How would your priest read it?

I turn my black pen cap around and around in my fingers.

Why do my classmates like dating? I see them sometimes at the mall, holding hands with boys from Saint Dominic's and Oaks Magnus and Thousand Oaks High, sharing cinnamon buns and frozen yogurt and smoothies. So much sweetness. Maybe right now the girls are writing about mall snacks and holding hands. Maybe they're thinking about the ways they've already sinned with boys, becoming Scott stories. Maybe they want a marriage that was better than their divorced parents'. Or maybe the lucky ones are writing that they want a marriage as good as their parents'—like my parents'.

I'm one of the lucky ones. I grew up in a house where no one ever yelled. They just laughed, or pouted, or got stern sometimes. Like my dad did this morning.

Even then. My parents always seemed to understand each other. There was an order to the way they always were with each other. Knowing. Teasing. Full of affection.

I know what *intrinsically disordered* means.

It means I'll never have a happy church wedding. I'll never have all my friends and family near me at a pretty place, crying and smiling at my holy transition into matrimony. I'll never keep a garden with a man, or go to church with him. I'll never date in any honest way. It doesn't matter what any laws say, as long as the Church says this. *Intrinsically disordered* means I'll always have to fake it. It means I'll always be alone, banned from making my own family.

Mrs. Scott leans over me. She smells like a combination of all the perfume samples at the Oaks Mall.

"You won't have to turn this assignment in, Cory," she says. "It's just for you to think about."

I realize she's trying to reassure me. What can she see in me right now? I glance up at her concerned face and nod. She walks down the rest of my aisle. I look at my right hand and open it. There's a huge black mark on my palm where I'd started gripping the bottom of my pen without noticing.

I get up and go to Mrs. Scott at her podium now. She frowns like my mom, suspicious.

"I think my stomach is a little upset," I whisper.

I know, by how freaked out I feel, that I look weird already. Probably pale, as much as a brown girl can look pale.

"Go ahead," Mrs. Scott says.

I leave my classmates' dreams of Catholic-approved love and go into the hallway. It's empty there, but the air is filled with voices from other classrooms: teachers projecting their voices, murmurs of group activities. I know I should go to the nearest bathroom. But I walk four classrooms away from Morality class, stop near a broom closet, then lean against a locker. I slide down the locker until I'm sitting on the floor.

Then the broom closet opens. I look up, then scramble to stand.

"Hey, Cory! I didn't mean to freak you out, sorry."

It's Ms. Holden. The broom closet isn't a closet. It's a tiny, windowless office, with a small green lamp, one desk, and two rolling chairs. She's sitting in one, her tattooed arm holding the door open.

"You supposed to be out here, Tagubio?" she asks.

"I was in class. Then, uh, I wasn't feeling too well."

Her forehead wrinkles with beautiful concern. "Need to go to the nurse?"

"No! I just—just needed some air," I say.

"Okay. Well, you're welcome to join me. Not much air in here. But a chair's slightly more comfortable than the floor, at least."

I stand up. Ms. Holden stands too, and drops a small stopper to keep the door ajar. I sit in the other chair.

"So what class suffocated you?" Ms. Holden asks, and smiles to one side.

"Morality," I said.

"Ahhhh." Her smile gets full. "I remember Morality class. I had Sister Perpetua, though. A bit more stringent than Mrs. Scott seems. Lots of . . . interesting material, in that class."

I don't know if it's safe to agree. I just raise my eyebrows and nod, vaguely, the way I see my dad do sometimes when he's talking to our townhome association head, or rich clients.

I look around Ms. Holden's small office. She has a giant German-English dictionary, marked with Post-its, and a lot of books with long, complicated titles. There's an inch-thick manuscript with black plastic binding. A map taped up to the wall of Southern California surf spots, with blocks of coastline marked red.

"Mrs. Carmody didn't really have her own office," Ms. Holden says. "She just kept her stuff in one classroom. I like to have a small space for my research, so the sisters worked this out for me. Not fancy, but not bad."

I nod. Ms. Holden has only one framed photo on her desk. She looks ten years younger. She's wearing a short-sleeve wet suit. The young guy next to her has shaggy blond hair and a smooth face, and small muscles rippling across his torso. He holds a shortboard in one arm. With his other arm, he holds Ms. Holden around her shoulders. They're both wet with salt water. He smiles in that explosive way I'd expect someone to smile if they got to touch Ms. Holden.

"How are your other classes going?" Ms. Holden asks. "As well as mine?"

"I'm doing all my work. I finish everything on time."

I should stop here, I know, but my mouth disagrees with my brain, so I bumble on. "It's just—sometimes I don't know if it'll be enough, you know? Is anything ever enough? Especially in Morality. I mean even the name. Morality class. Having morals. How do you do that? The handouts? The exercises? Is it enough to just—do, and read and write, what they want?"

I stop before my voice starts shaking. I swing side to side in the chair and fake-smile, pretending it's fun. I wait for Ms. Holden to say something adult: something about needing to stay balanced, how stress and uncertainty are normal parts of high school, how this is one of the best times of my life, etc.

But she studies me. Usually, when teachers look at me, I take an inventory of what to hide about myself. I feel that way in class with Ms. Holden.

But right now, with just the two of us here, I like that she's looking at me. It feels like as long as she's holding me with her gaze, I'll be okay. For the first time in a long time, I feel calm. I don't want to hide or run. I just want to be here with her.

"There was a guy who worked for the pope around the year 1200 in Germany," Ms. Holden finally says. "Konrad von Marburg. Super-devout dude. The pope hired him to handle a group that was disagreeing with the Church. The Albigenses. The Albigenses had their own canonical ideas, and they were protesting corrupt bishops in western Europe."

I like her pronunciation of the German and French names, the foreign languages making unexpected, graceful disruptions in her English. She drums her fingers against her desktop.

"So! Konrad von Marburg went to the Albigenses. He sat them down. Served them dinner. Had a reasonable dialogue with them. By the end, they were all friends, they understood their mutual differences, and peace reigned."

"Really?"

She grins. "No. Von Marburg tortured and massacred them. He tortured and massacred a lot of people who disagreed with the Church. When folks heard Meister Konrad was coming to town, they'd panic. He said he'd happily murder one hundred innocents if it meant one might be a heretic. Even the corrupt bishops protested his excessive brutality. But, Pope Innocent was a huge fan.

"So Konrad kept at it until he was murdered, of course, in 1233. I could tell you some of the methods Konrad used against heretics. But it's almost lunchtime so I'll spare you. Let's just say you'll never look at a wheel the same way again."

I imagine terrible screaming, pleading. An angry man smiling through it all.

"The Church is a very old, very powerful institution," Ms. Holden says. "It has undergone its own particular evolutions. Thankfully, Meister Konrad and his ilk are out of business. But it makes you wonder what else might change in the Church, with enough time."

"They do not mention that stuff in Morality class," I say.

Ms. Holden laughs. "No, Tagubio, I suppose they don't. There are only so many weeks in the semester, after all, to teach you how to be a moral person in the modern day."

"You don't mention this stuff in History, either," I say.

Ms. Holden tilts her head. She's still smiling, but I've challenged her. I feel heat creep into my cheeks.

"You have an AP test to prepare for," she says. "The content predetermined by the College Board."

"Totally, I'm sorry, I didn't mean—"

"But are you interested in history?" Ms. Holden asks. "Is it something you might want to pursue as a major?"

I hadn't thought about that at all. I'd tried to imagine going to college, what I might do or be, how I might look. But my mind always came up with a panicky blank. I couldn't think beyond my mediocre grade point average. I wasn't smart at math like my mom, or smart at mechanics like my dad. The only thing I liked to do was doodle in my notebook sometimes, but that didn't seem like a career at all—nothing they advertised to us at Saint Agatha's, anyway.

But I can see my chance now: to study something that matters to her.

I say, "I'm interested in the story you just told. I think I want to hear more stories."

Ms. Holden nods. She likes that answer, and inside myself, I dance like I never do in life. "That's what history is, after all," she says. "A whole series of stories we tell ourselves about what came before, and what might come afterward."

The bell rings. We hear hundreds of feet shuffling along the hallway, girls shouting to each other, an announcement about the lunch menu on the intercom.

"If you don't mind the closet," Ms. Holden says, "we can talk about characters like Konrad von Marburg. We can call it extra credit."

"Whoa! That'd be awesome!" I check myself. "Uh, I mean. If it's not too much work for you. Don't you go to the beach after school?"

She smiles. "I can skip one session a week, if it's for the betterment of the eager youth."

"Is that who you surf with?" I blurt, looking at the framed photo. "Your, uh, Valentine?"

Ms. Holden laughs loud, a short, sweet sound. She looks at the shirtless surfer. Her laugh turns into a sad smile.

"My brother," she says.

"Oh." I am so embarrassed. So of course I keep talking. "I always wondered, you know, what it would be like. To have a sibling."

Then I remember my Skype calls with Kuya Jun. Technically I have a half brother. But it seems like too much to explain to Ms. Holden. And anyway, he's not really someone who lived with me the way her brother grew up with her. I've never even met him in person.

Ms. Holden keeps looking at the photo. "'Wovon man nicht sprechen kann, darüber muss man schweigen,'" she says.

I wait for her to translate. "Wittgenstein," she says. "Tragic guy. Germans. We can talk about him later." Then she looks worried. "Though the nuns might not like me sharing unflattering stories of the Church. Or controversial philosophers."

"What stories?" I joke. "What philosophers? I don't know what you're talking about."

We smile, our first shared conspiracy. "Good," says Ms. Holden. "Sehr gut."

The bell rings, and our first history tutoring session ends.

I'm not thinking of Mary when I go back to Morality class to get my stuff. I don't even feel nervous around Mrs. Scott when she asks me how my digestive issues are. I tell her I feel better.

Because I do. I'm fueled by new knowledge, new plans, new hints of Ms. Holden and what she wants to share with me. Just me!

But I can't avoid Mary forever. I have to pass by her to get to my next class, English, the last one of the day.

It occurs to me, though, that I feel blessed. Therefore, I should thank Mary.

I should tell Mary: It's for my grades. It's for my GPA. My parents both had mentors who helped them: My mom had a college math professor; my dad had his brother, a handyman who taught him how to fix anything and everything. Now I have a mentor too!

And I'm just about at the walkway near Mary's courtyard, having the kind of faith in Her love and acceptance and nurturing and gifts that the sisters and my parents always say will lead to Great Joy and Peace and Righteousness. I'm going through more of the acronyms that will determine my destiny—SAT! ACT!

AP!—thinking of how tutoring with Ms. Holden will launch me to success with all of them. I'm happy, full of faith. I believe in whatever happens next.

And then I hear my name over the intercom, telling me to come to the front office right away.

I freeze.

I walk slow.

I imagine Mrs. Scott's disappointment and calculation. My new status as a Scott story. The sisters' fingers on their crosses as they look at me, their eyes damp with prayer for my soul.

How do they know? What evidence did I leave behind?

Through the open glass doors of the office, I see my mom.

"Corazon," she calls to me.

I freeze again.

My mom is using the kind of voice I've never heard before.

Somehow, I recognize it when I hear it. It's the kind of voice that announces a break in time. A life-size, inescapable change.

I force myself to keep looking her way. My mother's face is as altered as her voice. It's filled with a kind of horror and fear that's never been there before.

"Ma?" I say.

Now she's a torrent of action and commands, her voice hard.

"Corazon, your papa fell from the roof. Let's go."

And before I can ask my questions—What roof? Where are we going? Papa's fine, right?—my mom's hard voice shoves us toward her idling Corolla, into a new, terrible future. "Come, come now!"

THE END OF OUR ORDINARY TIME

I was expecting a black eye, maybe. An arm in a sling. Both
ankles sprained. My dad grinning through it all. Maybe missing
a tooth and making a joke about whistling better. Not this.

Not the machines helping my dad breathe, raising his chest up
and down automatically. The plastic cuff around his neck. The
tight bandage around his left wrist. His face locked in a grimace.

My father almost never shows pain. He does everything to
hide it. For us.

I'm sure this is not my father.

And in a way I'm right. It isn't.

But I'm not me right now, either. Part of me isn't in this too-
dark, too-cold room. I'm still back at In-N-Out, listening to my
dad tell me a funny story. I'm still at school, keeping my eyes to
the floor, away from the sun that is Ms. Holden.

I'm downstairs with my mom, waiting for my dad to be done with a computer conversation. Sitting in the truck with him, waiting for his blessing.

All of me is not ready to be here and worry on a scale this big. On a scale so big, the worry is useless.

The worry does nothing.

My mother shuts her eyes, opens them. Her face crumples for the briefest moment, and then smooths.

I know I'm supposed to comfort her. Say the right thing. Touch her arm.

I stay frozen, waiting for a stronger, better version of myself to know what to do, and how.

A social worker tells us. He was working alone on the roof. A guy walking his dog on Potrera Street found him. A few more minutes of bleeding, and he might have—

It's a miracle, considering—

I think of Mary's face.

I get angry.

The anger surprises me.

I try to stomp it back down.

It's weird. My parents met because of a roof.

If you zipped around the world a few times—seventeen

and a half rotations, to be exact—and ran about twenty miles north, to a bland office building in Oxnard, you'd see where my parents met.

My mom, estranged from her parents in the Philippines, working a freelance programming job for cheap bosses. My dad, giggling with his crew, there to repair the leaky roof for under-market rates.

My mom complaining my dad laughed too loud. Turning up the volume of her radio.

My mom's radio breaking. My mom throwing it in the trash, sad and frustrated. My dad fishing it out. Fixing it for her. Leaving it playing on her desk, so she'd have music as soon as she arrived.

His voice plays in my head like he's speaking now.

"I didn't have toys when I was small. We could not afford. My toys were the broken things the rich throw away."

My dad fixing everything in the house for us. Fixing our old cars, our hot water heater, our TV remote, our fridge.

All the laughing and fixing things my parents did together, from the moment my mom saw that resurrected radio.

Do those moments still exist? Will there be more?

My mom reaches for his left hand, the one with no needles plugged into it. He's shirtless. I wonder if he's cold. *We need heat,* he said, just a few hours ago. *Sana umitin.* Hopefully it warms up.

The tubes, carrying his breath for him, are dark blue.

"Para kang cyborg, o," my mom jokes to him.

* * *

I don't want to touch him. Touching him would make this real.

Doctors and nurses confer. Then they wheel Papa away for a scan. My mom follows close behind the head of his bed. I stand near a lobby couch.

The neurologist's office. Dr. Chiu. She's rushed over from a hospital in LA.

She picks up the model of a brain, passes it back and forth between her hands, takes it apart to show us layers. She says "precarious state."

I want to throw up. My mom's gaze stays steady.

The doctor says "neurons and axons" and "stretching injury." She says "still waiting to determine" and "increased intracranial pressure" and "lack of oxygen."

We drown in words. Mine jump up before I can stop them.

"Is he coming back or not?" I yell.

I feel my mom's grip on my upper arm. The doctor pauses. She avoids my eyes and opens a brown envelope and sets a black sheet against a projection screen.

Papa's brain.

Ma leans forward, a new shine in her eyes.

"We use something called the Glasgow Coma Scale, to measure where a patient is in terms of possible recovery," Dr. Chiu says. "The best rating is a fifteen."

"And?" I demand.

There's no annoyance in the doctor's face at me. Just sympathy and sadness. Which feels worse.

"Today I'd place him at a three. There is no lower score."

We don't move. We don't speak.

The doctor goes on.

"We can't be certain if—when he'll wake. He may have deficits."

Ma repeats the word "deficits" back to her.

I stop hearing her full sentences again.

Difficulty swallowing. Trouble recognizing. Speaking. Eating.

My father under the tubes, in the truck, at our kitchen table making my mom laugh, praying at Mass, limping, falling.

Monitor. Tests and scans.

My mom touches the edge of the CT scan, looking at the shadows across my dad's brain.

"Rom's mind," she says.

Her voice stays steady, but water spills over from her eyes, leaving wet tracks on her cheeks. "It's my favorite mind."

Papa's back in his ICU room, today's tests done for now.

My mom and I are silent, listening to the murmurs of nurses, the hiss of machines. It's like we're leaving room where Papa's consciousness should be.

A pale, older doctor steps through the door. He looks like a human mix of melting butter and a pug. His plastic name tag says JOHN MILLER, MD.

"Nurse Emilia?" he asks my mom. "I thought your shift was later."

He looks at me, then back at my mom, who isn't wearing hospital scrubs, and whose name is not Emilia.

"Emilia, is this someone close to you?" he asks.

I want to throw something, but there's nothing to throw. I yell instead.

"Her name is Maxine! Christ!"

"Corazon!" My mom's voice slaps me.

The doctor's eyes cloud with shame. "Oh," he says. "Sorry. You resemble one of the other. . ." His voice dies. "Excuse me." He hurries out the room, down the hall.

My mom asks if I'm tired. I can't answer. I'm awake with watching, and anger.

My feet ache but I can't sit.

My mom taps her phone. Taps and deletes a text. Finally sends it.

She doesn't leave our dad's left side.

I don't stop standing at the foot of the bed.

My mom leans her forehead on the bed next to Papa's hand. Maybe she's napping. But then I hear the familiar whispers of her prayers.

I still can't pray. I can only watch. Inside, I burn.

* * *

Toward midnight, a nurse—not the mysterious Emilia—tells us we have family in the waiting room.

"Go na," my mom says, sending me ahead.

I hesitate, then leave the ICU. The automatic doors whisper and shut.

When I see Tita Baby and my cousin Bea and my uncle Dan, I know I should be grateful. But a prayer finally comes to me instead: Please, God, make Tita Baby leave me alone.

Of course, God does what He wants, and He inspires Tita Baby to reject my hand for my elder's blessing. She seizes my whole face instead, which she then presses into her combination jade-and-pearl necklace in her version of a hug. My mom's younger sister has always been a hugger.

"Cory! Anak, naku, what a shock, what a shock for you—" The pearls make indentations on my right cheek. "I always told your daddy, he should get a safer job, go to an office so your mom can stay home, keep the house, and now this injury, naku God, why did your mom wait hours before texting us what happened? Have you eaten?"

"Mom, don't suffocate Tito Rom's only descendant," my cousin Bea says dryly. "The family's been through enough today."

"I'm not the only descendant," I mutter.

The full thought of him comes to me then: Kuya Jun, on the other side of the computer.

I assume my mom will tell him. I don't want to be the one to face him.

Tita Baby releases me; she doesn't seem to have heard my reminder. Or maybe she didn't want to hear.

I rub my cheek. I look at Bea, as self-possessed here as she is on stages and runways. Lifelong example, standing tall, green-eyed, dark-haired, between her pale, sunburned dad and my bejeweled aunt.

"We brought you doughnuts," she says, and holds out a greasy bag to me.

"Good thing it's open twenty-four hours," Uncle Dan says, and pats my shoulder exactly once. "I wanted to rush here, but you know your auntie, she can't come empty-handed. You okay, kiddo?"

Of course I'm not. I mumble thanks and take the doughnuts.

Bea yawns and covers her mouth.

I hate her. Here with her intact parents, looking forward to bed. Besting me now even in family wholeness.

The ICU doors slide open. My mom looks from her younger sister to me. My mom's short dark bob is, for the first time, mussed. Long shadows droop under her eyes. She's been crying in the room without me, I realize, her hands probably gripping her own hair.

She interrupts whatever Tita Baby is about to say.

"Ading. Cory needs to go to school tomorrow," my mom says, calm.

Tita Baby nods. "Jerome is away at Stanford. Cory can take his room."

I feel stunned, betrayed, that my mom is sending me away.

Then I feel more tired than I've ever been in my life.

My mom says, "When Papa wakes, anak, I'll call you right away." She doesn't say "if." "The school is just two blocks. You can run. You have your Nokia. Keep it on."

I think of school, that distant planet.

With the Mary statue. With European History. With Ms. Holden.

Maybe, if I arrive back at school, I can be in a world where none of this happened. Where the brightness I feel in her presence carries me past this horrible night.

The shame of my hope makes my head heavier.

I look at my feet. I nod.

I hand the doughnuts to my mom.

Then I follow my aunt and uncle and cousin into whatever new world this is.

FEBRUARY 13, 2009
FRIDAY THE THIRTEENTH

I lie awake under my cousin Jerome's Stanford pennant. His lacrosse medals and trophies glint in the dark. His digital clock blinks 2:13 a.m.

My aunt and uncle's house is just a few miles away from us. But those miles are uphill, in a huge development, and this house is four times the size of our townhome. It's too quiet and huge. The sheets smell like fresh, flowery, unfamiliar detergent.

My tears pool on one of Jerome's pillows. I wipe my face.

They brought me back to my house to collect a change of uniform and my homework.

Tita Baby insisted on coming with me inside.

I saw my dad's flip-flops and the magnets of my parents' moms on the fridge.

I wondered if my dad would be on a memorial magnet too.

I crossed myself in front of Jesus to hide my tears. Tita Baby rubbed my back, and talked a lot. More sentences I couldn't hear.

I don't cross myself now. My emotions crowd out any urge to pray in the dark. I kick Jerome's sheets into a tangle.

I dream that my dad is a little kid selling candy and cigarettes to drivers along Moorpark Road. He's ten, maybe, but I can tell he's my dad. He's wearing my dad's paint-splattered shirt. He has my dad's buzz cut. He's walking with open wounds all over his bare feet. I try to yell, to warn him in time, but a truck that looks like his truck rushes toward him, the driver faceless, not looking, not caring to look—it's going so fast, there'll be nothing left to him—

"Ow! Shit," a voice cries.

I open my eyes and sit up. My cousin Bea—skinny like a clothes hanger, huge eyes, the planes of her face perfectly symmetrical, like God carved her on one of His best days—clutches her arm and winces.

"You kicked me," she says. "Were you winning a football game in your sleep or something?"

"Sorry," I say. My voice is cracked and strangled. I cough.

"Hope this doesn't bruise," she says, checking the skin of her arm, and I wonder what she'll be photographed for next. "My mom's going to take us to school. We'll drop you off first."

Bea goes to Oaks Magnus, the private high school with double the tuition and triple the prestige of Saint Agatha's. I hear a loud coffee grinder from downstairs. "I'll just shower," I say.

Bea points her chin toward a folded clean towel and travel-size body wash from a fancy Manila hotel. My aunt still takes all the available toiletries home from their vacations, even though she clearly doesn't need the freebies. My dad supports it, though, says it's good not to waste.

My dad. His absence is still so new. I check my phone. My mom hasn't texted or called. My dream anxiety sinks into the heavy thought of my dad still there, silent, not responding to my mom's crying or praying or jokes.

I can't bring myself to eat anything, so in the buttery-leather back seat of Tita Baby's Lexus, I hold a brown-bagged bagel with cream cheese and a thermos full of coffee I think is too bitter. My dad hates bagels.

The route is almost the same one as my dad drove yesterday: chilly, with a salt tang somewhere in the air. But Tita Baby glides downhill, past other enormous homes, and lets Uncle Dan's favorite conservative talk radio channel play.

"Ay, Cory, another challenge for you. I know your parents are struggling right now, the downturn, no? And your mama, freelance, your papa, also freelance—you know I always told your mom, your dad should—"

"Nanay," Bea says with a bad Tagalog accent, interrupting her.

"My dad is super good at what he does," I say.

"Of course, dear! He can be good at any job he does, and now—ay, I hope he gets up soon, no? But the head injury, so serious, of course we'll help any way we can, and then when he's better he can change career, finally—"

"What about your dad? Will he help?"

This is my secret-weapon interruption.

Anytime I ask about my mysterious grandpa in the Philippines, my aunt gets really quiet and careful. I think I see Bea bite her lip, but then her face goes model-neutral again.

The radio announcer says something about big government and family values. The bass in this car is really strong. I can feel the guy's anger vibrate through the speakers.

"You know, Cory, your lola Irma was sick a long time before she passed," she says. "And your lolo Joe—well—he has much to worry about. He's good at business, calculation. Like your uncle Dan."

"Uncle Dan is like your dad. Cool," I say.

"Bea, how are your studies?" Her voice flows toward my cousin, smooth. Then she talks back at me. "Sayang because Bea is bored with the violin na, I wish music would be part of her life always. But she's so busy with preparing for Stanford, joining her brother, and in between, modeling in Manila. Your schedule is so packed, but exciting, no?" She pinches Bea's cheek. In the rearview mirror, I see Bea roll her eyes.

"Nice to see Bea thriving," I mutter.

Tita Baby slows a few blocks away from school.

"This is kinda far from the Saint Agatha campus, Mom," Bea says.

"Exercise is good, no? Especially when you're stressed. And the traffic is so bad there."

That's her Tita way of saying she's done dealing with me for the morning. She's not my mom, after all.

I slam out of the Lexus before she can say anything more, and I walk toward my homeroom classroom without saying thank you.

I make it to the parking lot. I see the familiar streams of students, all wearing the same plaid gray uniform I am, heeding the same morning bell.

I stop, thinking of how my dad never drove into this parking lot. He never said why, and I never asked him to. His Tacoma was so much older than the other sedans and convertibles owned by students, his truck bed filled with tools other parents never used themselves.

The Nokia buzzes in my skirt pocket. I fumble for it.

Papa d same. Just come after class.

I can't bring myself to go to class like this is a normal day. It feels like betraying my dad: moving through a usual day, when he can't move at all.

I wait until the parking lot is quiet and the final morning bell has rung. The classes will begin without me.

I cross a couple of lawns and sidewalks, passing empty picnic tables and industrious classroom scenes.

I stop at the courtyard in front of the Mary statue. I look at her open, empty hands. Her gaze turned downward.

Looking at her makes me feel the truth.

I'm still hoping to see Ms. Holden.

The shame rises up in me, hotter than any anger, heavier than any sadness or fear. I sit on the bench below Mary. My dad might never return to me, might not even be my dad anymore, and I'm still thinking intrinsically disordered thoughts about my history teacher.

Then I feel another truth, something coming up from somewhere deeper.

I was hoping that this huge worry—Will my dad survive or not?—maybe would be the Thing. Maybe that would finally dislodge my thoughts about Ms. Holden. Maybe the disorder of my dad falling off a roof would finally make order fall into my heart.

"Is that why it happened?"

My whisper is small and choked.

"Tell me a reason," I say.

I cover both eyes with my palms. I can hear remnants of students' and teachers' voices, the wind through branches pushing away the fog. Even a bit of sun starts to touch me. But there's no voice. No answer from Mary or any saints.

I stay there until the bell rings again, until the courtyard fills again with students passing through. I ignore them. Until—

"Cory?"

I pull my hands from my eyes.

Of course it's Ms. Holden. Of course she's standing in front of me, in her sensible slacks and black cardigan and flats, every inch a teacher except for her hair, still tangled from salt water—today she surfed in the morning instead. She's holding a thick stack of handouts.

"You okay?" she asks. "Ready for more AP test practice?"

I look up toward the school's one-story roof, so I don't have to look at Ms. Holden, and shock bolts through me when I think of my dad falling from it.

"Hey," Ms. Holden says, and she rushes toward me with more tenderness than I've ever seen from anyone outside my family. "Hey, hey." She just sits next to me. I feel other teachers and students looking. Someone murmurs to Ms. Holden, and she says she's got me. I try to breathe in and a sob coughs up from me instead.

"Come on," she says after a long moment, when my breathing returns to a normal speed. She stands up, tilting her head for me to follow her to her little office.

If I weren't crying, I might say going back to Ms. Holden's office feels like going home. I might wonder about getting to my next class on time, or if I'll have points taken off my school citizenship grade for skipping my first class.

But my whole gaze falls to her keys, which I haven't noticed before. I've never seen her unlock a door.

There's a small, square-shaped rainbow.

I've seen these square rainbows before. Last year some protestors put some square rainbows up on the directional signs of the Oaks Mall parking lot. My dad glimpsed some and said, "Bakla signal. Like a bat signal for gays." Then he giggled. My mom scolded a familiar scold at him. I sat frozen in the back seat, hoping the moment would pass fast.

Even though that was months ago, before Ms. Holden arrived, I knew.

I was both mortified, and glad, to be at an all-girls school. I liked the smell of my classmates' wet hair in the morning. The way girls smiled and had steady, buoyant voices that never broke or deepened. I liked the graceful and awkward ways girls moved, all sharp elbows and soft torsos and strong limbs.

I liked to think that if I pried Ms. Holden out of my mind, that part of me would leave me too. But I knew. I know.

Seeing the rainbow key chain, in the hands that already hold so much power for me, the office suddenly feels holy. I feel what I'm supposed to feel in the cool calm of a chapel. I feel seen, settled, in quiet communication with someone, somewhere I'm supposed to belong.

But like I do in any chapel, I also feel nervous.

She drops her keys onto her desk and sits. She's waiting for me to talk, looking at my face. But I look straight at the floor, sniffing away the last moments of my weeping. How is it that I can feel someone smile without looking at them?

She closes the door.

"Want to share that coffee, Tagubio? I'm assuming it's coffee."

I remember I'm still gripping the thermos and the brown bag with a bagel.

She opens the bottom drawer of her desk. She pulls out a mug, a packet of chocolate cookies, and some potato chips.

"Always have to have sweet and salty," she says. "For snack emergencies."

We sip the bitter coffee. She laughs, watching me. "You don't seem used to it," she says, and hands me a cookie. "Wait ten years."

"Till I'm twenty-seven like you?" I sniff.

She rolls her eyes. "Cory, I'm twenty-five," she says, and toasts the cap of my borrowed thermos with her mug.

I calculate. Eight years between us.

I do finally feel hungry. I chew the bagel.

"You must need to teach," I apologize.

She shakes her head and picks up a cookie. "Not till the afternoon," she says. "Anyway. Seems like a lot happened since we discussed heretics yesterday."

I nod. Then I start talking. I try to keep my voice strong in my throat, but I feel it wobble a few times. She gasps a little. She stops eating and leans toward me, listening. She says she's so sorry. I feel like I'm in confession.

"The thing is," I say.

She nods.

"I never upset my dad. But I did yesterday, somehow. Then he—"

I can't go on with what I want to say. That he must have been distracted on that roof, thinking of how I'd disappointed him.

I definitely can't go on with the deeper thing I want to say: that maybe this is my punishment. My lesson. For everything I can't stop feeling, can't stop wanting.

Ms. Holden sits back in her chair. She seems stunned. For a

moment I think I've horrified her. She closes her eyes and takes her glasses off, thinking.

In the next moment she takes my right hand with both her hands.

My whole world sways. Only the part where Ms. Holden is touching me feels still and stable. I'll never shiver or fear or want again, as long as she keeps holding my hand. I want time to stop. I want school and the cars outside and electricity all to stop.

This is what I was supposed to feel with a boy, with any boy, but I feel it now and I don't want to stop feeling it. All the doctrines disappear for me in that moment. To my shock, all my shame disappears too.

"I'm going to tell you something I don't tell a lot of people. But it's not about me. It's about you. Okay?"

I nod. I don't want her to let go.

"My brother died about a year after that photo. I thought it was my fault."

I want to hold her face. I've never wanted to hold someone's face before. I want to tell her she's only capable of good things in the world and of course it wasn't her fault no matter what happened. I want to put her glasses gently on her desk and climb into her lap and wrap my arms around her shoulders. I want to say the perfect, pain-banishing phrase, the thing that will heal her once and for all.

"I'm so sorry," I say. "Why? It couldn't—"

She lets go of my hand and waves my words away. My heart drops.

"My brother and I got into a huge argument right before he moved up to Santa Cruz. Broken dishes, broken windows kind of argument. So my parents—they'd been divorced since we were toddlers—they decided it was better that he live with my dad. The way I saw it for a long time, if there was no me, there would be no tree, no brother running into it in Santa Cruz."

I don't say anything. I look at the ground, not sure what feelings will erupt if I look up at her.

"But I had to learn after a long time," Ms. Holden says, "sometimes . . . sometimes there are brothers."

"And sometimes there are trees," I say.

She nods. She's quiet, deciding what to say next.

"Yeah. I want you to know that now. Because I didn't know it then. There's no grand scheme of fault designed to punish us. You don't have to take that on. Sometimes there are roofs. Sometimes there are trees."

My throat closes up. I talk to clear it. "Your tree tattoo," I say.

Ms. Holden smiles. She pulls up her sleeve. It's more detailed than I'd first glimpsed—a snaking, wounded trunk, the leaves still blooming along the skin of her upper forearm.

The details cover raised scars. I can see that close up now.

She tugs her sleeve back down toward her wrist.

"Do you hear me?" Ms. Holden says, solemn. "No matter how bad this might feel. This is not your fault."

I nod. Though I'm not sure if I do hear her yet.

Then my body moves ahead of me.

I lean my head against her right shoulder and hear myself sob before I feel it coming. She wraps her arms around me and hums. It reminds me of my dad singing hymns while he and my mom worked in our little herb garden, pulling away dead leaves. But I don't know what Ms. Holden is humming. I listen anyway. I close my eyes.

I enter the Emergency and Trauma Care lobby, then go down to the lobby of the ICU. My mom's hair is still disheveled. But she's wearing a sparkly gold sweater now—Tita Baby must have brought her a change of clothes from her own closet.

They look tense. Tita Baby's face is cautious but pleading and insisting. My mom's is set and hard.

"Not now," my mom says in Tagalog. "Don't trouble me with this now."

"Xi-xi, we have to tell him," Tita Baby says in Tagalog. "Maybe he'll help, you need help—Dan and I can only help so much—and what about Junior?"

"You know he won't lift a finger for me," she says. "He'd rather die."

"Maybe I can ask. Maybe he'll help as a favor for me."

"Stop, ading," my mom says.

"Don't let your pride—"

"She understands," my mom reminds Tita Baby. My aunt is always forgetting, since she didn't teach Bea Tagalog—she didn't want Uncle Dan to feel left out of any family conversations, so

59

her kids went English-only like him.

But Tita Baby's pleading mission isn't done, even with me overhearing.

"Kausapin mo na siya," she says to my mom in a high whisper.

"Talk to who?" I ask. "Who should Ma talk to?"

"And what, ading?" my mom yells at her sister in English, ignoring my question. It's a rare break in Ma's stern cool. I jump. "You think if I ask, if I prostrate myself, he'll suddenly change? He'll show generosity? He'll support his eldest daughter? That man will find a way to hurt me with it again, the whole family this time. Oh, ano? Gusto mo ba ng patunay? Kitang-kita naman sa buhay namin, eh! You have your relationship with our father, I have mine. Corazon, let's go to Papa," my mom commands, and we leave Tita Baby behind.

My mom walks straight into my dad's dark hospital room, ahead of any of my questions. But I'm not that determined. I'm not that good. I pause in the doorway, frozen again, seeing him under all the tubes and braces.

I can only see half his face, his nose and bruised, closed eyes.

I forget about all the machinery and muscle that makes us move around every moment of the day, until I see how many machines my dad needs to keep all that movement going for his life. Maybe, instead of being mad, I should express more gratitude to God, for keeping my dad alive. Maybe if I'm grateful enough, He'll let us keep Papa.

I remember Ms. Holden telling me it's not my fault. But I

still feel like I can do more.

My mom doesn't pray, and she doesn't ask me to, either, which surprises me. She talks to my dad like he's awake. I feel too weird to talk to him—he still seems like an unrecognizable version of my dad, not my true dad, and I don't know how to talk to this version. But my mom seems to know how.

"Baby wants Tatay to help us," she says in Tagalog. "I keep telling her . . . I know, I shouldn't complain about her too much, you always say she's my family."

My mysterious grandfather. The guy she never discusses with me, except to say they don't talk. She rushes on, talking to my dad.

"Ay, Rom, I have to complain again. That client of yours, Manolo. I won't take the calls of that man. He keeps leaving messages about the Potrera house. I told you he was a bad one. But you should tell me, no, if there are other clients I should call? I will take Cory with me to Mass today. I made sure she went back to school, I know you want for her to stay with her studies. Cory, talk to your dad."

I try to visualize yesterday's version of my dad—God, it was only yesterday.

I imagine how it might be if our roles were reversed, if it were me under all those tubes. I've never seen him cry. Not even when he got news from Manila that his mom had died. He just went into the garden by himself, not saying anything, and my mom joined him there until late into the night. They went to Mass every weeknight for two weeks, and then my dad never mentioned her again.

Maybe if it were me in there, under all the tubes, he'd try to make me laugh.

"Want to hear a joke?" I ask him.

I worry my mom will think this is the wrong thing to try, but she looks toward his swollen eyes. "Oh, mahal, Cory has a joke for you."

"Yeah. What's black and white and red all over?"

"A newspaper," my mom guesses.

"Ah, no," I say. "It's a nun. A nun that fell down the stairs."

My mom stares at me. This is the kind of joke my dad and I would have laughed at while my mom scolded us. The silence where his laughter should be is the worst.

"I mean, it doesn't really work at Saint Ag's because the nuns don't wear habits since they usually wear plain skirts, and I think I heard that joke in a play somewhere, uh—" I keep talking nonsense to try to cover up the horrible silence.

And then my dad blinks.

I'm so used to hiding a lot of my feelings from my mom—I think she doesn't show everything she's feeling to me, either. But when she says, "Rom?" in a high, breathy voice that's not her usual voice, I know we're feeling the same wild hope. I wait for Papa to sit up. Maybe he'll even unplug all his tubes and ask us why we look so worried.

We lean close. But my dad's eyes can't seem to settle on anything. They flick around.

The heart rate monitor sprints. And then there's a horrible

choking sound. And a tear trailing wet down his face. Now I've seen my dad cry.

"Nurse!" my mom cries out at the air. "Nurse! Tulong!" She finds a remote and presses call buttons. The doctor from yesterday, Dr. Miller, and more nurses rush into the room. They hustle me and my mom out.

We wait, both of us crossing our arms, hugging ourselves, not speaking to each other. My mom prays again.

Dr. Miller comes out, crouches near us, and asks my mom's name. His explanation swims toward both of us.

A seizure. Immediate operation to relieve pressure on the brain. Induced medical coma. Intracranial pressure monitor. Preventing infection. Could be weeks. Indeterminate amount of time.

Then someone from the billing department asks to meet with my mom. She closes her eyes, nods, and follows her into another office. She doesn't ask that I come with her, and I don't offer to go.

We arrive home together for the first time since Papa fell.

His truck is in the driveway. Uncle Dan drove it home from my dad's last work site sometime yesterday.

Is it his last work site? Will he work again?

My dad's stainless-steel mug is still upside down near the sink, dry now against a dish towel after his last coffee. The last necklace of flowers he left around Jesus's neck is dry too.

The word torments me: last, last, last.

My mom goes upstairs, fast, like she's on her way to work. Her speed surprises me.

But she doesn't go into their room right away. I hear her hesitate.

Then, when she opens the bedroom door, she sniffs and then weeps.

I hear the computer starting up. Then the dialing. The call doesn't go through at first. She dials again. There's the delayed, hollow sound of Jun's voice. "Tita?" he says. "What's wrong?"

She gets up and closes the bedroom door. I hear her murmur. Then, even through the closed door upstairs, I hear Jun's voice rise.

"How?" he asks in Tagalog. "Paano nangyari?"

I can't stand the sound of his hurt, his shock. It sounds too much like mine.

I go outside to sit and shiver near the little herb garden.

THE WEEKS OF WAITING

Someone—maybe the Filipina nurses, maybe my Saint Ag's teachers—alerts our church. So the first few weeks, there are visitors at the house every day.

I'd been on the other side of these crisis visits before: Someone would get terrible news, and then the whole community would descend on the house of bad fortune. Which I guess is our house now.

Titos and Titas—I can hardly keep track of who was who—drop off huge wheels of pancit, chicken and pork adobo, spaghetti with banana ketchup and hotdogs in it, bags of dry rice, boxes of doughnuts, bags of siopao. Even toiletries and cleaning supplies and clothes that don't fit us.

Flowers fill glasses and old jars on the counter. We get prayer cards from my mom's former bosses, my dad's former clients, and stack them on top of the fridge.

We get bills too. They pile on the countertop near Jesus's

head. Bills for our utilities, the mortgage, from the hospital. My mom stops opening Excel to calculate our budget.

As weeks pass, the flowers get brittle. The food stops arriving. My dad doesn't wake.

Only Tita Baby and Uncle Dan keep dropping off takeout for us, or, eventually, leftovers from their own dinners.

My mom accepts some remote programming jobs, taking her laptop to use the hospital's wireless, cursing in Tagalog when the connection isn't fast enough.

"Why don't I apply to In-N-Out?" I ask one night, sitting next to her in the hospital. "To help."

I thought the offer might make her happy, but it seems to inflame her. "Your job is school," she snaps. "My job is the finances. Make sure you keep your grades up."

At school, the teachers' sympathetic looks fade into routine reminders of my duties to study.

The nuns have me visit Mrs. Scott a few times. Just my holy luck that the Morality teacher doubles as the school counselor.

I sit on the scratchy brown couch in her spacious office, under Mrs. Scott's giant crucifix and motivational posters of kittens hanging by their paws from tree branches. I never quite know what to tell her. I wonder how soon I'll become one of her Scott stories, warning other students about suffering.

We end each session with a prayer. I lower my head, but I don't pray along.

* * *

The place where I feel most relieved is in Ms. Holden's office. Here, she gives me a tour of heretics.

There's the obvious one—Galileo, world being round and all. But there are other characters too. The bishop Nestorius, who didn't believe Christ could actually be born from a human woman. Marguerite Porete, who wrote a book about Divine Love and got literally burned by a bunch of men for it.

"Why were people so scared of these new ideas?" I ask her once. "Like, burn-them-with-fire scared? Of new information?"

"Why do you think?" she asks me.

I can't answer. She prods me. "How do you feel, when you're uncertain about something? When something you thought was true is challenged as untrue?"

"Uncomfortable, I guess," I say.

"Sometimes rage," she says, "is born from an incredibly intense feeling of discomfort. Rage is easier for some people than facing the discomfort of something new. And if that kind of person is in a position of power?" She rolls her eyes.

I'm facing something new, even as Papa's coma goes on. For seventeen years, my dad was my dad, whole and here every day. That used to be true. I thought it'd always be true.

Now my mom and I don't know if he'll ever come back. When I first saw him in the hospital, I wanted to destroy every religious statue I'd ever seen, and I yelled at a doctor. For the first time I felt something in me capable of wielding bad fire too.

* * *

Melissa and Rika invite me to an after-school AP study party out of the blue. My mom tells me to go.

Melissa and Rika live next door to each other in the same neighborhood as Tita Baby. Ten classmates sprawl around enormous couches and plush carpet in yoga pants and tank tops; I'm the only one who stays in the school uniform. They go through AP English and AP Chemistry and then on to AP European History, the only AP class I'm in. In between they gossip about guys from Saint Dominic's and Oaks Magnus. I don't try to join in.

"I'll be so glad when Ms. Holden is gone next year." Rika yawns.

"It's too bad Mrs. Carmody couldn't hold her liquor last semester," someone else says. "We wouldn't have ended up with the six-month sub from hell."

"Seriously," Melissa says. "Go surf away forever, Holden, and take your shitty quizzes with you."

Something hot enters my throat and then escapes.

"I dunno. It just seems like she wants us to care about history," I say.

Then, as usual, I wish I hadn't spoken. I swear I hear every pair of eyes roll across the room. Every time I talk to these girls, they look at me like I've grown four heads.

"Okay, Cory," Rika says, smiling down at her own index cards, and the studying goes on.

* * *

One day, I rise to leave Ms. Holden's office and fumble both my history notebook and my Morality textbook. They fall to the floor. We both reach to get them. I can smell her hair, something mint, and salt water, and coconut suntan lotion.

"What's this?" Ms. Holden says, picking up my Morality textbook.

I panic. She's noticed the doodles I made of the textbook's photo-illustration people. And she's reading the captions I wrote over my doodle-people's heads.

The more anxious I got in Morality class, the more I doodled. The margins are filled with my drawings of the wholesome, puzzled, praying humans in the book.

I haven't drawn much since Papa's accident. But still—weeks ago I defaced the word of God! And all His pictorial advice! I remember all of a sudden that she's still a teacher.

"Nothing," I say quickly, and I try to snatch the book back. She holds it away from me, grinning. She stands and reads. I sit, burning, and bounce both feet.

Then she reads the captions for my doodles aloud. "'I struggle with the temptation of evil, sensual hand-holding. Will you still have french fries with me?' 'I'm sorry your pet hippo died; Jesus will replace it.'" She giggles. She sits back down, continuing to read.

"These drawings are great," she says.

"You don't want to take points off my honor card?" I ask. "For vandalizing school property?"

"No way. I mean, I suppose I should, being your authority.

But I want to read more of these. We'll call it a special dispensation. Act of mercy."

She keeps reading, laughing at all the little scenes I drew. She pauses at one page and smiles a smile I've never seen before. She tips the book so I can see only the cover.

"What?" I ask.

"Nothing." She riffles the pages, closes the book, and hands it back to me. "You have a gift. It's very intelligent image revision and theme reinterpretation."

"Thanks? I guess?" But of course my whole body is abuzz with her approval. With the memory of her hand on my knee. I feel like I should run around all the bases of the outside softball field about twenty times.

That night, when we're back home from the hospital, I riffle through my doodles again, trying to see what she saw.

I catch a white boy with a scraggly goatee and a flannel shirt from ten years ago; a stock photograph. He has his fist under his chin. I'd sketched a cartoon version of him in the margin. In my drawing he was wearing a Saint Agatha's skirt, and I put my thought bubble over his eyes.

Siiiiiiigh . . . M.H.!! . . . Siiiiiiigh

I seize a pencil, mortified, and try to erase it. The indentations stay.

I tell myself she couldn't possibly have noticed—surely there were many M.H.s in the world.

APRIL 9, 2009
HOLY THURSDAY

All 565 of us stream into the gym today, bleachers pulled out and chairs arranged for Holy Thursday Mass before Easter break. We have one class in the morning, then Mass, then freedom. We're fidgety but obedient, sitting and standing for the readings and prayers.

The priest raises the Eucharist, commemorating Christ's gestures. We line up for Communion. I take it even though I'm not sure I should. I don't want to call more attention to myself by asking for a blessing instead.

At the end of Mass, walking behind a slow-moving crowd of restless classmates, I see the back of Ms. Holden's head near the gym entrance. She's talking animatedly with someone, nodding. I hear Ms. Holden's laugh drift toward me, the best music. Then I see: She's talking, and laughing, with my mom.

I stop breathing. Spending time with Ms. Holden always felt like a secret to me. I never brought my secrets to my parents.

Ms. Holden talking to my mom, at school, feels like a historical summit, with so much to potentially reveal.

I should pretend I'm more prepared for this. Instead I blink and stare.

Then Ms. Holden notices me watching. She calls over to me. "Magandang oo-maga, Cory!"

"Tanghali!" my mom corrects her. "Because it's noon now. But that was a good 'Good morning.'"

The guarded, worried, mourning version of my mom is gone for a moment, and this friendly, outgoing version of my mom is teaching Ms. Holden Tagalog. I feel a sense of gratitude calm me for a moment. I start breathing easy. Ms. Holden makes other people feel better, not just me. Ms. Holden is good. Even my mom can feel the goodness.

"Hi," I say.

"Your history teacher says you are very hardworking, earning extra credit. You didn't tell me and your papa."

Ms. Holden winks at me behind my mom's back. The wink that always wakes me up inside.

"I wanted to . . . surprise you?" I say.

"Cory has an excellent memory," Ms. Holden says. "She's able to absorb a lot of complexities and nuances of history. I'd say she's way ahead of her classmates."

"Her father also has a good memory," my mom says. "I think that's where she gets it. That, and her eyes. The shape."

The sadness comes back into my mom's face. Ms. Holden gets serious. "How is he, Mrs. Tagubio?" she asks.

My mom shakes her head a little. Then she brightens.

"Maybe we can have you for coffee at the house," she says. "Tomorrow, for Good Friday. You can tutor at our home, and then have merienda. A small thank-you, for your extra time with Cory."

"Ma, Ms. Holden's probably busy," I say. But I'm thrilled at the invitation. Then I wonder if my mom's offering just to be polite. But she looks eager to host someone for something other than sympathy.

Early on after Papa's accident, we had visitors almost every day—friends from church, or visitors from Manila, or younger guys from my dad's crew. But the kitchen has been quiet with our worry lately.

Ms. Holden looks between us. "I'm not busy tomorrow afternoon," she says. "That's so kind. I'd love to visit."

We spend the morning with Papa. His bruises have faded. The nurses have wrapped him in a gown. But he hasn't woken since his first seizure.

Dr. Chiu says one of her many acronyms at us: VS. Vegetative state. The next level up would be MCS: minimally conscious state. She walks in every day with the Glasgow checklist. She shines lights into Papa's eyes. She pinches him. The checklist doesn't change.

Ma tells him our plans for the day: the remote programming job she's working on with the hospital WiFi, Good Friday Mass later. "Cory," she says, "tell Papa about your teacher, your extra credit."

I'm a little more used to talking to him now. But I hesitate. My mom frowns. "The teacher is very young," she says to Papa for me. "But a PhD already. She says our daughter is talented in history. Maybe in a few years, Cory will also have her PhD."

"Maybe don't—" I say, embarrassed. But I don't quite know what I'm trying to stop. The machines beep on and on, and my mom's voice goes on too, hopeful and proud of me.

In the afternoon, I sweep the floor and put a towel over the mail on the counter and move the open cardboard boxes away from the doorway. My mom toasts sweet pan de sal from the freezer and sets out coconut jam. I boil water in a pot on the stovetop.

Our old electric kettle broke a couple of weeks ago, which filled both our eyes with tears. Papa could have fixed it in five minutes.

Ms. Holden arrives with wet hair again, her surfboard strapped to the top of her Civic. My heart jumps into my throat, to see her in a plain white V-neck T-shirt and jeans, her flip-flops still a little sandy.

"Don't mind the mess," my mom says, apologizing for the boxes. "Just some things my sister will take with her to Manila, for relatives."

"Your home is wonderful," Ms. Holden says. "I love how you've set it up."

She slips off her sandals and hands my mom a box of croissants from a nice bakery in Malibu. My mom prepares her Nescafé and apologizes, again, for not having fresh beans. "Any coffee is good coffee." Ms. Holden winks.

Our lesson today is just AP European History flash cards; no heretics while my mom overhears. Ms. Holden smiles a little between each flash card: Avignon Papacy, Ferdinands I and II,

Martin Luther, Prince Philip. My mom plays classical music in the living room and works on her own programming. "Prince Philippe named the Philippines," she calls to us, and Ms. Holden says, "Yes, Mrs. Tagubio! It's a strange omission from the AP curriculum, but an important historical point."

Our togetherness makes the house almost feel normal again. The ache of Papa's absence is dull, constant. But I like the lightness Ms. Holden's visit brings.

I glance around my kitchen, wondering how it must look to her. Every appliance used and repaired a few times, the boxes still half filled with clothes and canned goods and shoes to send to Kuya Jun in Manila. The old, frayed towel draped on the counter, covering the pile of bills my mom hasn't opened yet. The corded phone unplugged; collectors kept ringing the landline. But Ms. Holden's gestures are easy. She's comfortable. She looks like she belongs at our table.

My mom joins us when we're done with the flash cards. She and Ms. Holden do a few more Tagalog lessons; Ms. Holden takes notes on phrases, wonders aloud if she should do a surf trip to the Philippines. I watch her enthusiasm for language, wondering what I'll be that enthusiastic about in the future. My mom says the national hero of the Philippines, José Rizal, lived in Germany. She asks if surfing is dangerous. She wonders if I should have a sport.

Then my mom's cell phone rings. She excuses herself to the living room. Ms. Holden gives me a warm look and puts another croissant on my plate.

"Really?" Ma gasps. I can't tell if her gasp is relief or fear or

76

both. "When? Never mind, we'll go there."

I brace myself for the worst news. I think Ms. Holden looks scared too.

My mom says, "He's reacting to touch. He flinched when they replaced his IV today. The doctor says that's a good sign. I'm sorry, we must go—"

"Of course, you should go, that's great news!" Ms. Holden says. "Please." She gathers up the flash cards, spots mesh food covers above the counter, and places them atop the leftover croissants and pan de sal to protect them. I'm grateful for how ready she is, how much she wants to help. I join, rinsing our mugs quick in the sink.

We enter his room with so much hope, calling for him, asking him to tell us how he's feeling. We're ready for his return. We expect him to talk back; maybe he'd smile at us.

But Papa's still silent. His eyes stay closed.

Dr. Chiu shows us charts that indicate more brain activity, a steadier heart rate. She tells us we have reason to be hopeful.

But we can't hide our disappointment. My mom covers her face with her hands. I cross my arms against my chest. The surge of energy this new hope brought us makes us feel even sadder, a sadness we can't articulate to each other.

I leave the ICU for a drink of water at the fountain. In the waiting area I find the impossible: Ms. Holden, reading from one of her black binders.

I'm worried she's here for a different emergency. But she sees me and stands, and then I understand. She's here for me! For my family.

"My dissertation is somewhat portable," she says. "I can work anywhere. And I couldn't help but keep thinking of you. And your mom. How's your dad?"

The sliding doors of the ICU whisper open and shut behind me. "Ms. Holden," my mom says.

"Please, Mrs. Tagubio, you can call me Grace. Cory should still call me Ms. Holden, though."

"Very kind of you to check on us," Ma says. "I wish we had more to tell you about his condition."

Ms. Holden's presence makes me feel more hopeful. Her presence makes me want to emphasize everything good in my life, no matter how small, to meet everything good in her. I try to cover up our disappointment. "The neurologist says it's a small improvement," I say. "The EEG shows steadier activity."

My mom nods. She looks lost.

"Maybe you're hungry for dinner soon?" Ms. Holden says. "I'm happy to grab something for both of you."

My mom looks between me and Ms. Holden. Like she's deciding something.

I brace myself.

"Cory," she says, "why don't you go with your teacher for dinner?"

I didn't expect this. "But shouldn't I—?"

Ms. Holden gathers her binder. Maybe she senses that my

mom and me need to be alone. "I'll just pull around out front. Cory, just come out to let me know if you'll come with me, or if I should just bring you guys something. Happy to do either."

She steps away. I look toward my mom. She drapes an arm around my shoulder. I realize she hasn't done this in a while. It's like all the uncertainty kept us from hugging.

"We've been so stressed," she says. "You're more relaxed with your teacher, learning. You go ahead."

She presses some bills into my hand. I think she wants to be alone with my dad. Maybe to cry. Maybe to beg, or pray, or say some things she doesn't want me to hear. "I'm not so hungry. Go eat. Go na. I can ask your tita Baby for dinner later."

The classical music station. Sunlight. I watch Ms. Holden's hands as she guides the steering wheel. She lowers the driver's side window for a breeze to breathe in on us. We're silent for a bit.

"The AP test is in exactly a month," she says.

I think it's weird she brought this up, out of everything else she might have said.

"I know," I say. "You brought those cards to my house."

"Can't I give a teacherly reminder?" she murmurs.

She seems annoyed. Distracted and serious. Like bad weather has moved into her head, and she's hunkering down for a storm.

"Are you okay?" I ask.

My question doesn't seem to shift the climate. "Don't worry about it," she says.

Of course I worry. I freak out, silently, for the rest of the ten-minute drive.

She parks in front of Tres Hermanos, a bustling Mexican takeout place. She doesn't get out of the car right away.

"Uh-oh," she says. "The Cory X-ray gaze."

"The what?"

"You have a gaze. Where you see past whatever's happening on someone's face."

I'm self-conscious and thrilled, again, that Ms. Holden noticed something about me. Something I didn't even know.

She sighs.

"Hospitals remind me of my brother. We didn't spend as much time in the ICU waiting room as you guys. It was over quick. A long time ago. But I still get a feeling. It brings stuff up. I think I didn't even know it would happen till I walked in there."

"I'm sorry," I say, articulate as always.

"Nothing for you to apologize for! I mean—I'm sorry." She sighs again. "We all have our own secret history, yeah? Who knows what'll touch it off?" She opens her car door. "Come on. Taco time."

We join clusters of families, men in Hawaiian shirts and polos, women with bleached-blond blown-out hair, little kids staring at handheld screens. Ms. Holden orders us carnitas. I order my mom a takeout rice bowl. We wait in the noisy seating area, then take our tacos to eat outside on the ledge of a huge, decorative fountain out front.

"I should pay you back for all the food you've been treating us to today," I say.

"You have!" she says. "You've reimbursed me with good company."

She taps her taco against mine in a mock, funny toast. I watch water dancing out of the fountain sculptures: they're cheesy toddler angels, chasing each other and blowing through holes in their mouths.

"Religion is a mess," I say.

Ms. Holden laughs. "Why do you say so?"

I search for something to say, then decide on, "So many wars."

"That's true. Maybe you should nail a manifesto to some church doors yourself! What would it say? What would you want to change?"

I think. I notice again the grace in how Ms. Holden is sitting, true to her first name, the comfort with which she seems to occupy every muscle of her body. I notice her tan, renewed each day with her surfing regimen.

"Some things, I guess," I mumble.

A voice claps over us like fake-friendly thunder.

"Well, hiiiiii there, Cory and Grac—I mean, Ms. Holden!"

It's Mrs. Scott. My cross-wearing, story-telling Morality teacher and school counselor. Behind her is her husband in a plaid shirt. Behind that guy is a pale kid, maybe six years old, thumbing a game console. I stand. "Hi, hi!" I say, to hide my surprise and helplessness.

"Gosh," Ms. Holden says, and I have to stifle a laugh because she doesn't seem like the kind of person who would ever say "gosh." "This is a regular Saint Agatha's reunion spot. First Cory and I run into each other, and now you fine folks!"

I'm surprised Ms. Holden lied. Then I'm grateful to play along.

"Wow! Is your mom here too, Cory?" Mrs. Scott says.

"I'm—picking up tacos for her," I say. I decide it's not that much of a lie. "Just, uh, snacking first."

Mrs. Scott gives me her syrupy, warm look. "It's great that you can pick up the slack for your mom during this difficult time. You better get in line, it's out the door!"

"I will, thank you," I say.

"What a good daughter you are," Mr. Scott says, gruff. "Jared, when you're a few years older, maybe we'll send you here for tacos."

Jared doesn't look up. His thumbs stay busy on the screen. He wears a flaming-red T-shirt that says *I'm the Kind of Christian the Devil Would Fistfight.*

"Well, we're on our way to pick up some eggs for a nice little Easter hunt this weekend," Mrs. Scott says. "You guys have a blessed evening!"

"You too!" Ms. Holden says. "Good to see you, Jared."

He turns his back to us, and his parents roll their eyes, and then Mrs. Scott is gone inside the grocery next door.

I wait for Ms. Holden to say something witty and cutting to make fun of Mrs. Scott and her family. But she's quiet. She seems solemn and sad again.

"Are you okay?" I repeat, feeling useless.

She turns to me. She looks like she's going to say something weighty, important. Then she looks down, tucks her hair behind her ear, and looks up at me again.

"Your mom says you've never tried surfing," she says.

Now I'm confused. "Uh. No. My parents and I just walk on the sand when we go to the beach."

I remember my dad laughing, pointing across the waves, toward the Philippines. My eyes burn.

"Maybe you should try sometime," Ms. Holden says.

I clear my throat. "The ocean's, like, forty-five minutes away."

She glances at me, then looks toward her car roof. "We don't need ocean. We just need sand."

We pause together. I wonder what will happen next. I wait for her.

She shakes her head fast, like she's clearing it.

"Back to the hospital, yeah?" she says.

"Yeah," I say. "Back to the hospital."

She doesn't say anything more as we get back into her car, or as she drives. So I grip my mom's sack of Mexican food and fill the silence with my thoughts, telling myself the story of what's happened today. I am a dutiful daughter and a good student. Ms. Holden is my mentor, my teacher. She's helping me.

I wake early, before the fog has lifted from the lawn outside, before even the birds are too noisy. It's the deepest I've slept since the accident. I don't remember any dreams. It must be the new, good news about Papa, soothing me to sleep. And the dinner with Ms. Holden. I think of the surfboard on her car, and the last thing she said. What would it be like for her to teach me even more?

When I go downstairs, I hear the low voices of the DJs on a classical radio station, and the hiss of the iron. Mama's laundered Papa's clothes, and she's ironing his work button-ups. She's washed his flip-flops and leaned them against the door to dry. It's like she's preparing for his return home.

"Did you sleep?" she asks me.

I nod. "Did you, Ma?"

The barest smile crosses her face, and she nods. She picks up Papa's dark green shirt to examine by its shoulders. I hang the shirt on a hanger and take it upstairs to their closet.

Later she goes upstairs to Skype with Kuya Jun. She doesn't make me say hi to him. She just updates Jun on Papa. I can't hear all the words, but I think I hear a new lightness and relief in his voice.

We stop to pick up doughnuts. A cake doughnut with pink frosting and sprinkles for me, a long chocolate log for my mom, and a plain glazed for Papa. We eat ours at the side of Papa's hospital bed. We look at the beeping monitor, waiting for more of the hopeful reactions the doctors talked about.

Nurse Emilia, fifteen years older and four inches taller than my mom, stops in to say hi, and to check the pressure of Papa's bed. "Magandang umaga, sir," she calls to him.

Nurse Emilia lifts Papa's legs, massages his feet, and rotates his ankles gently. "Pressure okay, sir?" she calls.

My mom waits, looking Papa's way. She inhales and exhales, like she's adjusting her hope with each breath.

"Emilia," she says, "Gutom ka na ba?" She offers the plain glazed doughnut to Nurse Emilia.

"I can't take your breakfast, po!" Emilia says. She looks with warm eyes at Papa. During our first days here, we discovered they'd grown up not far from each other, back in the Philippines.

"You know he will go from VCS to MCS," Nurse Emilia says. "From vegetative to minimally conscious."

We don't respond. Nurse Emilia smiles.

"In time," she says to us. "He'll take his own breakfast."

* * *

85

Around noon, my Nokia buzzes. It usually only buzzes with texts from my mom.

How are things today, kid?

I grip the phone like it's a precious discovery, not the battered, secondhand thing Papa found at a garage sale.

Sorry, this is Ms. Holden. Got this number from your file!

I type back.

Hi!

Then I delete the exclamation point.

Hi—kinda same.

:-/ Need company again?

I look at my mom. She's on her laptop. In the intervals between typing, when she just needs to read or scroll, she reaches out to touch Papa's hand. His monitors beep, unchanging in their rhythm. I look at my backpack, filled with Easter break school-work from other classes.

Yeah, I type.

I can stop by whenever :) Just let me know.

I gauge what to tell Ma. Something in me hesitates to tell her I'll be going out with Ms. Holden again.

"Ma, I think I'll go to the library. Is that okay?"

She peers up at me. "What will you do there?"

"Just, look up stuff," I say. "For projects due when I get back."

"Very far," she says. "You want me to take you?"

I tell her there's a bus stop right outside, and it goes back and forth from the library; I won't even need to transfer. And I know she'll worry if I'll eat, so I say I'll just grab something from the counter at the grocery store.

She nods, straightens, and yawns. "Maybe I'll take a walk also," she says. "Nurse Emilia says there's a nice garden on the roof." She rolls her shoulders to stretch them. "Remember we have Mass at five," she says. "Holy Saturday."

I nod. "I know, Ma."

I walk fast to the end of the hospital driveway so no one will see her pick me up at the lobby. The wait feels like forever, and then I see it: the scratched gray Civic with a surfboard on top. It's a different board this time, made of old yellow foam.

"Magandang tanghali, Cory," Ms. Holden says. "Ready to learn?"

I get in.

Most playgrounds in town have been renovated, the sand replaced with rubber mats for safety. But we're at a playground near my neighborhood, one with blue slides and metal monkey bars, and the city hasn't offered this part of town the budget for a playground renovation yet.

We choose a spot of sand away from where a few little kids are playing. Ms. Holden sets the yellow surfboard down with a soft thump, fin up.

"This board is really long," I say.

"It is, in fact, called a longboard, Cory." Ms. Holden grins. "Now, before you get anywhere near the water, this is the most fundamental ability you need."

Ms. Holden drops to her stomach, her palms down on the board, her shoulders slightly up. Then, with one fluid motion, she's back on her feet, easy, knees bent low.

She talks some instructions at me, and I hear a few. But I've never learned from Ms. Holden in this way—watching her whole body move with pure, practiced, physical instinct. In our one-on-one sessions in the broom-closet office, or when she was driving, I'd always focus on a part of her—the swaying of her tree tattoo as she turned pages, the subtle wrinkles in the skin around her mouth when she was thinking through how to answer me. But I didn't know until now: those moments were like seeing droplets instead of the whole wave.

I love watching her move on her surfboard, and the sight of her now is the ocean knocking me down. I want to move like that with her.

"Now you," Ms. Holden says.

I slip off my sneakers, and then I'm on my own stomach, on her surfboard, my hands flat, preparing to press myself up. I can feel the scratches and smell the wax and salt on this board, once white, burned brown and yellow with use and salt water and sun, this platform Ms. Holden gives her whole body to every day. The thought bursts across my mind: I want to be Ms. Holden's surfboard!

I know how freaky that would sound if I said it out loud. So of course I don't.

Is it obvious, though? Is that why I'm so awkward getting up? I have nothing of Ms. Holden's grace and quickness. My legs tangle, and I land on my knees first instead of my feet.

"No, not just with your hands and wrists," she says. "You have to power from your shoulders and core too. Come on, I'm almost a decade older than you! You've got your youth, use it!"

"Don't I get, like, a permission slip to fail the first few times?" I ask.

"Yes, that's why we're not in the water. Your permission slip is sand."

I stand. "Show me again?"

She smiles and takes off her black cardigan, revealing her bare shoulders under her white tank top. She's even faster this time, powering down, then up, crouched. I can see the muscles ripple around her arms and shoulders. Her legs are so sure, her feet so stable.

"Again," she says.

I take off my own sweatshirt, and my socks. It's hard, getting down flat and then getting up, remembering all the details of where and how to be. I get sweaty and frustrated.

But something happens as I practice. I don't forget about my dad's injuries or my mom's fear. There's no way I can forget it. It feels like a sprain I'm walking on, and I have to be careful because the pain of it is always ready to shock me.

But. Now, practicing on Ms. Holden's surfboard, it's like I remember that my body works. I remember that I contain feelings other than worry and shock and pain. Is it too soon for me to be feeling that kind of relief? For me to be grateful for liking Ms. Holden, instead of afraid of it? For me to be having fun during a first surfing lesson?

After ten or so times, I press up, back foot down first, and rise, my knees still bent.

"Yes!" Ms. Holden claps once. "There it is. Did you feel the difference?"

I grin. I do feel the difference. I feel the stiffness in my face and realize I don't remember the last time I grinned that big.

My mom texts as Ms. Holden is putting her surfboard back on her car rack.

Papa d same. Tita Baby here. Mass 5pm St. Blaise. Come back to d hospital 430. I'll fetch u if bus is late

"Where to next, Tagubio?" Ms. Holden asks.

I think of my aunt and my mom and the hospital and Mass. I think of how I feel with Ms. Holden. Duty and desire go to war in my throat.

"Just back to the hospital by four thirty," I mumble. "We have 5 p.m. Mass. For Holy Saturday. With my aunt."

"You sound enthusiastic. You guys close with your aunt?"

We get into the car. I think of what to tell Ms. Holden. My mind travels over some scenes. How my dad would mimic Tita Baby's hand gestures and hugging behind her back, making us laugh. How Tita Baby always seemed to want to help, but it also seemed mean, like she always wanted to remind us of her money and her superior station. How at times I can see something in Tita Baby, a feeling like fear, always the youngest kid wanting to be on top of her smarter older sister.

"I think my aunt just kind of judges us?" I say. "For a bunch of reasons."

"Hm. Family crisis can intensify that kind of tension," she says. "I mean, whole empires have been compromised by family fights."

"The Guise family." I remember a flash card. "They espoused reactionary Catholicism, linked to the French monarchy during the wars of religion."

"Correct," Ms. Holden says.

She doesn't drive right away. I wait in the stillness.

"Curious about your history," she says.

"What?"

"You have a history," she says.

"I'm, like, seventeen."

I think of the sequence of my seventeen years. Uneventful until this year. Born, same townhome all my life, Catholic schools all my life. My aunt and uncle. My parents. Somewhere in the Philippines, my half brother.

"Hm. I should ask you a more focused research question," Ms. Holden says. "What was it like growing up with parents from another country? I don't know what that's like."

My mom, the computer programmer, the accountant. My dad, the handyman, landscaper, household repairman, mechanic.

I tell Ms. Holden what I know. That my mom learned to be a computer programmer at college in Manila. Her younger sister met this blond, American, resort CEO in Manila when he was on vacation there, married him, moved to California, and had my cousin Jerome, Bea's older brother. My mom went to the wedding on a tourist visa, then stayed for a programming job. Her sister was able to petition her for citizenship.

"My dad doesn't talk about growing up very much," I say. "Just little stories here and there."

I tell her how he used to be a street vendor. He didn't have a dad around. His brother got sick as an alcoholic and pretty much disappeared. I tell her about Papa's silence when his own mom died.

"But really, I think his mom was pretty mean to him?" I say, remembering his pained, held-in face back then. "He talked a few times about how she wouldn't, like, feed him sometimes, when she was mad. Which was a lot of the time."

I stop, thinking of all the versions of my dad before he was my dad. Always short and skinny, until he could afford to eat whatever he wanted, and then he got proudly muscly and bulky. An eighteen-year-old merchant seaman who docked in Long Beach after years on fishing boats, working odd jobs in Oxnard. A twenty-five-year-old meeting my mom in an office building. And then having me.

He was always gentle with me and my mom, even though no one was gentle to him when he was growing up.

I'd never really thought of that, how much it must have taken for him not to give in to anger.

I get so angry that he's still not awake.

I blink, feeling hot water begin in my eyes again. I breathe in.

Ms. Holden goes into her glove compartment to hand me a

small packet of tissues. I blow my nose into one.

"When my brother died, I was wild," she says. "Cutting classes, coming home drunk in the afternoon. My dad threw up his hands and thought we'd be lucky if I graduated high school."

I sniff. "So you rebelled by getting a PhD?"

She laughs low. "I'm ABD, remember."

"All . . . but dissertation."

"All but," she says. "That's what I am. All but."

I can sense her frustration. I remember her power on her surfboard, her ease with languages, everything about history she's teaching me. How she made my mom laugh even in the middle of our sorrow and fear.

You're not "all but," I want to say. You're everything, *and*.

"You'll get there!" I say, as if that's enough to hold her. "You'll be a doctor soon."

"Hey, I don't deserve reassurance, Tagubio. You do. Anything else I can do for you? Before going back to the hospital?"

I should want to rejoin my family at the ICU. I should want the duty of church after. That haloed, saint-like version of me, always hovering just beyond me, would rush back to my mom and dad and aunt.

But there's only fear and waiting there. Here I feel better. Here with Ms. Holden, my world feels warm, and small, like no injury or uncertainty could enter it, and I don't want to move. I don't want to answer my phone when it rings, and rings, and rings.

"I think you better get that," Ms. Holden says in teacherly tones.

So I do answer, even though I want to throw my phone—and any other interruption—away.

"Is this the daughter of Rommel Tagubio?"

It's a man with a Filipino accent. I have no idea who this is—some uncle? Do I call him Tito?

"Yes, po," I say. He sounds older, so maybe he deserves respect.

"I've been unable to reach your home line or the line of his wife," he says. "For many weeks now."

"You mean my mom, po?"

I'm so slow. I should have realized he was an asshole bill collector before I said that. I should hang up. Ms. Holden frowns a questioning frown. I glance away, embarrassed.

"How did you get my number?"

"Believe me, dear, I don't appreciate doing this," he says, and I hate this man for calling me "dear." "But the roofing for the Potrera house must be completed for the tenants. Your father did not finish the work. Therefore he must return the money. It's simple math, no?"

I remember my dad leaving In-N-Out to deal with this man. His sprained ankle. How my mom tried to argue him into rest. He would always smile off any pain, refusing to miss a day of work.

"My father's in the hospital—"

"I understand that, dear. But we are adults here, no? His company has, kuwan, certain obligations. Or did I make the mistake of hiring a landscaping and repair company with no proper license or insurance or budget? I'm sure some, kuwan, regulatory officials, would be interested to know that."

I hang up.

"I have a feeling that wasn't your mom," Ms. Holden says.

I strike my phone against the soft part of the passenger seat three times. I'm so angry, but I know I shouldn't damage this little brick of a phone—I don't know when we'll be able to afford another one.

The phone buzzes again. In one gentle, firm motion, Ms. Holden interlaces her fingers with mine, briefly, and takes the phone from me.

"This is Jennifer Gonzalez, an attorney with Gonzalez LLC. I'm representing the Tagubio family. Please identify yourself."

Her whole face is deadly serious. But she winks the barest, familiar wink at me. I feel a flood of gratitude that even in a moment like this, Ms. Holden can make it feel like play, like something a little fun, a shared conspiracy for just the two of us. Then, as she spends a few moments listening, I see her get angrier and more stern than I've ever seen her in class.

"Sir, let me repeat back to you the series of decisions you have made. The proprietor of a landscaping company you hired for its under-market rates suffered a grave, life-threatening injury at the unsecured site of a foreclosed home you purchased. Weeks later, you are harassing the man's daughter, a minor, for payment of a deposit that is likely a pittance compared to your overall income as a landlord."

I hear the man's voice rise. Ms. Holden keeps hers steady and hard. "You will cease and desist your harassment of this family immediately, or we will be filing suit against you. Communicate by certified mail through your own attorney from now on."

I can hear the man yelling until Ms. Holden hangs up and hands the phone back to me.

"Jennifer Gonzalez?" I ask.

"She's a real law student and paralegal," she says. "My ex's career decisions are slightly more lucrative than mine. I can enlist her to help if we really need it."

I get dizzy with this revelation. I look, again, at the tiny rainbow dangling from her car keychain.

"Is it okay that I told you that, Tagubio?"

"Yeah!" I rush to say. "Of course."

She smiles. "Good."

Then I feel a stab of jealousy and worry.

"She'll help you even though she's your ex?" I ask.

She laughs. "Women have a way of staying friends after break-ups." She puts her seat belt on and puts her hand to her keys in the ignition. She looks at me. "Any other questions?"

I want to ask everything. But my phone rings again. It's the guy again, wanting his money. I turn my phone off.

"Again? God dammit," Ms. Holden says. I've never heard her swear before. I'm startled at her anger before I realize she's angry for me, on my behalf.

Then I realize I'm angry for me too.

I don't know what to do with all my anger. It feels heavy and hot and I don't know where to throw it.

Then the place flashes across my mind. The place I've been avoiding for weeks.

It summons me then. I know I have to go there.

"Can we stop somewhere first?" I ask.

Ms. Holden cruises, slow, down Potrera Street, until I find it.

The house is all tan and white, casting long shadows on the asphalt in the afternoon light.

There are two garages to store an owner's hypothetical four cars. A lawn the quarter of a football field, the grass gone brown. Two white columns near the front door, which is ornate, carved glass and fake dark wood with brass handles. There might be three stories to this house.

The whole design looks cheap and repetitive and predictable to me. But I know my parents would prefer this over our own small townhome.

My parents always seem apologetic about our own home—how we don't have a guest bedroom, how we share a wall with the neighbors. When I was in elementary school, my parents always offered to have my birthday parties somewhere else. The community park or the beach. But I like how cozy our home is. Was.

I walk up the long, gray cement driveway, to one of the garages. There's still a ladder leaning against it. I see piles of roof tiles, red, Spanish-style, on the sidewalk and on the highest part of the roof. I see a scattering of broken tiles. I see the dark brown spots on the concrete.

"That must've been where," I say.

My voice sounds like cement, if cement could talk. A slab of words.

Ms. Holden doesn't say anything. She walks up just behind me.

"When they first bought our townhome my parents didn't have any money left for food," I say. "So they ate a plant growing on the side of the house. Sautéed. With rice. Sometimes soy sauce for flavor. Or ketchup."

My parents always laughed when they told me that story. Ms. Holden doesn't laugh. I feel her hand rest on my shoulder.

Usually I would love that. My whole world would stop to accept her affection. But right now I feel far from her and everyone.

I break away and pick up some broken tiles. I throw them. I throw the tiles and throw the tiles. A few shatter against the stucco of the house. One hits the aluminum garage door with a loud, tinny smack. I pick up another tile, and I aim it at the front doors. I want the cheap, stupid glass to explode.

A warm force stops me. Ms. Holden grips both my upper arms and pulls my back against her. She holds me there. Her mouth moves against my right ear.

"You don't have to," she whispers. "You don't have to. Let go, Cory. Let it go."

I feel tight and tense, ready to fight. Then I listen. I do let go.

I drop the last tile to the ground. I can't slow my breathing. I've been shaking without realizing. I grow still. I let my body's breathing feel Ms. Holden's breathing. She presses a hand flat against my collarbone and inhales slowly, teaching me. I breathe along with her. Something in her slowness, in the way she's holding me, tells me she's waiting for me.

I think, I don't know how to do this. But I do know how.

I turn my head right, feeling where her mouth was pressed against my ear. She moves her voice slowly to my neck. She speaks against my skin there, mouthing something without words. It's like prayer. Another way of speaking to something bigger than us. When I turn all the way around to face her, it doesn't feel like the first time. It feels like we've been doing this all along.

With the Morality class handouts on marriage, with my class-mates talking about boys—it was all trying to pull me into a weird, unfamiliar place, somewhere I was supposed to belong but never would.

Here, even though my eyes are closed, I feel like I know this place. I feel like I've landed where I should be. When my mouth meets hers, I feel at home.

We kiss. She puts her right hand to my right cheek. I worry for a moment she'll push me away. She moves her lips against mine, soft. I part my teeth, and my tongue finds her tongue. We find a rhythm. It's warmer than I thought warm could be. I trace the side of her neck with my fingertips, then touch down her forearm where I know her tattoo is. I feel her shiver. I never thought I could make someone shiver. I'm shivering too.

She stops our kiss and presses her forehead to mine. I open my eyes. She's looking down, some fear and hesitance mixed in with something else. A want I'm sure matches my own.

She nods. And I move forward just as she does, and we kiss

again. We speak against each other without words, answering questions we never asked aloud.

We lean against her car. It's like we're following some choreography I didn't know we rehearsed before. Her fingers lace with mine, and it's not taking me very long to learn different ways to kiss—every time I close my lips around her lower lip, she sighs halfway to a moan. She grips the hair just above my neck and somehow I know to kiss below her left ear—I smell that salt-and-mint smell that's hers and only hers. She lifts her head and turns my own face aside so she can kiss my throat, and a new kind of want erupts in me; I can hear my own moan and I'm almost embarrassed, but then she brushes the skin of my neck and I'm not embarrassed—I'm sure she feels what I feel. My body is doing what I'm meant to do. Our bodies are meeting the way we should. She runs her hands under my shirt, along my bare lower back and stomach. Her palms are rougher than I thought they'd be, from all her rising and descending on her surfboard, but her touch is soft, and I shake. She pauses, feeling me shake.

There's the hum of an approaching car.

We stop, frozen.

I see her face change. As if she's remembering just now where we are and who we are to each other and what we're doing. She crouches down on the sidewalk behind the car, and I crouch down with her.

I start to crane my head, but she holds the front of my shirt, stopping me.

I can see the rapid pulse in her neck, every nervous heartbeat like footsteps running into a future I can't see yet.

The car slows, then speeds and passes and disappears. We're alone again.

"Shit," she whispers. She stands and wipes sweat from her forehead.

I rise and look at her face. She doesn't look back at me. She looks past me.

I feel scared then. I try to think of something—a joke, maybe, to make this moment light. To make this a shared moment.

Instead I just stand there. She faces away from me.

She laces her fingers behind her head, like she's about to be arrested, and turns away.

She shows me her back.

All my hope, all my desire, my sense of belonging, flees me in that moment.

Here it is. Her turning away. The punishment and rejection I'm always waiting for.

I look from her back to the house. I leave the car and walk fast in the opposite direction, down the middle of the street. I don't know where I'm going. I just know I should be gone. I should quarantine myself. I'll contaminate anything I touch. I should start running.

Her footsteps pound behind me. She says my name. I do try to run but she's still faster and stronger than me. She turns me around to face her but I can't look in her eyes. I look away from her at the house, the black asphalt, the battered board on her car roof.

"Cory, don't feel bad. I—it's just—" She struggles. She pauses forever. She says, "We can't do that again."

I feel like the world is going to break apart. Like the ground is going to open up and I'm going to drop into something too deep for me to see or understand or imagine.

"Come on. I'll take you to the hospital. You can't walk from here. It's too far."

I still don't look at her. I'm still waiting to disappear.

"Corazon Tagubio," she says.

She touches the tops of my shoulders, searching my face with her eyes. I finally look at her. Her forehead and mouth have more wrinkles than I've ever seen. Her eyes are the color of deep brown wood, troubled and alive, filled with worry.

I decide her worry for me is real. It's a gift. She still cares about me. She still wants me around her.

"You said my name wrong," I say. "The pronunciation was weird."

She frowns. Then she slowly nods. "Yeah. Yeah, I could tell as soon as I tried to say it. Sorry."

I nod. She nods. We smile a little. We're both still shaky. She lets go of my shoulders. I wish she wouldn't, but I don't say so.

There's more traffic now, everyone out on a Saturday afternoon, maybe coming back from hikes or the beach or going to restaurants or filling the Oaks Mall. I wonder how many people will go to Mass for Holy Saturday like my family always does.

The sunlight is fading now, descending behind the dark foothills that look over the whole city like constant guards.

We don't say anything to each other. The silence feels like relief to me. Not as heavy as I thought it might feel.

But the closer we get to the hospital, the more I fill with worries and wants. I want to hold her hand. I want to listen to her say something wise to me. I want to tell her everything is okay, or will be okay. I want to say I didn't mean to freak her out; I didn't mean to go too far.

But more than that, I want to be back in the world we lived in together earlier today. When she was still just my teacher.

That's not really true.

I want all the moments before she turned away from me.

I want to kiss her again.

I want her to kiss me again.

The oak trees are as tall as always; the cars and bungalows all the same. But our kiss has refocused my world. Our kiss will define my history.

But I don't want to think of history. I don't want the past or the future or how I'll tell the story of it.

I just want to keep her.

She enters the hospital parking lot, and with every inch the car moves, I can feel the end of something coming nearer. I think she can too. She circles to the highest level of the parking lot, where there are no other cars. She parks in its farthest corner, near the hospital's prayer garden. She turns off her engine.

I can see the orange backlit squares of house windows below, black shadows where more trimmed trees cluster, the endless lines of cars pausing in Saturday traffic.

I wait for her to speak. I look from her radio to her keychain to her hands. I can feel her turn to face me. Then I can feel her hand, tucking my hair behind my ear.

"I'm sorry," she says.

"It's not your fault," I say, my voice heavy again.

I feel her shake her head. I hear the jingle of her keys shifting from her ignition to her lap. She doesn't believe me. I can feel her drowning in disgust with herself and I want to take her shame away somehow.

"You should go to your mom," she says. "You might be late for Mass."

She unlocks her car doors with an automatic click.

And sadness stabs me harder than I ever thought it could. I know after I leave her car, she won't visit us again. And when I get back to school, she won't be tutoring me about rebels against Church teachings.

I'll be alone at school, alone to face whatever happens with my dad, helpless to stop my mom from worrying, alone with how different and alone I am.

I can feel how empty the future is without her, and I don't want it. I don't want that future.

I face her then and reach to hold her cheek myself. How do I know to do that?

I'm worried she'll push me away. But she closes her eyes and leans her face against my palm. She blinks and I see my own sadness, reflected.

So I kiss her.

Every time I kiss her I learn something else. She's still teaching me.

I didn't know, before I learned from her, that a kiss could be more than a kiss. A kiss could be a question. Or a plea. And this kiss—a soft, slowly moving bridge between us, sharing tongue and lips, our hands on each other's necks, feeling each other's pulses, is all that. Don't leave me, my kiss tries to tell her. Please stay. Thank you for all you are to me. Please stay. Please.

I don't know how long the kiss goes on. I don't want to stop kissing her. I don't want the changes that will come once our kiss is over. I don't think she wants them either. We only stop when my car door opens, and I feel a different hand grip my arm, and somehow I know who it is before I see her—my mom.

It's a furious, awkward tangle with the seat belt but my mom unbuckles me and seizes my right arm with a strength I never knew she had, pulling me up and out of the car. I trip. I feel my heartbeat explode—I think I'm going to faint. I gasp, I stumble, my phone falls, clattering against the pavement, my mom picks it up without ever losing her grip on me and muscles me away from the car.

My mom moves so fast there's no time for any questions—Why isn't she saying anything? Where did my ability to form words go? Is Ms. Holden okay? Ms. Holden—

My mom pulls and then shoves me away from any questions. It's deadly silent except for her footsteps on the cement—hers fast and sure, mine shuffling, dragging, as if I've forgotten how to walk. I try turning my head to look back but my mom shakes me, forcing me to face forward and keep moving, seizing my shoulders and turning me whenever I seem to hesitate, like an unstoppable, mom-shaped wave pushing me back onto a shore I don't want to be on. We take the stinking parking garage stairs down two levels, reach my mom's old Corolla, and then she pulls open the metal door and finally lets go of my arm to shove me in, slamming the door shut, almost on my arm, and the motion, the brute force, is nearly enough, but not quite, to distract me from the fact that the world, as I know it, is truly over, has just exploded into nothing, has just been swept away by a flood, and then before my mom turns the engine on, I hear screeching tires and glimpse the surfboard on the roof of the car speeding away, and I lower my head to rest between my knees and I squeeze my eyes shut, hoping just the pressure of me closing my eyes and silently screaming inside will be enough for me to explode into nothing too.

AFTER THE END OF THE WORLD

This is one of those moments when I should be saying prayers. When I should be pleading with every saint, angel, statue, deity, being, ghost, spirit to please help me. Please intervene. Don't make me live these next moments alone. Take me away.

I should tell my mom to turn around so we can go to Mass like she planned. Should I ask for a priest? For confession? Would that make my mom calm down? I can't find my voice to ask.

I can't ask my mom for anything right now. Maybe not ever again.

I keep my gaze straight ahead. I don't look at my mom but I can sense her while she drives. I can sense all the reprimand in her silence. I feel condemned.

I remember that phrase—those who don't study history are doomed to repeat it, or something. But what if there's nothing about you in the history you study? What if what you've done is so off-the-charts bad, nothing you studied could have warned you or prepared you to avoid it?

I feel like jumping out of the car. I consider it. I consider leaping out the passenger side door to the road while the car is at its fastest. Taking all the injuries I deserve.

Ms. Holden hated that phrase anyway. "You can study history and still repeat plenty of bad stuff," she says in her broom-closet office. "Every step forward is a choice, informed or not."

"That's . . . cynical," I said, and it made her smile.

"You can be your own kind of historian when the time comes," she said then. "You can be the rare optimist."

Whenever I thought of Ms. Holden before our kiss, I would always feel better. I would feel like there was something to look forward to every day.

All I feel now, after our kiss, is a sharpness that makes it hard to breathe. A sharpness that adds to the pain of my dad in the hospital.

My dad. Could my dad see what was happening?

Was he somewhere in limbo? In the spirit realm? Somewhere between life and death, where he could see everything happening with the family?

No one speaks to me. No one answers.

"Come inside, Cory."

I didn't even notice she'd parked in front of our townhome. I don't know why my mom's voice is so calm. I don't move. I don't look at her. If it were my dad here, if it were both my parents here, what would I say or do? What would he say?

She opens her own car door and walks around to open mine.

"Cory, hali ka na. Come. Come now."

Her tone is still so gentle. I wait for her rage.

But her anger doesn't seem present. My mom just waits.

I move slow. One foot to the curb. Then the other.

APRIL 12, 2009
EASTER SUNDAY

3:12 A.M.

I can't sleep. I'm waiting for my mom's anger to break open my bedroom door.

I sit at the edge of my bed. I pace. I go to my desk and scribble notes.

I think of what I would text to Ms. Holden if I only had her phone number, and my phone. My mom hasn't given me back my phone. She probably never will.

I hold still in the moments when I hear my mom moving around her room, then up and down the stairs. I hear typing. Her door opening and closing. Rustling in my parents' shared closet.

5:14 A.M.

The dark turns dark blue.

I've never been in anything approaching this much trouble.

The worst was when I was around twelve. I was playing with a group of kids in Rika's rich-kid neighborhood, and Rika decided we'd cover a neighbor's tree with toilet paper. We thought it was hilarious. The neighbor called the police. When the officers got there—I remember them as ten feet tall—Rika and the other girls cried and said it was my idea. The other parents looked at me like I was a little demon.

Why did I accept her study session invitation just a few weeks ago? God.

My parents came to pick me up and my dad nodded and nodded at the police, saying sorry in as many ways as he could. When we got home I could hear my parents debating about what to do with me. I ended up grounded for a week, with no TV or desserts.

There are no voices from my parents' room now.

I'm making my mom go through something extra hard. Alone, without the one person who could talk her through it.

I miss Ms. Holden so much already. I want to know what she's thinking.

The car crash of my thoughts makes me so sick, I go to the bathroom and get on my knees in front of the toilet.

Nothing comes up.

I cross the hallway back to my room. My thoughts follow me.

Kissing Ms. Holden the first time—that felt like destiny, like something foretold, preordained. If we had stopped there, maybe we could have gone back to some kind of normal.

The second kiss, in the parking lot—that kiss I stole. That

kiss—a begging kiss—that was my fault.

I remember her telling me there's no grand design of fault in the world. That I shouldn't blame myself when something terrible happens.

The phrases from Morality class cut at me. *Intrinsically disordered. Contrary to Natural Law.*

I never understood those words like I do now.

Is there a patron saint who intercedes on behalf of Those Who Get Caught by Their Mom While Making Out with Their History Teacher?

If there is, I'm pretty sure that saint ended her human life burned at the stake. Cut in half. Thrown off a cliff. Tortured into the afterlife.

I keep seeing her turning away, showing me her back.

I keep seeing her car speeding away.

I write, like that might change something.

Don't, I scribble in my notebook. *Please.*

I tear up the page. I rest my forehead against my desk.

8:00 A.M.

I hear gentle knuckles rapping against my doorframe. I blink my eyes open. How did I sleep?

"Why do you still have your clothes on? Why not your pambahay?" my mom asks. I stay silent. I've spent all night braced for something bigger than scolding about no pajamas.

"Shower," she says, "we'll go spend the day with your papa before Easter Mass."

I imagine our other Sundays: Mass together, walking the beach, window shopping at the mall, watching basketball at Tita Baby's house.

Before I close the bathroom door, I hear the familiar ringtone of the computer calling Kuya Jun. The shower drowns out their conversation.

I jerk the temperature away from hot, hoping to cleanse myself of yesterday with a roar of cold.

I stand near Papa's bed. I'm too tense to sit again, like on his first day in the hospital.

I don't know what my mom will say today. If she'll report to him what she saw.

She starts talking right away, chatty and conversational as always. She tells him our plans for today. That Bea has another modeling job next week in Manila, so she and Tita Baby will be taking Jun's boxes with them.

She asks Papa if there's anything else we should send Jun. Then she falls silent.

I wonder if her silence is a test. If I should tell him. If she's expecting me to have the courage of my own confession.

"Tell your papa happy Easter," my mom says.

"Happy Easter, Tatay," I say, formal, stiff.

"Maybe you can rise for us today," Mama says, and kisses his thumb.

* * *

My aunt and uncle and cousins text that they're here. I don't wait for my mom to tell me what to do. I leave my dad's room alone to greet them.

I look for her. I can't help it. I want her to be there, waiting with her black binders.

Instead it's Tita Baby, Uncle Dan, Bea, and Jerome, home for spring break from Stanford. They carry plastic boxes filled with pork adobo and rice.

Jerome is the tall, muscle-bound, lacrosse-playing version of Bea, with huge dark eyes; high, sharp cheekbones; and dimples Bea doesn't have.

"Hey, Cory," he says, and pats my shoulder.

"Jerome, go greet Tito Rom. Bea, you also," Tita Baby says.

My cousins follow me into the quiet of my dad's room, where my mom sits beside him. I can feel their healthiness, their wholesomeness, the ideal teenagers they represent; their superiority stalks me so much worse today.

Bea stays standing. Jerome kisses my mom on both cheeks, then sits near my dad and says, "Hey, Tito," too loud. "How'd you end up all messed up! You get into a fight? How's the other guy?"

"Dude," Bea says to her brother, and Jerome grins, uncertain. My mom touches Jerome's shoulder and says, quieter, to Papa, "Oh, Rom, tell your pamangkin about your fight."

I don't like the contrast: Jerome's sporty strength, Bea's confident beauty, bathed with my mom's approval, next to my silent dad in the hospital bed.

It reminds me how Jerome and my dad would always greet each other, before the accident: with hearty handclaps and jokes about getting in trouble with girlfriends and basketball team stats.

It's been weeks, and I don't hate my dad's silence any less.

I have no idea what he would say, or do, about yesterday.

What would my cousins say if they knew? My aunt and uncle?

"He looks like he has more color," Bea says. "In his face."

I get annoyed, because I think Bea's lying. But my mom agrees, "Oo nga," and strokes the edge of Papa's hairline.

My cousins go back out to the lobby, leaving me and Ma alone with Papa.

"You stay with your papa," my mom says abruptly, rising with her purse. "I'll go with your tita for a while."

"For what? Why can't I go—" I start. She's never left me alone with Papa before. I've always had her voice to carry the room. I still don't know how to be alone with him this way.

Ma's eyes blaze at me, warning me, and I feel it—a hint of what she wants to do with me, under all her pretending normalcy.

"Stay with your papa," she says, her voice gentler than her eyes, and she leaves.

I sit at the foot of his bed. I move to my mom's usual chair next to his head. It feels weird to sit there. I stand again.

"Bea and Jerome look good," I say. "I'm sorry I'm not—"

My throat shuts. I can't go on.

The last time I felt like myself, like I was okay, was with her.

Will I ever see her again? Will I ever have that sense of belonging again?

What will Ma do with me?

Papa hated it when I cried. He'd try anything to soothe me. But now, not even the beeping of his heart rate changes.

4:00 P.M.

Any other Easter Sunday, I'd wear pants and a button-down polo as a kind of silent rebellion. And I'd wince away from any makeup.

But this afternoon I put on the dress my mom gave me. It's strapless and form-fitting green velvet, something from the clearance rack at Ross. I put on my blue uniform cardigan and strappy white leather sandals I know my mom would approve of.

My mom comes in wearing her own dark green dress and white flats. She carries a makeup bag.

"The sweater is very dark," she says. She digs through my closet and hands me a pink sweater instead, something I never wear. "Springtime colors are better for Easter. Here. Sit."

I sit on the edge of my bed. She opens her makeup bag and shows me how to open my mouth and pucker for lipstick. She gets out her eyeliner pencil. I half expect her to stab me with it, but I stay still.

"You look too tired," she says. "Let's make your eyes wake up."

I look for something she's about to tell me, in the focus on her face, but she's just looking at my eyes to make sure the makeup works.

She smudges stray lipstick away with her thumb. "Ayan," she says, approving.

Maybe what I did is so bad, it's gone beyond the realm of parental penalty. Maybe my penance is to just stew alone in my wrongness.

5:00 P.M.

We stand in the back hallway the whole long Mass, near the old baptismal font, since the twice-a-year Catholics had already filled all the pews before Mass started.

Most of them leave early, before Communion, but Ma stays and so do I. I don't line up to get the Eucharist, or a blessing. My mom doesn't ask why.

I glimpse some classmates and I look down at my sandals to avoid saying hi. My mom gets a lot of hugs from the other Filipinos. They touch my arm and say nice things to me too. I look down, playing the part of worried child, hiding the truth of what else is troubling us—the trouble and burden I added.

When we get outside to the parking lot I see an older gray Civic. I think about jumping in and asking her to drive away.

But there's no surf rack on top. And even though she never actually told me if she went to Mass or not, I don't think she would come to this Easter Mass. She knows it's the church most students and their families go to, including me and mine.

6:00 P.M.

On Easter Sundays, my mom used to make ham at home, and my

dad would invite other Filipinos and younger guys he'd hire when he could afford to pay a crew. He'd joke between Spanish and English and Tagalog and put on the rerun of a basketball game. He'd give me a chocolate bunny and pretend to be horrified at the bunny's new deafness when I ate the ears first.

This year Tita Baby and Uncle Dan and Bea and Jerome bring us roast pork and rice and small chocolate eggs in foil. We eat in the waiting room of the ICU, though I can't eat much, just enough so my mom doesn't scold me. I leave the chocolates in their wrappers.

I think I feel Papa grip my hand back for a bare second. But I'm probably dreaming it.

His eyes move underneath his closed lids.

I wonder where he is. I wonder what he sees.

8:00 P.M.

I sit at my desk again, staring at my notebook.

I open a blank page. I pick up a pen.

I want to draw her back when she turned away from me. I want to draw her hands tangled together behind her head.

Maybe if I draw it, the memory will stop tormenting me. I'll exorcise it.

My hand shakes too much.

It's just jagged-ink nothing.

I rip this page up too. I rest my forehead on my desk again.

10:00 P.M.

"Wake up, anak. Come downstairs."

This isn't the usual voice that wakes me. Tita Baby stands gazing at me from the doorway. She still wears her Easter outfit, a light green skirt suit.

There's something weird about her, just standing there looking at me.

I realize it's because she's silent. She's not asking why I fell asleep at my desk, in my dress, or why I'm sleeping the day away and not spending time with my mom. She's being gentle and careful and quiet.

This alarms me. For the first time in my life, I want my aunt to be as chatty as she usually is.

Did my mom tell her?

The possibility of Tita Baby knowing what my mom saw, knowing any hint of what went on—it's all a new knife in me.

I follow Tita Baby downstairs, still in my dress. I immediately wish I'd changed my clothes.

My mom is still in her Easter outfit too, with her shoes off. She's preparing to tape shut our two huge cardboard boxes. The masking tape makes a sharp screech I've never liked. My dad used to hold the bulging boxes shut for this ritual.

"Cory," my mom says, and I know to go to her and push the open flaps down flat and closed. She presses the stripe of tape down with her usual precision. She pulls out a fat black permanent marker from the ninety-nine-cent store and uncaps it, filling our nostrils with the chemical ink smell I strangely do like. She scratches an address in the Philippines on the tops and sides of the boxes. Then she adds my name.

"Tito Dan and Jerome will help you carry these to the airport," she says. "We'll check it under your name. You'll carry your clothes, since you'll have no more baggage allowance."

I'm so slow. "My name? What are you talking about?"

Now the blaze returns to my mom's eyes.

I grit my teeth against the rest of my questions, so I don't make her angrier. What is she talking about? Was she even talking to me? What did she mean, "baggage allowance"? Whose baggage? Who was going where?

I see an old duffel bag: navy blue, fuzzy and faded in parts, gaping empty on the floor next to the boxes. It smells like white vinegar. My mom wiped it down, I realize. Many years ago it was my dad's bag. He brought it here from Manila.

"You'll go with Bea and Tita Baby and stay there for two months. After, we'll see."

"Stay where?" I manage.

"In Quezon City. With your kuya Jun."

She says it like we're going to a new restaurant since we have a coupon, or we're going to a different church for Sunday, or going to the outlet malls.

"It's summer vacation in the Philippines na," she says, "so Kuya Jun has time to spend with you. No classes for him. Summer for students is April through June, back home."

"That's funny," I say. "Good prank, Ma."

Her eyes flash more anger, and then she looks away from me. She turns the box around once, to check that it's properly sealed.

120

My fear rises into my mouth, metallic and gross tasting. I swallow it back.

"It is. It's funny. Too bad I don't have a passport," I say.

My mom points with her chin to our kitchen table, then keeps fussing, or pretending to fuss, with the boxes.

Tita Baby finally finds her voice again.

"It's here, Cory," she says. "Your passport picture is very nice, did your mom put makeup on you that day? Like today. You look so nice today for Easter."

That's more compliments than she's ever given me. Tita Baby picks up two passports to show me. There's a dark blue American passport. The other passport is dark red. I have the same photo in both.

I forgot these passports existed. I've never left the country before, not even to go to Mexico for the school's volunteer weekend trips to build houses near Tijuana.

Then I remember the day we got my Philippines passport.

It was a couple of years ago, right before I started high school at Saint Agatha's. My mom said we would go to the Philippine embassy in LA on a Saturday morning, to renew their passports and apply for mine. I wondered if I would get in trouble for having two passports, but my mom said it was allowed, and my dad was quiet.

I expected the embassy to be a fancy building or diplomat's mansion, but it was a crowded old set of offices with Filipinos and occasional old white guys with their (always younger) Filipina girlfriends. A couple of TVs played Filipino game shows over everyone's heads. We sat in hard, once-white plastic chairs, waiting for what felt like days. I got bored and bratty but my parents ignored me, watching the shows.

When they finally called my number, an immigration agent in his midforties took my photograph and asked if I spoke Tagalog. I was shy and didn't respond, so he muttered something about FilAms always being so rude. I said I understood. The agent laughed at me, and then we were done.

My parents went to the Filipino grocery store nearby, where they stocked up on vinegar and rice and dried fish and I got my favorite—a dark purple ube milkshake.

I never saw my Philippine passport after that. When Tita Baby holds it out to me now, I don't take it.

Instead I turn to my mom and pepper her with more questions. Like my questions will change something. I ask and ask.

Don't I need to be here? What if Papa wakes up and needs to see me? Isn't the plane ticket too expensive for us now? What about my grades? Saint Ag's won't accept me being gone that long, right?

I thought my whole world ended twice this year. First my dad falling from a roof and disappearing into a hospital bed. Then my mom seeing us, and Ms. Holden speeding away, forever.

But now, this—this is the end of my world, and my mom is engineering it. This is my exile to another universe. I have nothing to try to stop it except for questions.

Sometimes Tita Baby joins in—her frequent-flier miles are paying for the ticket; Papa can always see me on the computer. I should work hard to study on my own.

I ignore her, keeping my gaze on my mom. My mom says nothing, just pushes the boxes with her feet toward the door.

Then I remember.

"The AP test," I say.

I say it like it's a prayer I've just remembered the words to.

"The AP test! There's no way I can miss that. If I go to the Philippines I'll miss the testing dates. College credits. College admissions. I need to take the AP History test!"

Ma stops and sighs, her hands on her waist, her eyes on her feet. She pushes her hair out of her eyes. I'm triumphant. She has no answer to that argument.

Until she does.

"I met with your history teacher," she says.

Her voice paralyzes me.

"She gave me your assignments. I told her you would pause your enrollment while you were back home. So she made you photocopies to bring with you. And she researched the date and location of the test in Manila. It's in a few weeks. I already told your kuya Jun. You'll study on your own. You'll take the AP test there. We have it scheduled na."

She inspects the empty pockets of the duffel bag.

My voice feels like someone else's. "You met with—"

"We had a talk. Your teacher and I. We had a talk. Earlier today."

My mom's voice is still calm, but it's harder now. Like when she's trying to appease an angry client on the phone, or when she's scolding a fellow temp who won't listen to her instructions. But the anger I hear is way deeper than anything I've heard before.

Had my mom gone after Ms. Holden with that voice? Like Ms. Holden was a dangerous threat to me?

I feel protective of Ms. Holden again. I want to call her and reassure her. Then I want her to rescue me from this impending exile.

But she gave my mom my assignments.

She's okay with my mom sending me away.

But did my mom really give her a choice?

I look at my mom. The person who holds my phone, my access to the computer, my ability to stay home. The person who's taking it all away.

"Go rest again, Cory." My mom sighs. "The flight is early."

"Five a.m.," Tita Baby says. "We'll drive to LAX at two."

My mom's not going to tell me what she and Ms. Holden said about me.

She's going to keep that story locked away.

I feel the urge to beg, and that urge makes me hate my mom.

I can hear Tita Baby saying how I'll need a light sweater for Manila's air-con, and good shoes but mostly summer clothes, and her voice, her Tita chatter—I want to drown it with my anger. So I do.

"It should have been you!" I yell at my mom.

I want to sound like I'm roaring but my voice is high and tight like a little kid's and it makes me angrier.

"It should be you in the hospital! It should be you dying! Not him! Papa wouldn't do this! He wouldn't—"

I hear the slap before I feel it. It's a hard clap, like my mom's hands trying to smack together to kill something flying in the air.

My face stays turned to one side and I sit on our couch, the plastic cover squeaking beneath me, and my vision turns all red, like the blood filling the stinging pain in my cheek makes its way into my eyes too.

When I can see again, I blink, and I realize I'm holding my face, and my mom is standing with an empty look I've never seen before.

"You are correct," she says, her voice low and formal. "Maybe. Maybe it should have been me. Maybe your papa could have guided you and cared for you and stayed with me at the hospital. Maybe he could take the extra jobs to pay the extra costs and raise you and support another child back home. But I cannot. It's true. It's too much."

I hear a wobble in her voice at the end of her sentence. She says it again. "Too much." Tita Baby rushes toward her and I feel my own tears start.

So I charge out the front door and past our garden, back into the street. I don't know where I plan to go, but I'm not going to the Philippines and I'm not going back to school and I'm not going back inside—maybe I'll run to the ocean, maybe I'll try to find her—

And I would keep going but I hear, "Yo, cuz," and coughing.

It's Bea and Jerome, sitting together on a park bench. They're both grinning. Jerome holds his hand behind his back.

At first I think they're making fun of me, and I get ready to yell again. Then I smell skunk and smoke.

"How's your night going?" Bea asks.

They keep grinning. I wonder how I must look, in my Easter dress, with my mascara running, half my face red.

"I think she's going to see the Easter Bunny," Jerome says. "He's that way."

He gestures with his hand, and I see he's holding something made of glass, with embers and smoke and colorful swirls. Bea shoves him with her shoulder. "Shit," Jerome says. "She's gonna narc!" He giggles.

"She's cool," Bea says. "Cory's cool."

I look away from my super-high cousins, back down the street. Tita Baby and my mom haven't come out to chase me. I bet they're talking to each other about me. I wonder if Tita Baby is comforting my mom. My mom hasn't ever seemed to find her sister comforting. Just mostly annoying.

I should be the one comforting my mom.

"Want some?" Jerome holds out the little glass pipe.

On any other day, I might have laughed in disbelief. Maybe even joined them.

But tonight, shame makes me dizzy. My mom's phrase rings in my head. *Too much.* I wonder how to tell all that to my cousins. How too-much I am. Maybe they already know.

"My mom's sending me to the Philippines," I say.

"Cool," Bea says. "You're flying to the homeland with me and my mom."

"Wish I were coming," Jerome says. "Hella good food in

Manila. Good weed too, even better than Stanford."

"Shut up about Stanford already, god," Bea says.

"I'm being a nationalist about the homeland!" Jerome says.

Homeland. It's not my home at all.

"Will you be okay being away from your dad?" Bea asks, serious.

"Oh yeah," Jerome says, trying to be serious too. He puts out the bowl, tapping it onto the grass behind the bench and grinding the ashes with his foot. "Shit. That's heavy."

I don't know what to say to my cousins. So light and happy, even in their transgressions, so comfortable in a world I'll never know.

How do I explain that I'm not wanted here anymore? How "too much" of a burden I am?

All my fight to flee leaves me, replaced with my shame.

They don't know—and I didn't really understand until now—that all my homes are gone. I destroyed them.

I won't run.

I'll take the duffel bag upstairs to fill with my clothes.

I'll carry the boxes under my name.

And when Uncle Dan comes to drive me and Bea and Tita Baby to the airport, I won't fight. I'll go.

I turn back toward my house and start walking, slow, alone.

Then I see my mom walking down the street. Her face is so tired. She stops, crosses her arms, and looks at me for a long time, like she's trying to find something she lost.

"What are you and your cousins doing there?" she calls out finally. "Bea, Jerome. Anak. Are you three hungry?"

PART TWO

METRO MANILA

SOMEWHERE OVER THE PACIFIC OCEAN

Dear ~~Grace~~ Ms. Holden,
Hi. This is my first time on a plane.
I think there's a phone on the plane but it's like a million dollars and my aunt would never pay for it even though she can afford it.
~~I wanted to~~
~~I~~
~~You~~
~~I wish~~

"Finally," my cousin sighs. "I thought my mom would never go to sleep."

Tita Baby snores softly. Her eye mask has happy faces all over it and her travel pillow is pink. She sat between us on the flight. I shudder to think she wanted to keep me separated from Bea.

Bea, in the aisle seat, only seems to care about the wine. I guess the drinking age doesn't matter over international waters?

She walks toward the middle of the plane, where the flight attendants are hanging out, and she returns with a tiny bottle of red.

"Cathay has the best free shit," Bea says. She flies back twice a year to the Philippines, to do modeling gigs and visit Lolo Joe, the dad my mom doesn't talk to anymore.

Little screens on the backs of seats play movies and TV shows but my consciousness won't let me settle on just one. There's a history documentary about Vikings and a show about home improvement. There's the president talking at a podium, and then random men saying angry things about his speech and the recession and the unemployment rate. Nothing onscreen makes me zone out.

I think about drawing a Viking. I start horns. But I lose the will to finish the face. I scribble waves on the page instead. Meaningless lines.

"This is a long flight, cuz," Bea says over her sleeping mom, sipping her wine from one of the clear plastic cups. "Are you not going to sleep? Are you actually studying?"

I rub my eyes. I didn't know the plane would be so loud. She must be used to it but whether or not I have the plasticky airplane headphones on, I can't get used to the roar.

I glance at Bea. Even in a gray sweatshirt, slip-on sparkly sneakers, and tight black exercise pants, she seems genetically engineered for a magazine feature. "How to Look Good on Your Long-Haul Flight to Your Next Modeling Gig."

Without a Catholic school uniform, I don't really know how to dress myself. When I finally packed some clothes, I sort of ended up with a new uniform. Just black shirts and jeans and black sneakers. I wish I were as comfortable as Bea. I don't deserve any feature, except maybe a gross one. "Student Exiled Because She Torments Her Mom and Her Dad's Probably Dying and She Made Out with the Only Person—"

"Shit, you look tense," Bea says. She goes into her pricey black handbag, pulls out a small square wrapped in foil, reaches over her snoring mom, and puts it on the corner of my tray table.

I sniff it. It smells sweet and grassy.

"What the hell, Bea!" I hiss. "A weed brownie on an international flight?"

"Oh em gee," she clucks. "Chill. It's herbal. Like, natural and organic. A gift from Jerome. I'm having one."

"With your free wine? In addition to smoking up with your brother?"

"Works every time," she says. "I sleep like a babe."

"Don't you guys have, like, four-point-five GPAs or whatever?"

"Because we know how to party when it's time to party, relax when it's time to relax," she says. "It's a skill. Don't waste it, though; give it back to me if you don't want it."

She swallows the rest of her wine, pulls on her own black eye mask, and wraps the memory-foam travel pillow around her neck. Her breathing slows. Soon I'm the only one of us three awake.

I unwrap the small square. It looks like familiar chocolate. I shrug and bite. It tastes musty and sugary. I finish it with a second bite. I wait for something to happen. I wait to sleep. I wonder if I should get wine too, but I'd have to climb over both my aunt and cousin and I don't feel like moving.

I sigh. Not even my cousin's drugs can distract me.

I flip through more channels. Angry politicians on stages. Reruns of musical sitcoms. Chinese language films with English subtitles. Korean heartthrobs sobbing. I dim the screen and keep the headphones on my ears.

I take out the sheaf of history papers from my dad's old duffel at my feet.

Ms. Holden touched these. Took time to photocopy and get them ready for me. I press my palm against each page. I glimpse the familiar headers. "Papal Power in the Middle Ages." "The Birth of Humanism."

I see random circles and underlines. Some of them are photocopied old marks. But some are blue, the color Ms. Holden used to grade papers.

The plane bumps. A touch of turbulence. I freeze. My whole consciousness slides sideways.

Tita Baby shifts and mumbles, her pillow now pressed against my shoulder. Everything feels fuzzy and slow. I flip the papers and laugh a little. I tap my finger against each underlined and circled word. I think maybe I should study more closely.

"Study," I say out loud, and I feel myself grin.

I trace my finger over some blue-marked letters.

DEAReSt C—

I stand with the papers. I clamber over my cousin and Tita

Baby, stepping gingerly on the armrests to make it to the aisle. I thump-land on my feet, making other passengers frown. Tita Baby and Bea don't wake.

I go to the lavatory and lock it and sit in the cold fluorescence. My eyes feel dry; so does my mouth. There's a Do Not Drink sign near the faucet.

I look at the random letters on the pages in my hand. Here it is. The key. The thing that will help me feel better. The message from Ms. Holden. I circle and circle. I underline. Then I ruffle the pages, reading, writing down letters one by one, deciphering the hidden messages.

Someone knocks on the lavatory door. "Uh, diarrhea," I call out.

The plane lurches again. I don't care. I read. I feel my own mouth moving, trying to make sense of the code I found.

I read it backward. I read it forward.

I slump over my knees.

g X H 0 13 A.D. POPE. H. C. 16

It's gibberish. I found random nonsense.

I hear it in my head then, like another voice has entered my hearing through the lavatory intercom. *You're not gonna get anything more from her.*

I'm trapped in thoughts of her. I think a message from her would free me.

Sometimes there's a message. Sometimes there's an answer. Sometimes there isn't.

Sometimes there are trees—

My mind slides sideways again. This time my stomach follows fast.

I stand and puke in the sink. I can't breathe for a second. I think of the tubes down my dad's nose and throat. How he must be stuck with that horrible feeling. It makes me puke again.

I think of my mom rubbing my back when I was nine, when I was sick with the flu and kneeling on the bathroom floor, saying practical, murmuring things about how my body was getting rid of the infection and it would be over soon, my dad hovering near the door with canned coconut water and menthol rub and paper towels.

When I can breathe again, I go back to my seat, wedging myself past my aunt's and cousin's knees. They shift but stay asleep.

Everything is so loud. All the plastic and metal and upholstery rattling. The engine a total racket, rumbling through everything. I feel dirty and tired and alone, stuck with my aunt and cousin some thousands of miles up. It feels like a waking purgatory. It doesn't seem possible I'll ever sleep, but then hours later I wake to a hard jolt and a roar.

NINOY AQUINO INTERNATIONAL AIRPORT

My half-awake brain looks for ways out, back into my old life. I think if I sprint across the tarmac, I might just make it back to California, back home with my parents, back to school.

But everyone around me claps. Some people cry. They're happy tears. Young passengers and old passengers wipe their faces with their palms, or put their hands over their brows to hide their eyes.

Tita Baby doesn't cry. She taps my wrist and scolds me, "You slept through your breakfast, oh." Bea doesn't cry either. She just wears fresh, perfect foundation, and wide blue-framed sunglasses. The cabin is bright with daylight. I squint.

As soon as the plane slows a little, passengers jump out of their seats even though flight attendants wave their arms in giant "no" gestures, even though someone on the intercom tells them to wait until the seat belt light is turned off. No one cares about lights or alerts or the plane still moving; they just want their bags, and they want to be in Manila. They crowd the aisle, pretending not to see each other, all their eyes on the exit. Tita Baby mutters in Tagalog about people having no shame. But she's up on her feet too, wanting to shove forward for her bag in the overhead compartment.

The plane smells like stale scrambled eggs. It gets hotter with the daylight and all the passengers crowding. I feel sick again and close my eyes. Bea stays sitting, checking her face by taking photos of herself with her smartphone. This trip was like a short car ride for her.

"That weed brownie was poison," I whisper at her. ·

She puts her sunglasses back on. "Maybe you should try smoking instead of edibles next time," she whispers.

The plane comes to a stop. A mumble on the intercom, and then the doors open. Tita Baby shakes my knee. "Tara na," she urges me, and I rise to join the crush of arrivals.

When I'm in the tunnel leading to the rest of the airport, I realize I'm not quite conscious yet. Everything comes to me in weird fragments. Clapping. Cries of Mabuhay! The clatter-roll of luggage wheels on the linoleum. A long glass-encased hallway. Too much light slamming through the windows. Passengers waiting for other planes, crowding hot dog and siopao stands. Passengers sleeping on plastic blue seats; browsing souvenir booths filled with bamboo carvings and banana chips and bags made of—dead frogs?

The tarmac. Old concrete and asphalt. Aren't we supposed to be on an island? What is this dry, city desert?

Guys skinnier and younger than my dad rush by me, pushing

old people in wheelchairs, gripping clipboards, doing airport errands. The guys grin secret jokes at each other over the passengers' heads, call to each other in Tagalog slang I don't know.

Tita Baby's pink travel pillow, still around her neck. A man wearing an *NRA Member + Navy Veteran* T-shirt who sort of looks like my dad. But this man's older, with more wrinkles and a beer belly. He cries with happiness. He doesn't shield his face.

Bea's voice cuts through to me. "Hey, Cory, where's your duffel?" and I realize I'm empty-handed. I wait to panic, but somehow it feels right not to be carrying anything. I grin instead. Bea shakes her head, then turns back through the terminal tunnel. The crowd parts for her, and one of the airport worker guys in a green vest jogs to her like he was destined to jog to her. He hands her my duffel bag, and she glides back to us and hangs it over my shoulder for me, and then we're at a little booth labeled HEALTH CHECK and I wonder, if I fail the health check, if officials knew how unwell and intrinsically disordered I am, would they send me back to California?

But the man and woman there aren't even looking at the little forms passengers hand them, they're just gossiping with each other, maybe flirting, and I time-travel a few months back and I hear my mom's voice muttering one day in frustration at the Seafood City supermarket in Northridge: "Filipinos aren't serious. We'd get further in life if we were more serious and disciplined." My dad argues with her a little bit, and she doesn't talk for the rest of the afternoon, and then he gets her new Sudoku puzzle books and starts singing Journey to her in the living room. "You think

I'm so easy," she says, and she laughs, because it is always that easy between them, and now we're down a short staircase and in another long line, the line for immigration.

I wander to the foreign passport line before Tita Baby steers me to the line marked OFW, and I realize I'm not holding my passports and I wonder if maybe they'll detain me and send me home, like angry commentators on Uncle Dan's conservative radio shows say America should do to immigrants, but Tita Baby stays with me when it's my turn and slides my red passport and my dark blue passport under the bulletproof glass, and a lady in a black uniform with long black hair tells me to press my thumb against a little scanner smeared with the ghosts of other thumbprints, and she flips pages and stamps stamps stamps, says "Maligayang pagbabalik," and in the baggage claim there are more Filipinos than I've ever seen at once, even at my parents' favorite Christmas thing, Simbang Gabi, where there are dozens, singing and eating pork in their nice barong tagalogs and dresses with puffy white sleeves, and now guys ask me if I need help carrying my stuff, but Tita Baby and Bea get a rolling cart and frown at the guys all mean, and they back off.

We're waiting there forever, near posters that advertise whiskey and expensive watches and chocolate bars, then I see a photo of some white guys carrying surfboards under the WOW Philippines slogan, and I think of Ms. Holden's surfing lesson, and I sway on my feet.

I see the boxes with my name on them on the carousel, and I grab at the corners of them, but I feel like throwing up again and they slip from my hands, and a heavyset, strong-looking lady frowns and grabs one box and sets it on Tita Baby and Bea's cart, then the other box too, and nods at me, and Tita Baby says "Maraming salamat, po" because I forget to thank the strong lady. Then my aunt's and cousin's own hard-case plastic suitcases come out, and we turn and wheel past the customs counter, where the employees don't even bother taking the white form Tita Baby filled out on the plane, they ignore us, and I don't get it, all these officials not looking, I wonder what else might escape their attention, if Bea has a million pot brownies she'll be handing out to friends here, but we're outside and it's hotter and brighter and I instantly start to sweat and I feel even sicker; whole families are crushed against metal barriers, they're carrying posters and banners with other names on them, we're just one small arrival surrounded by other arrivals; smiling strangers keep wanting to sell us something, rides, more luggage help, cell phone SIM cards, and Tita Baby and Bea keep frowning and not looking at them, then Tita Baby spots a white van with black-tinted windows at the curb, the kind of van I think a government might use to kidnap someone in a movie, and a man with a crew cut, wearing a blue polo shirt and faded jeans, jumps out of the driver's seat to load the boxes and suitcases for us, then we're in the van, cool with air-conditioning, and the man drives.

ALONG EDSA

Everything felt so tense. I didn't realize how tense until now, when we're in the car. Anyone not associated with our family seemed dangerous to Tita Baby and Bea. What are the rules here? I don't get it. I feel sick again.

Tita Baby complains to the guy driving the van. She complains for him to turn down the radio because it's too loud. She complains that it's too hot even though I'm freezing in the air-conditioning. She doesn't greet him at all, or ask him his name, or introduce him to us. He calls her "ma'am" and "po." I wonder if they already know each other. She tells him to get us home soon because we've been traveling so long. He presses the gas, and she complains that he needs to be careful. He smiles.

Bea dozes off, comfortable in not understanding any of this.

"Corazon Maria, listen to me," Tita Baby says in English. "This is very important."

I look out the tinted windows. The buildings are gray and too close together. So many street vendors wear basketball shorts and worn-thin sandals. Whole families sit under multicolored umbrellas, selling candy and cigarettes, or sleeping on the hard ground.

"Corazon," Tita Baby says, turning all the way around from the front passenger seat. I jump and snap to attention. Bea wakes up.

"We're about to meet your lolo Joe," she says, louder than she needs to be in the close quarters of the van. "My father. The father of your mother. We're going to the house for lunch. You make a good impression on him. You be polite. That is your job."

I've never heard her this authoritative before, all the smoothing-over gossip and chatter out of her voice.

Through the window I see a mom dunking her two kids' heads backward in a bucket to bathe them. It looks like they live in a falling-apart, wooden wheelbarrow. The streets are all so narrow. Sometimes we come to a stop and vendors walk the tiny space between cars, trying to sell us dustcloths made from old shirts, newspapers, random electronics, even a new-looking smartphone or two.

"Cory, do you hear me?"

"Mom, you're so loud," Bea says.

"She has to hear this," Tita Baby snaps. "It's very important."

"Be polite to Lolo Joe," I say. "Got it."

"Be serious, Cory. You can help your parents a lot if—if you're courteous. If you show him you're deserving."

A couple of little boys spray the windshield with dirty water to clean it. The van driver lowers the window and hisses them away, like they're stray dogs.

I was the poor kid in school. The one on scholarship who bought the oldest books and the used uniform blouses gone gray with too much bleaching. But I'm way better off compared to the kids outside my window. I'm practically a tycoon. God, what does that make Bea and Tita Baby?

Tita's voice goes on, telling me not to be mayabang, to say "po," to mano, to mind my language and my table manners. "Don't be with him the way you were to your mom."

Two kids knock on my window. The little girl wears only a dirty gray tank top, no shoes on her cut-up feet. The little boy wears a torn basketball jersey and huge black athletic shorts he holds around his hips with one hand. He holds his other hand out to the window.

I see a bread roll wrapped in plastic in Tita Baby's purse. She saved it from the breakfast I didn't eat.

I grab it, roll down the window, and hand the bread to the kids.

"Hoy! 'Wag! Don't do that!" Tita Baby snaps.

"Why not?" I snap back. "It's not like we need it. We're about to sit at the lunch table to mind our manners."

I hear more taps on the window. A half dozen more kids have run to the car. They can't see me through the black tint, I don't think, but they want more.

"That's why not," Bea says, and I hate my cousin more than I've ever hated her. Each of those kids could have been Papa. To her, they're no one.

They move away slowly, one by one, after holding their empty hands out longer and longer.

I wonder if one of the kids will make it to America one day. If he'll have a kid in California who gets in trouble and has to come back to the Philippines, to watch another kid knock on her window. The future-past thought loop makes me dizzy again.

I count the logos for Shakey's Pizza and McDonald's and Jollibee.

Side streets, alleyways, bigger avenues. So many people living their lives at the sides of roads. I see the giant red-and-white Jollibee face smiling over and over, and gas stations and motel signs, and rippling green metal roofs. Then we come to a bigger road with way bigger billboards. People hang off the doorways of giant buses, jumping on and off at quick random stops. White taxicabs with black lettering try to muscle past everyone else. I recognize a stylish hunk of rumbling metal with no glass in its windows, graffiti of Jesus on its sides; a jeepney, something I've only ever seen in my parents' photographs.

"This is EDSA," Bea says. "What passes for a highway here."

The billboards here sell me internet and cans of tuna and blue jeans and whitening cream and a short woman with short black hair and a mole. The president. The president here is a woman.

Then I see Bea.

She's on a billboard with three other pale, mixie-looking models. She wears tight black jeans and a spaghetti strap tank top and high heels. I gaze and gaze, turning my head all around to keep staring as we pass it.

"It's up now, anak!" Tita Baby says, her sternness breaking. "The shoot from Christmas."

"Why are you on a billboard?" I ask. "What are you selling me?"

"A dream, of course." Bea yawns.

"Bea, you look so pretty there with your hair big!" Tita Baby exclaims.

But Bea's words ring in my head. A dream. A dream. I'm alone, in some kind of waking dream world. The woman president is one of the gods of this world, maybe, and Bea is one of the little gods, a small saint, and I think of discussing a history of saints with Ms. Holden, and I start to feel sicker, my wrists tingle, and I wonder what prayers to say in this dream world, who I should send those prayers to—

"Dude, close your eyes," Bea says. She hands me a sealed water bottle.

My billboard cousin is right. Closing my eyes does feel better. Maybe I won't ever have to open them again.

APO

"Corazon," I hear, and when I open my eyes I expect to see my mom in the front seat and my dad opening the driver's side door of his truck.

No. We're at a two-story house surrounded by walls and a gate. Every house here has walls and gates. But it's quiet. No one here lives under an umbrella on the street. New-looking cars are parked here and there. This neighborhood looks like a version of Tita Baby's well-off street in California. Just with older trees, more humid air. Metal spikes menace us from the top of every wall, guarding every house.

"We're here," Tita Baby says. "Cory, remember what I said."

The driver unloads Tita Baby's and Bea's stuff. She never told us his name. He was meant to stay in the background doing stuff for us, I guess. I wonder what my mom would do if she were here, if she'd invite him in for lunch.

"Salamat po," I say to him.

He tightens his mouth and raises his eyebrows briefly, a polite, silent acknowledgment I recognize from my own dad's face, when he's dealing with strangers.

"Naku, Cory, come now," Tita Baby says.

An older woman, maybe in her sixties, holds the house's main metal gate open for us. She wears nurse's scrubs, but I don't think she's a nurse. The woman doesn't introduce herself, and Tita Baby doesn't introduce me to the woman, either. The woman stares at me, though, wide-eyed, and I feel weird at her scrutiny.

"Should I get the boxes from the car?" I ask.

"Bilisan mo na! Make sure you're presentable, change into something nice," Tita Baby snaps, and I take that as a no.

The woman in scrubs leads us into a living room with a low ceiling, antique wood and rattan furniture, and cool white tile. Tita Baby hisses at me to take off my shoes, like Bea does automatically. The woman drops a new pair of slippers in front of my feet for me to use, and stacks my sneakers on a dark wood shelf.

I see older family photos and newer family photos crowded on an old coffee table. I catch a glimpse of Bea as a kid, standing next to an older, grandpa-looking Filipino guy at a fancy Chinese restaurant. In the photo, the guy grins like Bea's the source of all his happiness in the world.

"Go with your cousin, shower, put on makeup if you have," Tita Baby says. I follow Bea up a narrow staircase. We're overlooking a dining room now, an old ceiling fan turning over several Filipino food dishes covered with plastic mesh lids to ward off flies—they look like the ones my parents keep for our own dining table; they're even the same color, dark blue. Another, younger woman in scrubs brings small dishes of ketchup and soy sauce to each place setting.

Bea leads me into a little bedroom with a twin bed. She shows me a bathroom.

"You should shower first, I think," she says.

"What are you trying to say?" I snap.

Bea rolls her eyes. "Cousin. Cuz. You clearly don't feel well. A shower will make you feel better. Then you can nap while I shower. Or! Keep feeling sick and wearing the same clothes you've been wearing for twenty hours if you want to; I'm not going to oppress your individual expression."

She closes the bedroom door behind her and pads down the stairs.

I go into the old duffel bag and find my clothes. I had just shoved them into my bag. But I see that sometime before I left, my mom reorganized for me. She folded my socks, underwear, pants, and shirts, and put them in separate plastic bags for me. I feel a sharpness in my throat.

I wish my mom were here with me.

Then I feel mad at the wish and mad again at her for sending me here.

I set out a black shirt and a pair of jeans and go into the shower.

The water is cold. I can't get it warm no matter how I mess with the knob. I shiver under the water for about thirty seconds before I can't take it anymore. Even though the country is hot I can't do a cold shower. My dad would take cold showers in the morning—he said it was healthier, some Chinese-medicine thing. But I ignore the soaps on the bathroom shelf and wrap myself in a towel, wanting the shower over ASAP. I brush my teeth and dress.

I do feel a little better.

I think about warning Bea about the shower when she comes back into the bedroom. But I'm still annoyed, so I lie down silent on the twin bed instead.

I can't sleep.

I watch as steam slips out from under Bea's bathroom door. Of course she got the hot water working, ugh. Everything works for her, so why not this, too?

After fifteen minutes she's done. She found a fluffy white robe that makes her look like she's on a billboard for white robes.

"Do I sleep on the floor?" I say, sitting up when she comes back into the room. "I'm assuming you get the bed here."

Bea pauses while pat-drying her hair. She opens her mouth to speak, then decides not to.

"What?" I say.

She rummages through her own suitcase, then goes back into the bathroom to finish changing into her clothes. I hear Tita Baby's scolding voice float up the stairs. Then I hear a quiet, apologetic knock.

I crack the door open; the older woman in scrubs is there. She has wavy black hair gone gray in places, and gold-rimmed glasses with a small crack in the left lens. I can't quite tell how old she is; only that she seems tired.

"Sorry, po," she says, ducking her head. "Are you the daughter of Xi-xi?"

I have to think for a moment, remembering who she means. Hardly anyone in California uses my mom's childhood nickname; my dad calls her "Mahal," Tita Baby calls her "Ate," I call her Ma.

"Yes. Uh, opo," I say, remembering respect.

The lady grins, all her weariness leaving her face for a brief moment. I can see that one of her bottom teeth is missing. She enters the bedroom and closes the door.

"Nagtatagalog ka ba?" she asks. "Tinuruan ka ba ng mama mo?"

I nod my head fast, trying to clear it, then answer in Tagalog. "Yes, I can speak. My mom taught me."

She laughs and answers in Tagalog too. "You sound so American! But it's good you can speak. I thought you are the daughter of Xi-xi; you have Xi-xi's chin, her hair, you walk like her into the house! Your eyes, though, that must be your father. How is your mother now? Ay, child, tell her thank you so much for the help. Tell her my youngest is in maritime college now, he'll be a seaman soon, higher salary. On ships, like your papa."

I don't know who this stranger is, this person who knows and already likes me, who's grateful to my mom for so much. She feels like a relative, though. I look for the word that would respect her best. "Ate—" I try.

"Manang!" she says, correcting me. "I'm so much older than Ate! Manang Merlie."

151

"I'm Corazon," I say.

"Of course, I know, child!" Manang Merlie says. "Cory. She told me in her messages. Are you still struggling in math? She says you are very good in history. Ay, you know, your mom was best at math in Ateneo, always talented, even in grade school! Maybe she can help you, no?"

Bea comes out of the bathroom. She's wearing tight gray slacks and a short-sleeve turtleneck. "Hi, Manang," she says. Manang Merlie gets more cautious and calls her "ma'am." She was obviously more excited to see me. With me, Manang acts warm; with Bea, she goes back to being a careful employee.

Tita Baby calls upstairs again. I see the tiredness return to Manang Merlie's face. "Po," she calls back. Then to us: "Lunch, po." She ducks her head and goes downstairs.

"Manang Merlie's been with the house forever," Bea says. "Since our moms were kids. I think she misses your mom; she must be happy to meet you."

I'm stuck on Bea's first phrase. "'Been with the house'? Is a family maid like furniture?"

Bea looks at the ceiling and sighs a huge, frustrated sigh. Then she goes downstairs. I pad behind her in my socks and the borrowed slippers.

Tita Baby is sitting at the table, her face newly made up. She's changed into a stylish striped tunic and white trousers. She puts down her mug of green tea and frowns at me. "I thought I told you to dress nice."

"This is all I have," I say.

"Bea, can she borrow?"

Bea stares at her iPhone in response, ignoring her mom. "I'm at least double Bea's size," I say. "I'll ruin her stuff." I change the subject. "Are we staying here tonight? Do I take a couch, or—?"

Tita Baby lifts a mesh plastic food cover. "Look, oh, humba, your favorite, Cory." Manang Merlie returns with glasses of ice water for us, and a Coke for me.

"My favorite is adobo," I say. "Humba's my mom's favorite." I see Manang Merlie smile before she heads back into the kitchen.

"Humba is like adobo," Tita Baby says.

I feel suddenly tired again, then. Like I'll fall asleep in the humba.

Bea's phone buzzes with a text. "It's Tita Maxine," she says. "Wanting to know if we landed already."

"Just say we did and Cory is fine," Tita Baby says.

"So . . . don't say we're in Valle—"

"Sst!"

Bea rolls her eyes and taps a reply. She waits, then reads my mom's response aloud. Her voice is gentler now.

"She says your dad is showing good signs," she says. "And he's blinking more. He's opening his eyes, sometimes, when people enter the room. It's a really good sign for his brain functioning. They call it purposeful movement. And his vitals are still stable."

Tears prick my eyes. I look at the white couch, trying to get myself under control. Tita Baby walks over to me and puts her arm around my shoulder, the motion making her jewelry jingle in that

153

familiar aunt way. "It's all right, Cory," she says. "It's good news."

A door opens from somewhere within the kitchen. An entrance to the house different from the front door. Manang Merlie rushes out to our table to set out a tall glass of water with no ice, a cup of hot green tea, a plastic case full of pills, and a small brass bell. Tita Baby releases me and stands at attention, watching the kitchen door.

The grandpa-aged man from the photograph—older now, curved forward from between his broad shoulders—walks into the dining room.

No, he doesn't walk. He shuffles, leaning a little on a cane in his left hand. Someone else might make shuffling look weak. But this old man brings all the gravity of the room with him. He wears a sharp-pressed, short-sleeve, white tailored shirt. He sweeps what's left of his hair across his scalp with perfect grease. He keeps his shoes on—dark black, tasseled slip-on loafers, gleaming with new shine. Everyone snaps to obedience in his presence. Manang Merlie and a couple of younger women rush to the table to arrange his place setting, pulling out his chair for him, hanging his cane on a wall hook.

Tita Baby pinches my sleeve for me to stand. Only Bea stays relaxed and smiles.

"Lolo Joe!" Bea cries, and though the man doesn't smile, I see a look of years-long adoration cross his serious face.

Bea takes his hand and presses it to her own forehead, then gives him a hug. He pecks the top of her head and pats her shoulder. He sits, stiff, careful, and sighs. Manang Merlie pushes his chair in for him. Tita Baby leans down and kisses his cheeks. She frowns and flaps a hand at me for me to greet him.

The old man fixes his watery gaze on me. For a second I think I see something warm there.

Then something hard comes down over his eyes. A door closing. A wall coming up.

Tita Baby looks from him to me and back again. "Your third apo," she says. "Corazon."

I take Lolo Joe's hand for the blessing that would show him respect. His fingers are cold. He stiffens before the back of his hand reaches my forehead. He withdraws his arm, then rests his palm flat on the tabletop instead.

"You must be hungry, Tatay," Tita Baby singsongs. "After going to the office so early. I'm sure you're so busy after Easter, po."

He unclicks two lids of his medicine case, takes one pill, and then another. He rings the bell, and a young woman rushes out of the kitchen. "Didn't I tell you the water should be warm?" he says in Tagalog, his first words in our presence. "Not cold, not hot, warm. Why is that so difficult?"

She whispers an apology and takes back the tall glass.

Lolo Joe pushes the bowl of rice toward Bea. She thanks him and takes about five grains of it. He pushes the humba toward Tita Baby. He ignores me.

I search the man's face for something that resembles my mom. His eyes stay unsmiling and low, the corners of his mouth turned down. My mom's eyes are usually wide-open, observing everything and everyone, her face calm and perceptive, like a scientist or an investigator.

"Bea," he says, his voice rumbling warmly toward her. "What brings my apo back home? Where's your brother?"

Bea tells Lolo Joe about her modeling job this week, in a place called Makati. She says the name of the company, how long the drive might be, how she and Jerome would be back during American summer. Tita Baby joins in too, talking about Bea's good grades and her early-decision applications, about Jerome's lacrosse club stats and pre-law grades.

I reach across the table and pile rice and a little ketchup and a piece of fried chicken on my plate. Tita Baby squints at me for reaching. I eat a mouthful of rice and realize I'm not hungry. I look around the room while the voices brag on. I see the pristine white leather couch, the ornate vases and copper urns lining shelves, an ancient treadmill, an old stereo and record player. This is a man with money—more money, I think, than my dad ever grew up with.

No one mentions my parents. Where are the family photos with my mom?

"Corazon is also a very good student," Tita Baby says. "She'll be going to university soon."

"I don't think I can go far from home," I say, with a burst of loyalty, "because of my dad. And his recovery."

A quiet descends on the table. Lolo Joe coughs. Or is it a laugh?

"Was your father still fixing toilets on ships," he says in English, "when he met his . . . unfortunate fall." It's a mocking statement, not a question. "Is he still a palikero?"

I don't know the word "palikero," but I decide to say something.

"He can fix anything. Sir," I say in Tagalog. "He has his own business. Thank you for your kind interest in my father."

"Corazon," Tita Baby whispers, warning me.

Lolo Joe stares at me. He smiles a little, amused.

"Oh. You understand," he says in Tagalog. "You can speak."

"Cory's, like, fluent, Lolo," Bea says. "Way better than me."

"No one's better than you," Lolo Joe says in English.

A second wave of weariness hits me, taking me under. I feel my head nod low. I'm tired of it all—tired of the journey already, tired of knowing my low status, tired of this game of manners Tita Baby wants me to play.

I barely manage to stay awake until the end of the meal. I sip my Coke, hoping the sugar and caffeine might sustain me. I feel Tita Baby nudge my foot with hers a few times. I don't hear my own robotic answers.

After forever, Tita Baby says they'll just drop me off. I follow their lead to stand, finally, too tired to ask where we're going. I'm just glad to be leaving, though I'd rather lie down on the floor and sleep.

Manang Merlie brings Lolo Joe his cane. He rises, both hands on the head of his cane, and I go to him to say goodbye. This time he half hugs me with one arm. I smell must and menthol and pomade and age. Bad teeth. He murmurs Tagalog into my ear.

"I've thought of your father and mother often, these many years. Now he's in the hospital. The Lord works in His own time, no?"

I think, at first, that he's wishing Papa well. Then he releases his hug. I look in his eyes. There's old anger there, and old sorrow. And amusement.

He's happy my dad got hurt.

My tiredness turns into flame.

I turn back to the table, full of just one purpose. I use one arm to sweep everything off. Dishware shatters. The humba bleeds black onto the ground. Ice and glass skitter away toward the bleach-white couch. Bea and Tita Baby jump back, as if from a surprise tsunami. The maids gasp and cry out from the kitchen.

Only Lolo Joe stays still, standing with the support of his cane. He's smiling now, even more pleased. As if I've just proven something he suspected of me all along.

I run for the front door, a machine in me overheating. I kick off the stupid house slippers. I stand outside in my socks. I look at the green gate, the ferns and orchids and little fountain. The world slides sideways again.

I want her to pick me up in her car. Take me somewhere quiet. Teach me something so this whole scene makes sense.

I pitch forward, gripping the edge of the fountain. I vomit rice into the burbling water. I cough.

"Nice final touch," Bea says behind me.

I turn. She's holding my duffel bag and my sneakers.

"You okay?" she asks.

I cough again. "Are you sure that's my grandfather too?" I ask, my voice strangled. "Are we in the wrong house?"

Bea sighs, puts the bag down, and crosses her arms. "What did he say to you?"

I shake my head. "He's happy my dad's in the hospital."

"That's fucked up. I'm so sorry."

"You won't say anything to him, though," I accuse her.

Bea sits next to my bag. "You're right. I probably won't."

I spit into the fountain.

I don't expect Bea to say anything more. But she does.

"I don't know if I really have the whole story," she says. "Actually, I'm sure I don't. But, you know *Romeo and Juliet*? It's like, if Romeo and Juliet got older and had a kid. And Juliet's rich dad stayed angry at her forever for her husband choices. But . . . I don't know. It might be deeper than that."

I thought I was the one in the family with secrets. I take this one in.

"Why do you know that and I don't?"

"I don't know. My mom likes to gossip?"

"Why didn't you tell me all this?"

"We hardly talk! It's not like you're my biggest fan."

"I didn't know you needed any more fans," I mutter.

Bea lets my snark go.

"I thought Lola Irma dying, and Lolo Joe getting older . . ." she trails off. "I sort of wondered if maybe he'd soften, about your mom."

A memory from before high school: my mom in the bathroom, crying, hiding her grief from me. My dad sitting on the floor in front of the closed door, saying gentle things to her. Her mom's photograph going up on our fridge a few days later, a candle next to the bust of Jesus.

Tita Baby rushes outside. "Get in the car," she says to me in Tagalog. "If you were my child I'd never let you leave the house again. I'd slap you till you had no face. Bea, dito ka lang."

"What?" Bea says.

"Hay naku," Tita Baby says, and repeats the instructions in English. "You stay here with Lolo Joe. Diyos, you're the only one who can make him calm after this. Corazon Tagubio, those poor maids, those poor maids. This was not your house to destroy!"

The maids. I catch a glimpse of them before the door closes behind Tita Baby.

Manang Merlie and the younger maids, whose names I never learned, pick through the scraps of my mess, finding stray shards of glass with their bare hands. Manang Merlie's on her hands and knees now, looking at the mess through the cracked lens of her glasses.

I want to stop them. I should clean it up myself. A flood of shame makes me feel sick again.

I follow Tita Baby out the home's gate. I let her angry words wash over me.

"He disinherited your mother; she's too proud to ask him, but I was hoping, meeting you, meeting his apo, seeing the person you are—grabe, you don't know, anak—" she says.

I feel my stomach clutch. "Don't call me that."

The driver opens the door for me. I get into the back seat and lean my head against the window. I see Tita Baby in the rearview mirror. Her eyes are red. She dabs at them with a tissue. We move away from the quiet neighborhood, back into more crowded streets.

JUNIOR

I sway, sick, between sleep and waking, talking to them in my head.

Ma, how did you survive such an asshole?

Dad, please come back . . .

Ms. Holden—

We're at a Jollibee.

In California my parents would drive over an hour to Jollibee in Cerritos when they wanted to celebrate and In-N-Out wasn't enough. My dad always insisted on a picture of us with the statue of the bright-red Jollibee. He must have seven years' worth of photos with us and Jollibee.

At this Jollibee there's no parking lot, so the driver teeters the van on a tiny ledge of sidewalk. Cars from the street swerve to avoid hitting him. Little motorbikes with sidecars veer around us. More little barefoot kids come up to the window. They dart away when a shotgun-clad security guard hisses at them. Everyone seems to know how to hiss, how to shoo, and who deserves dismissing.

There is a bee statue, but he's standing alone right now.

"Stay here." Tita Baby growls at me now, like she thinks I'll go into Jollibee and set it on fire.

The driver looks at me in the rearview mirror. Then he ignores me and texts on his own little Nokia.

I close my eyes against the window until Tita Baby returns with an enormous paper sack. The oily, meaty smell of fried chicken fills the car. Something sweet, too: maybe some pocket pies, maybe spaghetti.

Then we're moving again. I feel hungry and sick. My parents should be here; the three of us should have been doing this together. But I don't think my parents ever wanted to come back. Our future together was never here. Just their past.

We pause near a sandstone-red statue of mother Mary. It looks huge and handmade, and her face is peaceful, but her garments are filled with lumps. I look closer. The lumps are dead little limbs. Fetuses. I don't realize I've groaned out loud until Tita Baby turns fully around to glare at me and says in Tagalog, "Don't you dare. Don't you dare make more of a mess in your lolo's car." She shoves an empty plastic bag at me.

We go uphill a little, and then right. The streets here are quieter. There are actual sidewalks, more trees. Every house has a gate. But there are no security guards, none that I can see.

We stop at a three-story building with a giant, pastel ocean mural on its three garage doors. A pastel mermaid and a few dolphins smile at me. We stop at a small black gate to the right of the mural, lined with barbed wire.

"Get down na," Tita Baby orders me. She commands the driver to get the cardboard boxes out of the trunk for us. I get my own duffel bag and keep the plastic would-be puke bag gripped in my right hand. I step out onto cracked concrete. I feel like I have sea legs, like I'll wobble for the rest of my life.

A gray box hangs near the gate from some frayed wires. To me it looks dangerous, but the driver presses a button inside the box, and I realize it's a buzzer. I hear the shuffle of sandals down the driveway, a *thock* and slam of metal against metal. A small door in the gate opens a crack. A short, straight-backed, older woman in green basketball shorts and a pink T-shirt, her black-and-gray hair cut close to her scalp, looks through the crack at my aunt, wary. Tita Baby says, "Anak ni Rommel."

Papa's name, and the fact of me as his kid, is the key that opens the gate. Again, no one tells me this woman's name, but she nods and takes the Jollibee sacks my aunt pushes at her. The driver and Tita Baby follow her, and I follow them, ducking through the gate and into the driveway it's guarding.

Behind the dolphin building, three two-story apartments, cast in shadow, rest next to each other, framed by clotheslines and little box gardens. It's like a smaller version of my townhome neighborhood in California. Except here, shards of broken glass spike from the tops of surrounding concrete walls. Rusty barbed wire curls sinister on the roofs. Each home is powered by a bunch of black electrical lines bound together, snaking in and out of the second-story windows. It doesn't seem legal. But maybe "legal" is different here, less important than what works.

We stop at the second apartment, the only one with a makeshift aluminum roof over its box garden. There are vertical metal bars over the windows. The older woman slips off her sandals and steps past a swinging screen door. The driver slips off his own shoes and deposits the cardboard boxes just inside. He takes my duffel bag from me and puts it on top of a box. Then he puts his shoes back on and goes out to the car.

Tita Baby doesn't go inside. She stops next to me at the doorway and rummages through her purse.

"You be helpful to your kuya," Tita Baby hisses. "Don't wreck his house. Here. From your mom. You give it to them when they need."

"What?" I ask.

She presses a roll of blue-colored money into my hand. I have no idea how much it is. I look at it, and Tita Baby scolds me to put it away. I shove it in my jeans pocket. She turns to leave, then remembers something else in her bag.

"Here, oh. The old phone of your cousin. There's load there. You just go to the sari-sari for more."

Maybe, if I weren't swaying on my feet, I'd ask what the hell "load" and "sari-sari" are. Also: Why isn't Tita staying behind to do introductions like a good tita? Why won't she stay a little longer with me? I hate to admit it, but suddenly, for the first time in my life, I don't want her to go.

She presses a scratched Nokia into my hand, a model even older than mine in California. Then she rushes back toward the car.

"Are you serious?" I call out. I sound brattier than I should. The gate slams shut behind her, metal on metal echoing down the driveway.

I stand there blinking, gripping the phone.

I can't see any of the neighbors, but I hear their house sounds. Tagalog news, pet roosters, running water from someone's sink, American pop songs. It doesn't sound anything like my quiet neighborhood, where the walls are thick and we don't hear much besides ourselves. I don't know what's waiting for me inside this home.

The woman swings the screen door open and looks at me. "Pasok," she says, and I do, crossing the threshold for the first time. Anak ni Rommel.

The apartment smells like the ghosts of many Filipino meals' past, vinegar and rice and stewed meats. And under that, old plastic, and dried flowers. It's familiar.

The living room I've stepped into has a cozy mismatch of furniture. Two wooden side tables with plastic tablecloths. Under the window, a flower-patterned, foam rectangle on a bamboo mat. Two white, monobloc chairs. One tall black standing fan, and a squat blue desk fan. An old tube TV with a long antenna, resting on a table made of plastic black crates and a two-by-four.

Old photos are tacked up on a bulletin board near an old desktop computer, set on a scratched, wooden folding table.

"Upo ka," says the woman. I stay standing. She presses a button on the fan and it whirs awake.

"Nakatagalog ka?"

"Opo," I say.

"Ay, ang galing," she says, mock-impressed I understand.

Is it her teasing welcome, and the strange familiarity of the house, that makes me pass out into an instant sleep? I lie down flat on the foam mat and everything fades from me.

She shakes me awake.

Not the woman who let me into the house.

Ms. Holden. Her hand is warm on my shoulder.

"Cory," she says, and we're instantly together again.

She keeps her hand on my shoulder while I sit up on the flat mat. It's twilight. My parents are in the garden outside. I can hear their happy voices float in. They know she's here with me. We'll have dinner together soon.

"Hear how happy they are?" Ms. Holden says. "We'll have that too."

I look in her dark eyes. They welcome me home. I lean toward her.

The edge of a side table bangs me awake. I'd sat up and leaned forward in my sleep.

I press my palm against my aching forehead. My cheeks are wet. I press my hands against my eyes. When I open them, I notice the biggest photo tacked up on the bulletin board.

It's my dad, looking gloriously nineties. He wears a red flannel open over a crewneck white T-shirt, slightly baggy blue jeans, black sneakers with white toes. There's a duffel at his foot and one over his shoulder—the same bag my mom packed for me.

It's twilight now, like it was in my dream. I don't know which twilight, how many hours I've been here. The air is filled with the smell of oil and garlic, the voices of cooks chatting with each other between other houses, the sizzle of food tossing in woks. I hear the shuffle of someone walking just outside the window, then keys jingling at the door. It opens.

And it's my dad.

I stand and stare.

There are differences, of course. He's stronger and thinner than he was in California, before his accident. He's wearing all black—a tight black shirt, slouchy, skinny black jeans. His black hair is cut close on both sides of his head, longer and combed left on top. He wears those glasses with thick black frames—Papa never needed glasses.

But in all those years of video chatting with Kuya Jun, I didn't notice this: his resemblance, the way he moves, the way he summons Papa in all his gestures.

Why didn't I notice, during all those video chats? Was it because he was sitting, stuck in the electric square? If he'd gotten up and danced or laughed, would I have seen it then? But I was always stiff, obeying my dad's insistence that we talk through the screen.

I wait for him to grin at me like Papa always did when he came home. This near-copy of Papa doesn't smile, though. And

168

his voice, when he speaks, is not my dad's, always ready to joke and play.

"Hello, Corazon," he says. There's a heaviness in his tone. A seriousness, a sadness. "Welcome to Teachers' Village, QC."

"Jun. Kuya Jun," I say.

"Yup," he says.

A Saint Agatha's–branded messenger bag hangs across his chest. Last year it was a freebie Christmas gift for the parents of Saint Agatha's scholars. My dad stuck it into that year's December cardboard box.

"You've met Ate Nene," he says.

The woman who let me in. She opens the paper sacks of Jollibee food, puts some spaghetti in the microwave, and sets placemats out—the blue-bordered, brown cotton placemats my mom bought at Ross a long time ago. Ate Nene's a maid, I know now. A younger version of Manang Merlie, for Jun.

Now I notice other stuff around the house. Throw pillows and thin cotton blankets we sent, discounted from Target and TJ Maxx. The black Reebok sneakers Jun just took off. I remember my dad stopping at a roadside garage sale, checking the size, holding the box up to me—"Look, oh! Brand-new!"

"Jun, ayaw niya kumain. Natulog lang siya," says Ate Nene.

He lifts his eyebrows in acknowledgment. "Well, of course you'd prefer to sleep over eating," he says to me in English. "It's a long trip. I imagine, anyway."

I think I detect something else in his courtesy. Bitterness? Regret?

He puts his messenger bag down near the computer desk, turns on the monitor, then goes to the kitchen and picks up scissors. "Do you mind?" he asks, standing over the boxes. I shrug. He stabs carefully into the lines of tape.

I try not to stare, but I can't stop watching his face. It's like he's a never-ending, updated movie of Papa. Young and capable. No wounds. It almost feels like relief, seeing him there with the box, instead of gray and immobile in hospital-bed limbo.

But it's a new ache, too. The pain of missing my dad is sharper, meeting Kuya Jun in person.

I remember the last update from my dad's condition. The phrase Bea used. "Purposeful movement."

Jun pulls out a plastic bag, peers into it, and tells Ate Nene he thinks it's for her. She says, "Yehey," then pulls out some of my mom's work blouses that she doesn't wear anymore. Ate Nene holds a light blue oxford against herself, admiring the cotton and the ruffled sleeves. She holds the same shirt against Jun's shoulders. "Maybe for you, very pretty," she says, and he smiles at the joke. "Not my style."

He sets body lotion and toothpaste and shampoo and conditioner and bar soap on the floor next to the box. Beef jerky and graham crackers and dry pasta go on the counter next to the sink. It seems like a usual ritual, one he and Ate Nene have practiced a lot. She takes the bottles from the floor and organizes them in a little bathroom off the kitchen.

He pulls out a roll of new pens and highlighters. I think my mom collected those from her freelance jobs, over the weeks before Papa's accident. She wound a rubber band around them so they weren't loose in transit.

"Salamat, Papa," Kuya Jun says, crouched, holding the pens, and in Tagalog, "I'm almost out of highlighter ink."

I watch him unfold from his crouch, and the literal translation of the word "kuya"—a word I've said casually to the computer screen all my life—repeats in my head. A word I thought I understood, but didn't really until now, meeting him in person. Older brother, older brother, older brother.

The sound of loud karaoke somewhere. Bottles clinking. Men's laughter. Heavy trucks rumbling on asphalt. Footsteps just outside. Lights shining on and off.

I shift in and out of sleep. Doors open and close somewhere else.

The morning light gets brighter. Something buzzes near the mat I'm sleeping on. The old phone Tita Baby left me.

Hey C.

I fumble letters on the faded number pad.

Hu r u.

LOL. Bea. Damn. Cold.

Hi sry

Are you still sick? was it the brownie :(

No just cant sleep

**Come to my shoot tomorrow. We'll pick you up tomorrow
morning.**

K

Ate Nene strides toward me before I can text if Tita Baby
would be okay with that. "Gising ka na?" She neatens my duffels
into a corner and calls me over. "Tara."

There are fried eggs and rice and Vienna sausage on the table,
alongside banana ketchup. "Saging muna," she says, putting a
tiny fresh banana on my plate. I sort of like how she's instructing
me. There's something calming about it. I peel the banana and
press it against a bite of white rice with each bite, like I always
watched Papa do.

Slippers slap against the stairs. "Hey," Kuya Jun says. "Your
mom is gonna Skype us."

My mom. I wonder what she knows about my arrival here.

I wonder where Kuya Jun's mom is. My dad never mentioned
her. I never asked him.

I bet my mom would know. But I'm nervous on top of all the
nervousness I still feel.

Another unwelcome pang. I miss my mom. I want to talk to
her, but I also don't.

"Okay," I say.

He sits me on a plastic chair in front of his desktop. He checks
a power cord and an old Ethernet cord. He calls my dad's user-
name, RTagub. I didn't realize he'd still been using that to talk
to us after Papa's accident.

"Hello, po," Jun says quickly to the screen, leaning over the desk near me. Papa always smells a little like flowers, dirt, plaster, paint. Jun smells like hair pomade and a strong, chemical deodorant.

My mom is there by the hospital bed, pixelated and hollow-sounding. "Hello, Jun, kumusta?"

He answers with his own polite question. "Kayo po kumusta?"

I try to remember the last time I asked my mom how she was. More shame for my shame.

My mom moves her laptop camera to face Papa. I see the tape holding his feeding tube in place. The familiar beeping is fainter from here.

"Hello, Ro-Ro," Ate Nene calls. She stands behind us, looking at the screen. I'm startled she knows my dad's nickname. I wonder how she's related to us, if she is. "Junior and I miss you so much. Please wake up na."

Ate Nene gazes. All of us do. She shakes her head and clicks her tongue. "Wala." She goes to the kitchen and washes dishes.

My mom turns the computer so that both she and my dad are in the frame.

"He's exhausted," my mom explains to us. "Dr. Chiu says he might be moving from the vegetative state to the minimally conscious state. But he needs to rest his brain, still. And we must watch his blood tests for infection. The doctor mentioned his white blood cell count seemed a little high, the other day."

"Is it okay now, po?" Jun asks.

"For now, Jun," my mom says.

He nods. I gaze at my parents.

Jun stands suddenly. "Oh, here is Corazon," he says. "I'll take a bath."

He bounds up the stairs, leaving me alone with the computer. I see him wiping his eyes as he goes.

I look at my parents. My silent father. My mom in a white shirt and dark blue pants. She still looks so tired.

"How are you there?" she asks.

I shrug.

"You've met Ate Nene," she says. "She's like a second mother to Jun. Worked for the family all her life, raising him like her own."

"Like Manang Merlie?" I ask.

I see her straighten. "You met Manang Merlie?"

I remember: Tita Baby didn't want my mom to know we'd seen Lolo Joe.

My mom swears under her breath. "Diyos ko. I told your tita Baby to leave it alone," she mutters. She shakes her head. Then she smiles, wry. "So. How was he?"

I wonder if she means Jun. Then I realize she means Lolo Joe. I shake my own head. "Why is he so . . . mean?" I ask.

She glances at Papa. I imagine how they might have checked in with each other with just their eyes, if he were awake. She sighs.

"Some men," she begins. "Sometimes, the only way they relate . . . all they know how to do, is control. If you try to be away from their control, in any small way, they punish. I was not like my sister, ready to please, ready to obey. If you must always reshape yourself, contort yourself, for their love, anak, it is not love."

175

She sighs. She reaches for Papa's hand.

"Near your age," Ma continues, "I saw that if I did not get away from him, I would always be punished for being me."

Her phrase crosses thousands of miles and then hangs, suspending and stinking, between us.

"Is that why I'm here?"

My voice wavers. Maybe she missed it. I still my face so my chin doesn't shake. My mom must see. She talks in her most soothing voice.

"When your papa had his accident," she says, "I researched bringing Jun to the US to be with us. But the visa is too hard. He's a single man, twenty, no longer a dependent. The States will reject him. I thought, kawawa naman siya, all alone there, away from us, also worried for your dad. And then—"

She stops.

Pain and embarrassment well up under my skin, like body-size bruises.

"What do I do here? How do I—"

I want to know if there's a system of penance, a way to earn my way back. But I don't know how to ask.

My mom exhales. "You spend time with your brother. You—teka. Read."

She types into the chat window of Skype, looking down at her own keyboard. A message pops up.

You have the money Tita Baby gave you? The pesos?

I nod at the screen. Another message appears.

Give them 12 per month.

"Twelve . . . pesos?" I ask the screen.

My mom exhales, annoyed, and types again.

12 thousand, Corazon. Anticipate a little. They don't have much there. Papa bought the townhouse, they just need for utilities & food.

"So I'm just here for—for that? What else? What about school?" I ask.

My mom starts to talk again. "You study on your own. You take your AP test. Then we'll see."

My throat burns with the mention of the AP test.

"Where's Jun's mom?" I ask.

I hear Ate Nene open and close the kitchen door—not quite a slam, but loud.

I wait for my mom to slap me with her voice. She lets the pause between us go on too long.

"In Cavite, Corazon. A bus ride from QC."

My mom's eyes fill with tears.

"Anak. Love—love is—" She sniffs and wipes her face with the back of her hand. She can't go on. "You'll know someday," she finally says.

If I were more careful, if I were the one-month-ago version of me, maybe I wouldn't say this out loud. But I mumble, "Maybe I do know."

Even through a staticky screen, I see her lips get thin and stern.

"Anak," she says, her voice full of warnings, "that wasn't love."

I click the chat window closed. My mom disappears from the screen.

I cover my eyes with my palms.

Then I remember: I have internet now. The browser. Email. Facebook. I could look her up. See if she has updates.

I log into my email. Nothing, just newsletters from Saint Agatha's, some study-at-home worksheets from my other subjects, and spam.

I click to Facebook. I don't even look at my feed. I search for the name I want.

There are eight Grace Holdens. I know which one is her profile picture. Just the beach at sunset, not her face. Zuma Beach, probably.

I click it. Nothing there, no update. She was never active on social media anyway. Her last post was a violin concerto by a German composer four months ago. Max Bruch.

Heavy steps down the stairs. "You done?"

I click away from Facebook, but he's seen it.

"Hey, let me show you how Wi-Fi works here," he says. A new weariness weighs down his voice.

He points to a USB stick jutting out from the blinking black box on the floor.

"See that stick? It's pay-as-you-go. I go to the sari-sari and give them pesos, and then we get to go online. We have to save pesos to Skype with your ma. We can't afford our own router, not with Papa's condition. And Tita Maxine won't like if we get cut off midsentence, no? Because we're wasting pesos doing other stuff online."

"Sorry," I mumble.

"You want to go online, spend your own pesos at the internet cafe on Maginhawa."

I think of the drive from the airport, all the makeshift lives and crowded streets. "Is it safe here?" I blurt.

For the first time since I met him, Jun laughs. I can hear a hint of our dad's high-pitched giggle. Jun's laugh, though, is tinged with scorn. "Safe as the US! With all your guns. Fine, stay here."

I'm dismissed. I get up and go to my mat.

I take out the cash Tita Baby gave me, and count it with my back turned. I leave twelve blue bills on the kitchen table. Jun doesn't watch me do it. He watches the screen.

Jet lag keeps stealing my consciousness. I keep falling asleep, then waking under the window to Ate Nene's and Jun's departures or arrivals. I blink my eyes open, and Jun is crushing graham crackers and rolling them into cookie balls. I sleep, then wake to Ate Nene returning from somewhere with fresh garlic and greens. I hear Jun talking to someone outside; I rise to my knees and see him through the barred windows, tutoring a six- or seven-year-old kid in math. Side hustles, like Papa has. Had?

Ate Nene makes rice and garlic spinach and dried fish for lunch. I barely taste it.

I sleep again.

BANDMATE

I wake into a hot afternoon. Ate Nene sits at the kitchen table. She puts eyedrops into her eyes, turns on a game show, and shuffles a deck of cards to herself.

I look at the stairs, feeling restless and awake. Ate Nene nods at me and jerks her chin upward. "You want a tour?" she says in English, and grin-frowns. She adds in Tagalog, "Your older brother's room stinks like boy! No matter how much I clean. But if you want to smell, go ahead!"

The TV switches to news. It plays protestors against the woman president, car crashes, petty crimes.

I climb the stairs. At the top is a narrow landing with two doors facing each other.

I open the door to the right. It's Kuya Jun's door. Ate Nene is right; here's the musty, sweaty smell of boy, foreign to me.

But his room is pretty neat, otherwise. Stacks of photocopies and a pile of highlighters under a seat of windows with vertical bars on them. Two cheap wood beds, like a bunk bed sawed in half, have been pushed against each other to make one bigger bed in the middle of the room. I see a pair of shiny black dress shoes; nicer, low-top brown leather sneakers; and a battered pair of running shoes. Piles of circular weights and two small bars stacked near his bed. And a device with once-white little knobs.

It's a four-track recorder. And a set of headphones repaired, over and over again, with black electrical tape. Piles of CDs and cassettes.

No photos on his walls. His class schedule from last semester at University of the Philippines Diliman is still up, filled with acronyms and numbers I don't understand. I see his full name: ROMMEL EMMANUEL TAGUBIO JUNIOR. This print-out is right above a dresser, its one drawer sagging with age. On the dresser there's a bunch of peso coins, a cologne, and an underarm-whitening deodorant. Why would Jun or anyone need whiter underarms?

I look at the sum of Kuya Jun's routine in his room. Even though he doesn't have parents, he has his life together. Going to college, keeping a schedule. Making music on his own. Not like me, exploding my own life after a few hard weeks.

I leave his room and go into the door facing his. Ate Nene must stay here. This room is smaller and brighter and hotter. There's a foam mat on the floor, narrower than mine downstairs. Resting near it are prescription pill bottles and more eye drops. On the wall are some photos—three girls cross-legged on a concrete floor, a graduation photo of one of the girls ten-ish years later. An older man wearing a baseball cap, standing solemn in a rice field. And an old family photo of my mom, me as a baby, and my dad. These two photographs are set near a half-melted Virgin Mary candle.

I look at the painted face of Mary, and my family photo, and I turn away.

The screen door bangs open and shut. Jun greets Ate Nene. I dart down the stairs.

"Find something up there?" he asks. His voice is light but I can hear annoyance. I see myself through his eyes for a moment. Intruder, stranger. Someone he's forced to host, when probably the only one he wants is Papa.

I think of something to say, an apology, an excuse, but a voice calls through the window. "Hoy, Junior, when's band practice?"

Jun swears under his breath. "Iggy, I told you, band's over." But he opens the screen door for a girl around my age.

She's browner than me by maybe three shades, with both sides of her head shaved even shorter than Jun's hair. Thick curls spill in every direction from her crown and down her neck. She squares her shoulders under a white tee with cutoff sleeves. Even while she moves slow, with a limp from her left leg, I can sense a steely cool in her. Like a fire could start, or invaders could take over, and she'd know what to do.

"Ligaya," he says. "Iggy. Our kapitbahay. Soon-to-be UP classmate."

She half smiles at me, dark eyes sharp. She juts her chin into the air in brief greeting, then keeps talking at Jun. "You forgot bandmate."

"Ex-bandmate," Jun shoots back.

"You have a band?" I ask. I think of the CDs and headphones upstairs.

"Junior, come on, we gotta get back in it," Iggy says. She sits, stiff-legged, and thrums her hands against the kitchen table in sharp, sure rhythms. "Ang ingay!" Ate Nene scolds her, then sets a packet of Jun's cookie balls out for us.

"You look like your brother," she says.

Her face is so confident, her presence so sure, she seems to demand I be the same. I feel too tired to be that. I wish I could hide. I wonder what Jun said about me. I shrug.

She nods and nods, like I gave the right answer. "Sorry, yeah, about your papa's accident. Really sucks. Doesn't mean your brother should give up music, though."

"Enough," Jun says, glaring from the computer. "You wanna hang out, stop it."

"Tangina," Iggy says. "So touchy, Kuya."

"Price of the cookies is respecting your lead singer's decisions," he says.

She eats a cookie ball and shrugs. I look between them for any hint of flirting, of more-than-friends. But Jun seems to be in older-brother mode, the tension between them instantly gone, like it would be between siblings. I didn't realize exactly how stiff we're being with each other, until I see him with Iggy. He's so much more relaxed with her than he is with me, the Papa-style joking in him emerging.

"You text Luna back yet?"

"How's your ex from Poveda?" Jun shoots back.

"She's seeing someone from Poveda now," Iggy sighs. "Some tycoon's daughter. So you and Luna are exes now?"

I look at Iggy and look back down again, fast. Iggy dates girls.

"Tanginang mga taga-Poveda," he mutters. "They always return to their own."

I try to find my way into the conversation somehow.

"Is Poveda a school?" I ask.

"Yes, ading, a high school. For exceptional girls," Jun deadpans.

Iggy's about to jump in with something else, but an older woman calls from somewhere outside.

"Iggy? Ligaya? Nasaan na yung batang 'yun?"

"She's here, Tita," Jun calls.

"Later," Iggy says, then, to me, "Tell your kuya to get a new guitar. Use those American dollars." Jun raises his hand, threatening her with the back of it. But it's just a joke, like how Papa would do to feign being annoyed. I glimpse an older woman leading Iggy back to the place next door.

"Is that her mom?" I ask.

"Her aunt," Jun says, stiff again. "She doesn't have a mom or a dad."

For the millionth time I want to ask more questions. But Jun's done talking. He goes to the kitchen counter and rips open another box of graham crackers. He dumps the sugary rectangles on the table, grips a knife, then smashes the crackers to crumbs with its handle.

THE SHOOT

The next morning, a car honks ten times outside, no one bother-ing to disembark to get me. Jun, extra grumpy at the noise, walks me out the gate. The shiny SUV with dark tinted windows idles curbside, spewing exhaust.

When I get into the SUV, it's like I'm back in another world. The air-conditioning is icy, and Bea looks her usual elegant self again, ready to step in front of any camera, even in a T-shirt and jeans. She's not even made up for her shoot yet. "Hey, cuz," she says.

Tita Baby sits in the front seat. She doesn't look at me when I get in. I look at Bea. She rolls her eyes toward her mom, then types something on her phone to aim at me.

She insisted on coming, sorry. At least I won the argument to have you come along.

Soon we're in the worst traffic I've ever seen. We seem to move less than a foot every ten minutes.

I see more kids along the road. They're playing a game, though, in between begging. One throws his broken slipper at an empty aluminum can; the others run and laugh. I think of Papa laughing.

Ma called us earlier to say he's making some verbal sounds now. Papa's white blood cell count is still of some concern, so the room is staying extra dark and cool for his rest, and Ma and the nurses are wearing gloves as a precaution before touching him.

"I thought rush hour was over by now," Tita Baby complains to the driver. This is a different guy; I wonder if the other one was fired. Still, no one tells me this driver's name.

"Heavy traffic everywhere, ma'am," he says in English.

"Are you modeling jeans today?" I ask Bea.

"Don't distract her, this is an important day," Tita Baby says.

Bea's the aloof version of herself now, not as casual as she was when she texted me or talked to me outside Lolo Joe's house. She coolly ignores her mom.

"No, I just wear whatever when I get there," she says. "I like to be comfy first."

I look out at the road. The exit signs are green, like in California. But they seem older, more battered. We finally get to a bridge and turn off at a sign that says Buendia, but it takes us another hour of crawling before we make it to a cluster of high-rise buildings. The streets are as busy and wide as downtown Los Angeles, with hundreds of workers in business-casual clothes crowding the huge, clean sidewalks.

"We're in Makati," Bea says, then sits up ramrod straight and waves one cupped hand like a sarcastic queen. "The Manhattan of the Philippines!"

The driver pauses at the parking lot of a shimmering hotel. Three guards pass a metal-detector device under the car, then a Labrador sniffs and sniffs the trunk. They let us drive forward to the building lobby entrance. The guards here wear crisp white long-sleeve shirts with Mandarin collars, and microphones in their ears, like secret agents. They hurry to open our car doors, and their gazes stay on Bea's pale face. Bea ignores their greetings and goes straight for the front desk.

Who gets ignored, and who gets ordered around? Who gets courtesy? It's like there are people here whose service is automatically expected, then ignored. It makes me even more tired and annoyed. I wonder why Bea buys into it now.

Bea signs in at the front desk, and we follow her into a silent, metallic elevator. It's like we're her entourage. A lady elevator attendant—I've never been in an elevator with an attendant before—sits on a stool, swipes an electric card, and presses a button for our silent, fast ride to the top floor.

The doors open, finally, into a penthouse. But really, it's another world. Like a Filipino minimalist hipster kingdom. There are ferns and marble counters and low-set, blocky furniture. Some young assistants offer Tita Baby a seat on a clear plastic chair that's nearly invisible. All the walls are windows. We can see the city stretch forever around us. I didn't realize it had so many green trees.

A tall, regal figure with long, elegant gray hair and an all-black, flowing caftan, carries an enormous, multilevel toolbox of makeup, and kisses Bea on both cheeks.

"Mother! How are you, po?" Bea pecks the makeup artist on both cheeks.

"Oh, anak, you only get more graceful each year," Mother gushes. "I swear you are taller, brighter. Ang ganda-ganda mo."

They walk ahead of me, overcomplimenting each other. Mother shows Bea a rack of clothes, explains the day's schedule, hands her one outfit, then shows her to a dressing room—just a circular wire rack with a curtain.

"My cousin will be my dressing assistant today, Mother," Bea announces, and Mother nods warmly and opens the curtain for me too. "Proceed, po, pinsan."

I join Bea behind the curtain. I think I see Tita Baby rising to object, but Bea shoves the curtain closed, and I know Tita Baby won't want to make a scene in front of strangers.

"Uh, I'm not trained for this," I say, looking at the glittery piece Bea's somehow supposed to shove onto herself.

"God, finally," Bea says, then lowers her voice. "Listen. I stayed awake last night because I couldn't stop thinking about it. I have to say it. I'm sorry, all this stuff with your dad, Lolo Joe being a dick to you and your mom, it sucks. I wanted to help."

The tension in my heart unclenches a little. "Thanks," I say.

"And I have to say it, I have to say it. It was wrong. That teacher was wrong to you. She took advantage of you. She was selfish. That was fucked up."

All the air goes out of me.

Bea gets gentle, seeing my face. "Before we left, I heard your mom talking to my mom. She was, like, almost crying with worry. Saying she told that teacher to stay away from you. She shouldn't have been like that with you."

"Been like what." My voice is flat, deflated.

Bea looks like she wants to hug me. I flinch away.

"Did she say what—did she say what the teacher said?" My voice gets high and frantic in the way I hate.

Bea exhales. She regrets mentioning what she heard.

"The teacher said . . . she said she cared deeply for you."

Hope surges up in my chest. It must show on my face, too.

"Are you all right, girls?" Mother's voice calls out.

"Bea?" Tita Baby calls.

Bea turns away and takes off her T-shirt. She lowers her voice to a whisper.

"Look, I actually don't think your mom, like, cares if you like girls, or whatever. But that teacher is—how old is she?"

"Twenty-five," I say. "Eight years older."

I answered too quick. Bea stares at me and says, "Can you imagine kissing someone eight years younger than you? A nine-year-old?"

"It's not like that!" I cry.

"Girls?" Tita Baby says.

"Cory was just worried she was going to damage the dress!" Bea calls. "But we figured it out! Almost done!"

She whispers, "The teacher also said it was the worst mistake of her life. That it would never happen again. Ever."

I want to find an open window.

I want to jump out.

To care for me is a mistake.

To return my affection is a mistake.

An intrinsically disordered mistake.

"I'm just glad it didn't get worse for you," Bea says. "We all are."

I turn to the opposite wall, away from my cousin. I'm like a dunce in time-out. Except my sense of humiliation is so strong, I'm sure it's going to murder me. I gaze at the curtain, waiting to die.

"Can you help me latch?" Bea asks.

She's changed into what turned out to be a glittering, tight, golden dress. She breathes in with her back to me. I help her hook the final hook. "Take my slippers to my mom?" she says. "And, dude. It'll be okay." She stares into my eyes. Then she opens the curtain and is the model, celebrity Bea, a force field of self-assured beauty, stepping into heels Mother put out for her.

I move, stiff, like I've just been hit by a car. Tita Baby grabs the sandals from my hands, then pulls out a plastic grocery bag from her massive purse and wraps them up. She scolds me to sit. I don't.

I stand behind Tita Baby, near the elevator door. I watch photographers set up a white screen. Bea sits at the edge of an armless, white leather couch. Mother the makeup artist perfects her, together with a hair assistant, using beauty tools I don't know the names for.

Then when they're done with her, Bea looks out over the city like it's hers.

I didn't know until this moment that Bea isn't modeling the

dress. She's modeling the building. The penthouse. The place. She's probably going to be the person on the cover of a real estate or hotel brochure.

There's so much pride on Tita Baby's face. Pride, and wonder—feelings she probably wouldn't ever say out loud to Bea, but that show on her face.

GOD BLESS JESUS WINSOME TAXI

It was easy to leave the shoot. So much motion, and so much focus on Bea. No one even looked when the elevator dinged open.

Now I'm walking out alone, down the hill of the parking lot, past the guards and the sniffing dogs. It's my first time walking here in the Philippines alone, doing anything here alone, and I pause, feeling free and lost and reckless.

I walk to a corner and find it fenced off against a busy avenue. I see office workers heading down an underground escalator. I take it, and then another escalator up.

I walk down a quieter back street. I pass food carts setting out trays of adobo and menudo and other stews I don't know, piles of meat and sauce my parents never made at home.

I get really tired. I move to sit on the curb.

A man in a tattered green tank top sits at the next corner, sorting through the contents of discarded plastic bags. He looks up at me, then down again, like he's ashamed, or scared of me. I realize, if I sit, people here might think I'm like the trash sorter. People in suits and uniforms might look down on me the way this man thinks I'm looking down on him.

The thought makes me even more tired. What are the rules here?

I stand there, not knowing what to do next, sweat soaking my shirt.

A once-white car slows near me. It's adorned with hand-painted black words: *God Bless Jesus Winsome Taxi*. The driver rolls down the window. A gray-haired man in a tired red polo shirt, someone who might have been forty or sixty, calls out to me. "Taxi, po? Taxi?"

"Sige, po," I say, and I get into the back seat.

It smells like a whole stadium of people have sat and sweated and smoked and farted on the vinyl.

"Saan, po?" the man asks.

"Uh." I search my memory for where Jun and Iggy said we were. "Teachers' Village. Po. QC."

"Sa may UP, po?" the man asks.

I don't know where to tell him to go, so I just say, "Opo."

He frowns at me in the rearview mirror, then drives.

Papa turns to me in the front seat.

"Did she hurt you, anak?" he asks.

He starts bleeding from his head. He doesn't wince. He just keeps looking at me.

* * *

A hard brake jolts me awake. I gasp.

"Your phone, ma'am," the driver says.

I look. There are half a dozen missed calls from Tita Baby, and ten from Bea. It vibrates again.

"Maybe it's your husband," the driver muses in English.

I freeze, creeped out. Then I decide I still feel reckless. "I don't have a husband. Or a boyfriend," I say.

The driver lowers the corners of his mouth. "My daughter also," he says. "She's thirty already. T-bird. You know T-bird?"

He guffaws. I see a small rosary dangling from his rearview mirror.

I look through the contact list of the Nokia. I see the name JUN.

"Tomboy! Short hair, always wearing pants. She work in Hong Kong as a helper. She have a friend," the driver continues.

I've never heard the term "T-bird" before, though girls at school have called me a tomboy. I never knew why—I didn't even play any sports or cut my hair higher than my shoulders.

I can't tell if the driver is being gross and flirting. Or if he's lying. He seems to just be grandfatherly. I think about telling him everything—Ms. Holden, my dad, my cousin. Maybe he's my confessor. Like a taxi priest.

I think of my cousin and I think of Jun. I stop myself and say in Tagalog, "Maybe you can talk to my brother. For directions."

He agrees right away. "Sige!"

The first call doesn't go through. The taxi driver keeps musing aloud.

"Too bad, my daughter," he says in English. "I want another grandchild. But bahala siya. At least my son have a wife, two boys."

I try again. I recognize Jun's low, familiar voice.

"Hey. It's me. Corazon. Cory."

"Your tita says you left the shoot; she keeps calling me."

"Sorry—can you tell this taxi driver how to take me home?"

The driver aims his bare hand at me. "I'll talk to your brother, po!"

"You just got into a random taxi?" Jun's low voice gets faster. I haven't heard this frantic tone from him yet. "Stop speaking English—ay, puta, he heard you na. Tell me what's on the window. The cab code."

It looks like numbers have been scraped off the right window, so I look at the left. "'God Bless Jesus Winsome Taxi Corp. UVN 1594. Telephone 576-5551.'"

"Don't worry, ma'am," the driver says, cheery. "I'll bring you home. You're safe here!"

"If the doors aren't locked," Jun orders, "lock them all now. Then give the phone to the driver."

I lean around the car and flip the plastic tabs of the doors closed. The driver grins but says nothing. He seems wistful and pained. I hand him the Nokia.

They have a short talk. The driver's voice is cheery, obedient, singsong. "Yes, sir," he says. "I know the place. Yes, of course, of course. It's okay, it's okay. All right. Here she is again."

The driver hands the phone back to me.

"Hey," Jun says, "if he tries anything, just get out and go to a gas station or a Jollibee. Make sure all the doors stay locked. I'm low on load, I'm having him bring you to me at UP. If I text you, text back right away."

Now I'm finally fully scared. I clear my throat, trying to hide it. "Okay." He hangs up.

The driver turns the radio on. Something called Love Radio, with a screeching, baby-voiced announcer. *Like mo? Share mo!* I keep my hand on the right door handle, and I eye the lock, in case I need to jump out. I have no idea what this driver would try.

We end up in a place with a lot of trees. There's a statue of a man with his arms outstretched. He's looking skyward, like he's preparing to dive. He's naked, with the columns of a huge building behind him as his backdrop.

We pass roadside snack stands and two-story, gray school buildings. The driver stops at a small, one-story building with a green metal roof. I see Jun next to an ice cream vendor.

The driver grins at me in the rearview mirror. "Okay!" he says. "Safe and sound!"

I dig into my pocket. I take out a blue bill. He flaps a hand back and forth. "No change, ma'am," he says, and smiles again, hopeful and sheepish. "It's okay?"

Jun opens the driver's door and hisses some sharp words to him, too fast for me to catch. The driver finds a yellow-colored bill in his pocket and hands it to Jun. I get out. When the taxi drives away, I think the driver looks a little wounded, a little tired. I feel guilty for being scared of him.

Jun is still tense, though. "Hey, don't do that again," he says to me. "A lot of crazy shit happens in this country."

I should be startled, I guess—I just met Jun in person, and now he's not just annoyed, he is truly pissed off at me.

But his protectiveness. The fear and gentleness under his low voice. It feels familiar. It calms me.

"Sorry," I mumble. "And thanks."

"Just don't want you to get kidnapped," he mutters. "Papa would be pissed. I'm keeping this, by the way. As commission for your safety." He waves the yellow, five-hundred-peso bill at me.

"I thought you said it was safer here than California," I mutter.

"It's dangerous for ignorant FilAms everywhere," he shoots back.

We look away from each other, not knowing what to say next. Jun stuffs the bill into the pocket of his black jeans. I look around us at the food the vendors are selling. Green mangoes with shrimp paste in plastic bags. Ice cream flavors in a yellow cart with metal compartments. In a bigger green stall, little orange orbs and pale white discs fry to brown in bubbly oil.

Jun sees me looking. "Fish balls," he says. "You want to try? Will it give you the shits?"

I shrug. "Sure, probably. Let's get some."

He smirks. "I'll order. You pay."

Jun gets us two half-dozen orders of fish balls on sticks, on paper-and-foil trays. He slathers some mysterious sweet brown sauce, then adds an oniony vinegar. He gets a bright green soda too. I use another blue bill to pay. I remember what my mom said, and I hand Jun the change. He shrugs and takes it.

"Your mom texted earlier. Papa's blood is normal," he says. "They don't have to wear gloves na. The white cell count is okay."

I nod, relieved. We stand at the cart's narrow green counter, not speaking, eating together. The fish balls are sour and salty and good. It makes me wish my parents were here with us. I think they'd like the vinegar. I want to know if my dad ever came here, if he taught Jun the ritual of ordering fish balls.

Jun says, as if he heard me, "Papa says this is his favorite. He can't find this in California. Even as a kid he'd come here, beg for someone to buy one stick for him. He'd dance, sing, laugh. To make himself different from the other kids. Better sales pitch."

I think of my dad singing to my mom. He'd sing Journey and Phil Collins and Carly Simon so loud and off-key. Tears sting me. I blink fast, try to pretend it's the vinegar. I look into the concrete hallway of the building next to the fish ball stand. Little groups of kids are running and clapping, in between sticking their hands out toward students and university employees who ignore them.

I want to bombard Jun with questions. I could do it for weeks, I think. But I feel like I already asked too much of him today. I decide on just one.

"Did Papa grow up around here?"

Jun nods. He chews his final orange disc, takes a sip of soda. "With my mom. Nearby. In a barangay where you'd probably be mugged."

I frown. His mom. Jun's whole family history, parallel to mine.

PINSAN

That night the bell rings. Kuya Jun thumps down the stairs and looks at me. "Expecting someone?" he asks. Ate Nene moves to the front door. "Baka si Luna," she says. Maybe it's Luna. Jun stops Ate Nene and goes out on his own.

I hear his voice approach the front door a few moments later. "Cory, your pinsan."

My cousin? Bea's here? I hesitate. I'm not sure I want to see her.

They don't come inside. I smell smoke. I open the door. Bea and Jun have lit cigarettes together. They sit next to each other on plastic chairs in the fading light, easy, familiar.

"You guys know each other?" I ask.

Bea exhales. "My mom and I bring him balikbayan boxes every year," she says.

"We chat for like five minutes each time," Jun says. "Adds up over the years. Maybe we've known each other for an hour now."

Bea laughs. I ask, "How'd you get here without your mom?"

"I lied that I had a dinner meeting with a new ad firm," she says. "Lying is efficient. I don't think she'll speak to you ever again, by the way, after the panic you caused her by leaving the shoot. Wrecking a dinner table, then peacing out in Makati without telling her. Damn, cuz, way to be in the Philippines."

"You wrecked a dinner table?" Jun asks me.

I don't respond. I wonder if Bea wants me to feel guilty, if she'll spill the whole Lolo Joe story. She just smiles in my direction, like she's pleased with me.

"You still playing the violin?" Jun asks Bea, somehow knowing to change the subject.

Bea shrugs. "Here and there. How's the guitar?"

Jun stubs out his butt. "It's not. Sold it. Will leave you guys to it."

He goes inside.

Bea hands her cigarette to me. I shake my head no. I feel calmer with her here, though, even though I ran from the shoot earlier. Someone familiar amid all this newness. We sit for a minute.

"Just wanted to check in," she says. "See if you need anything. We go back to California tomorrow. Mom and Dad don't want modeling to disrupt my school year too much, of course."

I nod. I wish she were staying, but I don't say so.

She puts out her cigarette against the dirt of the garden. "I didn't mean to freak you out by telling you," she said.

I say nothing. I hear Jun typing on the computer inside.

"So?" Bea asks. "How are you? Do you need anything?"

"I'm fine," I say, automatic.

She watches me, disbelieving. "What?" I ask.

She inhales, thinking.

"There can be times," she says, slowly, "when you're vulnerable. It leaves you open to . . . the wrong things. The wrong people. The wrong people, making the wrong choices."

She goes quiet. I get cold and angry and embarrassed and armored again.

Bea goes on. Now she reminds me of her mom: not knowing when to stop.

"It's happened to me too, kind of," she says. "Older guys, in their twenties and thirties, saying they want to mentor me in acting, or 'take me to the next level.' Here in Manila and in LA. They're always charming. Talented and hot and, like, nice, even."

"Stop," I say. "It's not—you don't know—"

She does stop now, sensing the volcano in me.

After a few moments, Bea tries again. "If you ever want to talk . . ."

"There's nothing to talk about," I snap.

Pots and pans bang somewhere, cooks bantering with each other. A karaoke machine plays a triumphant fake trumpet sound, and a man laughs, then coughs into the mic. Another diesel engine buzzes.

"Those guys," Bea says. "Those creeps. It sucks. It really sucks."

I look at her, still angry. "Come on," I say. "Your life is pretty awesome. That's just one thing, out of, like, a million great things."

Bea doesn't respond right away. She rubs her upper arms and

looks toward the gate, then at the ground.

"I used to wish I were Jerome," she says. "He's not monitored. He's pretty, I guess, as a guy. Those damn dimples. But he's not, like, required to be pretty. No one guards him like they guard me."

Something shifts in Bea's voice. It's unfamiliar, the kind of voice you use to reveal something deep and important that you never say. I don't know how to deal with it. So I joke.

"You wanna be a guy?"

"I wanna be free," she says. "I need to be free."

My anger dissipates. I don't know what to say. I never imagined my cousin wanting, or needing, anything. The longing in her voice lingers in the air between us.

Bea's phone rings. Then it dings with several texts.

"Shit. My mom. She figured out my agent's not with me in Megamall."

She stands and gets on the phone with Tita Baby. She pretends the reception is bad, and says she'll be home soon.

"Jun?" she calls into the house. "Would you be okay calling me a cab?"

"Sige," he calls back. "You don't want to stay and party?"

"I do," she says, "but my mother calls."

I feel a pang.

"We'll visit your mom and dad in the hospital," she says. "And if you want to chat or whatever, just text me. You have that old phone, yeah?"

"Yeah," I say.

I think about asking a final question. I think, wildly: maybe if I ask just the right question, my cousin can answer something for me.

But I stay wordless, not knowing quite what to say, and I watch Bea leave the gate and get into a cab. Whatever it is, I'll have to ask and answer myself.

UNSENT

~~Dear Ms. Holden,~~
~~It wasn't a mistake~~
~~It wasn't a mistake~~
~~I wasn't a mista~~

Dear Ms. Holden,
Dammit. Dammit. Shouldn't I want to be quiet now? Shouldn't I leave
you behind? Like you want. But here I am writing again
Trying to draw your tattoo again
~~again and again~~
Are you really what Bea says you are?
~~Did you~~

Please, if it's what I'm supposed to do
Please teach me something, from somewhere, anywhere in history
that will help me forget you

REVELATIONS

For the next few days I study on my mat and eat the food Ate Nene makes us. I underline the first and last paragraphs, where the main ideas are, in the history handouts. I barely skim the rest. I look at the few photos and paintings in the text, marred by photocopying.

I get some ideas to draw. An imperialist. A white man with a burden.

But whenever I start, I rip the page out and face another blank one.

On Skype, the nurses put down mats under Papa's heels to prevent pressure sores. Ma learns how to gently move his arm and leg joints so his muscles don't get too stiff. Dr. Miller and Dr. Chiu shine lights into Papa's eyes to make sure the pressure in his skull hasn't increased. He winces after they do that, but the doctors say some of the winces could be involuntary.

There isn't much news. Just more watching and waiting.

* * *

One morning, Jun fills a plastic bag with a few cans of Vienna sausage, a shirt, and bar soap from the boxes I brought. "I'll go for dinner with my mom in Cavite," Jun says. "I'll take the bus, be back late. Just text me if there's news of Papa."

His mom. Jun brings her stuff from the boxes. I feel like I should be taking notes, piecing everything together. But he seems like he's in a hurry to leave.

Ate Nene sees his rush too. "Your dinner is not for so many hours, Jun," she says in Tagalog. "So many buses for you to take on EDSA. Have lunch with your ading. Go take her outside."

I hesitate, sort of wanting to be alone and quiet, not wanting to trouble Jun. Jun hesitates too. "I dunno if she can handle the dangerous streets," he drawls in English.

I scowl. Ate Nene pulls out a tattered little umbrella from under the sink and gives it to me. "Then you protect your ading," she says, then to me, in English, "but don't get sunburn."

I wonder why Ate Nene is so insistent. Then I realize she's never alone in the house. She's always looking after us. She basically lives at her workplace. Maybe she wants some time to relax.

I take the umbrella.

"Be careful," Jun mocks me as we walk out of the gate. "We don't want you kidnapped and sold into FilAm slavery."

When we walk outside our door, the afternoon daylight's gotten stronger. It feels like it's punching me in the face. Jun doesn't seem to mind it. "You're okay to walk even though it's hot, right? Teachers' Village has trees and sidewalks, unlike the rest of this city." He points to our blue street sign. "Know what that means?"

"Matahimik," I say. "'Quiet.' But . . . it's noisy here."

"The streets here are all named for virtues. But probably all the streets are opposite. Madasalin might have a gambling den. Mabait has hostile neighbors."

"Prayerful. Kind," I say.

"Bery good," Jun says, emphasizing his own accent, making it sound like our dad's.

"Do mostly teachers live here?"

"Nah. Used to be mostly UP professors, but now it's whoever can manage the rent. Students. NGOs. Gentrifiers. Ignorant FilAms. Whoever. Open your umbrella," he says. "You'll feel better. Init kasi."

I scowl at him but I open the old umbrella above myself. He's right, it is better in the heat. The shade halts my squinting and sweating.

"Sige," he says, and we walk, single file.

We turn right, past the dolphin mural building in front of our apartments. We walk in the street, close to parked cars. I want to try walking on the sidewalks Jun mentioned, but there's always some obstacle—a pothole, a tree growing through the cracked concrete, a car using the sidewalk as a parking space. Blue motorbikes with sidecars zip by, then slow near us, calling out, "Tri-si-kel, ma'am?" before speeding off again when Jun shakes his head. It makes me nervous that guys keep pulling up next to us with their loud motorbikes, but Jun just walks on. We turn left onto a street called Malingap, a word I don't know.

At each corner, wooden poles are marked Tubero, Lipat Bahay, Bedspacer. I recognize the words "plumber" and "moving house"; they're some of the tasks our dad does. Did. Does?

I look up. The poles are heavy with countless crisscrossed power lines.

We pass a music school and a car wash and a barbecue place where guys without shirts watch news on an old TV and chew zigzaggy meat off sticks. We pass a small stall selling goat stew, surrounded by skateboarders hopping onto spray-painted concrete blocks. We pass a little shop where kids crouch and chat with each other, sipping soda from straws stuck into plastic bags. Chip bags and candy hang on wires tied to a mesh-cage window. The shopkeeper sits behind it, fanning herself.

We turn right on a street called Maginhawa, another word I don't know. We walk past nail salons and a small gym and a café and a bakery for pan de sal. I glimpse an alleyway where shoeless little kids are playing on the asphalt, where the two-story homes look like precarious, temporary, patched-together sheds.

"Don't walk down that way alone," Jun says. "You'll get robbed. Or kidnapped."

"Does everyone here joke about that stuff?" I ask.

"I'm not joking," Jun says. I listen for his sarcasm, but I don't find any.

We get to the end of Maginhawa. At this intersection, cars are paralyzed, waiting to turn. Hulking jeepneys try to muscle past shiny new sedans. Motorbikes and tricycles lurch onto cracked sidewalks and then back into the gutter, shooting past the tangle.

I see some mobile phone shops and a blue-and-yellow sign for a huge supermarket. Then I smell the familiar grill and grease of a burger joint.

I remember my last meal at In-N-Out with Ma and Pa, when I got the hundred percent on the quiz, and my dad was still up telling jokes, and my crush on Ms. Holden was still a secret. It feels like a million years ago.

"Buy one, take one burgers," Jun says. "You want? Or you need air-con? Americans usually need air-con."

I hear his mocking now, and I say, "We can eat outside."

He leads us to Burger Machine, a tiny trailer with a griddle and a few stools outside. "Take out or dine-in, po?" asks a teenage-dude cook.

"Dine-in," Jun says. "Cheesy bacon and longganisa."

We sit on the stools. I turn and watch the street. It's electric and tense and full of motion. I've never seen this in California. I feel like there's going to be a car accident every second.

But we don't see any accidents. Just people driving and motor-biking and walking and selling and buying. Doing their lives.

Jun texts on his own Nokia for a moment. Then he points out a place called a ukay-ukay, for used clothes. "Those donations meant as foreign aid for disasters here? They end up there," he says.

"Do you ever shop there?" I ask.

"Nah, I just wait for Papa to send . . ." He stops, clears his throat, and doesn't go on.

I see a place to get shoes repaired and keys replicated, next to another cell phone shop. I see a man with a machete next to a wooden wheelbarrow, selling buko. My parents only ever got coconuts in aluminum cans from Seafood City. I wonder what a fresh green one is like.

"So it's summer right now here," he says. "Your mom says we'll take you for your AP test soon. If you need a book or something, I can get for you from the library at UP."

I flinch. "I have printouts," I say.

"But maybe you need more books. Supplement. Do you study Philippine history in California?"

"I'm doing European."

"Of course you are," he mutters. I wonder if he's annoyed at me or at California. I look at the ground, not knowing what to say.

The grill guy hands us our burgers in white paper. I don't unwrap mine. Jun polishes one off in about two seconds. I bite my burger. It tastes weird and sweet. The meat is like mealy cardboard.

I wonder what Ms. Holden would say about all this. How she would talk to Jun. She'd be easier with him, more joking with him, offer to take him surfing.

I feel that stab again. That wanting-to-tell-her-everything.

I remember Bea talking about creepy guys. I shudder.

"You said Papa and—and your mom, they grew up here," I ask Jun. "Where?"

Jun smiles a little. "Where we passed. The dangerous part."

We watch the street a little longer. I turn this new knowledge around in my head. Every question opens more questions. I think of cruel Lolo Joe and obedient Manag Merlie, my cousin and Tita Baby used to visiting them. My mom grew up in a gated community.

My dad grew up in—a shed? A dangerous alley? The worlds here seem so far apart. Would my parents ever have met here?

"That's why they worked abroad," Jun says. "Different countries. My mom was in Saudi. Papa on ships, then the US. If they stayed here?" He makes a face. "Maybe he'd be a tricycle driver. Maybe she'd be a maid, a yaya."

"Like Ate Nene?" I ask.

Jun snort-laughs. I've made him angry. He thinks I'm judging him. Maybe I am.

A man in jean shorts and a white tank top pauses near us, showing armfuls of belts and wallets. We shake our heads and he walks on.

"What does your mom do?" I ask, feeling like I'm risking something dangerous.

The side of Jun's mouth turns up, not really a smile.

"She stays at home in Cavite. Has a new husband she met in Saudi, some other kids, younger than me. But you know. Papa leveled up in the States with your mom. Like the Beyoncé song. 'Upgrade.' Good for him, leaving my mom. Sucked for her, though. For a while."

I sit very still, my hands suddenly sweaty around the burger wrappers.

"My dad left . . ."

Jun shows his teeth to me, a bitter grin. "Oh," he says. "They left that part out of their love story?"

"I thought . . ."

Jun swears in Tagalog under his breath, the grin never leaving his face. He seems tired in a years-long way.

I think of my parents meeting in my mom's office building, my dad singing to her, fixing everything for us. I had always assumed Papa had been single when he met Ma. That he'd had the breakup already. Or that his ex-wife had left him first. My parents never mentioned Jun's mom, and I never asked.

I knew Jun and I didn't share a mom. But I never thought about Papa leaving Jun's mom. He was someone who repaired, never someone who broke.

"Ah, huwag kang mag-alala, ading," he says. Don't worry, little sister. "Not like it all happened today."

I think of my parents in the hospital, waiting. If my dad stayed in the bed forever, would she find someone else? Would she leave me behind in the Philippines with Ate Nene, like our dad left Jun?

"Sorry," I say. "I can't finish this." I give Jun my burgers.

"What's wrong?" he asks. "Papa's past choices stole your appetite?"

I say nothing. He calls to some kids pushing a makeshift wooden cart full of plastic bottles, hands them the burgers. They grab them and sprint away like Jun might change his mind. Some other little kids come near us, asking for burgers, but Jun shakes his head, like he did at the motorbike drivers.

"I better go to Cavite soon," Jun says.

We stand. I feel that want, that stab, that restlessness in me again. I eye the mobile phone shop next to the grocery store.

"One more stop? Need a new phone?" Jun asks. "Nokias are bulletproof—I don't see why you'd want a different one." But he leads me toward the shop and I follow.

Jun waits outside, texting on his own phone, while I enter into a blast of air-conditioning. I'm not sure how much cash Tita Baby left me, and I have no idea what the rate from pesos to dollars is. Every phone is in the thousands. I know I should save the money because so much of it is meant for Jun and Ate Nene—their utilities, their food, their pay-as-you-go internet connection. But I'm not really here to buy. I just need to look.

I pick up a random, shiny new phone with a touch screen, some brand I've never seen in the US. The two employees in yellow polo shirts ignore me, gossiping with each other instead.

"Does this one have a working Wi-Fi connection?" I ask in a loud, American English voice. I don't know how I know to speak English to get their attention, but I do.

"Yes, ma'am," says one of the woman employees. She points out the curved bars on the screen, showing that the Wi-Fi's on. She says to her coworker, "Inglisera pero mukha namang Pinoy." She speaks English but she looks Filipino.

I go to my email. More spam and prayer newsletters.

I go to Facebook. It loads slow with my log-in. I search for her name.

It's the same stuff, no updates. Just the Max Bruch link again, the same beach profile pic.

"Do you want to buy, ma'am?" the saleslady asks me. Outside, Jun's started to pace.

I'm about to put the phone down when I remember another name. The name Ms. Holden mentioned in her car. Her ex.

There are more than a dozen Jennifer Gonzalez profiles.

213

A bunch here in the Philippines. I narrow it down to Jennifer Gonzalez around LA. There are still so many.

But I find the Jennifer Gonzalez I'm looking for right away, because of her profile picture.

It's a couple-y profile picture, like the annoying ones girls at Saint Ag's post, to brag about their off-campus boyfriends. Except this Jennifer is a lawyer, and she's showing off Ms. Holden.

I click on the picture. I look at the date.

Two days. Two days after we kissed.

I read the caption.

It's a quote.

I don't know if it's from a poem or whatever.

"I missed my beautiful friend. I had to send her away to bring her back again."

Someone commented with a bunch of hearts.

Someone else commented, "I had a feeling this would happen," with a wink.

Ms. Holden looks tanned and happy.

She wears a blue windbreaker I've never seen before.

Her right cheek presses against Jennifer Gonzalez's left cheek.

She looks at home. She looks proud.

I stare and stare, feeling that old, nervous desire again, turning into something new and lethal inside me.

I remember how our kisses felt inevitable.

I remember kissing her, and her kissing me back, each time.

I remember her sadness in her car.

All of it—my missing her, my memories, my love—

Yes—my love—

Love—love is—

All of it churns in me like poison.

I stare at the screen.

It's shaking now, because I'm shaking.

"Ma'am—" one of the employees says.

"No, I'm not going to buy anything," I snap in English.

I drop the phone with a clatter. It hangs from the counter by a little metal string. The employees swear at me in low murmurs to each other.

"Mga pangit kayo!" I shout, and bang the door open. You're so ugly.

I don't know what direction I'm walking, only that I need to be fast. I need to outrun myself, outrun all my history, all the parts of me capable of feeling anything at all.

"Hoy!" Jun cries.

I stop in the middle of the street. A car honks at me and nudges me forward, touching its bumper to my hip. The insistent plastic and metal of the bumper is almost gentle.

The heat, the fumes, the poison rising in me. I stop and put my hands on my knees. Car horns roar. Someone—a security guard?—trills a whistle.

Jun holds a hand out at the cars, palm up. The cars all slow for him like magic. He tugs my shirtsleeve and leads me out of the street, toward the supermarket entrance. A uniformed guard asks if I'm sick. Jun says in Tagalog that I'm just dizzy.

It's still too bright and crowded and the speakers are playing a maddening, repetitive jingle. But it's air-conditioned.

"What is it?" Jun asks in Tagalog. "Is it Papa? Did your mom tell you something?"

I shake my head but I can't speak. We stand near a gigantic stack of eggs in gray crates. People are staring but I still lean down, keeping my hands on my knees. Jun asks if I need to go to the clinic. The jingle, Jun's voice, all of it seems distorted in my ears.

I look for something in my memory to calm me. But all the usual scenes, the ones that soothed me or filled me with longing—now they contaminate my insides more and more.

Sitting in her office, riding in her car, listening to some wisdom about history, about school. The surfboard, her voice in my ear, telling me sometimes there are trees, nothing is my fault.

Jun sits me onto the tile and crouches next to me.

I try to obliterate my memory of her, burn it down. I try to think of my parents instead, replace the transgression and betrayal of her with their hard work and their love for each other. But my dad is gray, floating somewhere I can't reach him, forever disappointed in me. My mom can hardly look at me, onscreen or in person.

I think of praying, I think of replacing my mortal parents with saints and Mary. But they're still quiet. They're still so far from me. There's no guide for me. There's no one.

"Easy," Jun says. "Easy lang."

"There's no one," I say, and my voice sounds sick, like I'm about to puke.

Jun waits, crouching near me and the eggs. "Easy," he keeps saying. "Steady lang."

ALBULARYO

Jun finally gets me home, asking the tricycle driver to go slow because I'm sick. He tells Ate Nene to watch me. He goes and returns from his Cavite dinner with his mom. And a fever comes for me and stays for days.

I shiver and ache on my mat in the living room. Ate Nene makes me a weird, grassy tea. Jun brings me buko juice—now I know what a fresh coconut tastes like.

The three of us Skype with my mom and with Papa each night, still, and on the third day, soon after my mom sees me onscreen, we take a cab to a nearby clinic. A doctor pokes me with a needle to draw blood. I flinch and yelp and then cry a little. The doctor frowns at me, thinking I'm a baby. But I'm thinking of Papa and all his needles.

The blood test tells us I don't have dengue fever.

"She's just adjusting," the doctor tells Jun and Ate Nene. "It's hard for some FilAms here, always sick." She sends me back home, to rest and hydrate with more buko juice.

Papa undergoes more tests. An EEG shows he's not having seizures. His blood pressure stays within the normal range.

His bed angles up. He starts to blink more. His pupils start dilating more normally in response to light. He opens and closes his hands when noises in the room get louder.

Jun and I gaze at the motion of our father's hands. I think of how much his hands can fix. My eyes fill up with water and I shiver more. Jun stays silent, hiding whatever's happening behind his eyes.

Our dad sleeps, but his sleep seems to turn less dangerous.

"You back yet?" Jun asks me, nudging his foot against the mat.

I blink my eyes open. It's midmorning. I hear a rhythmic tapping.

"When I first got to my aunt's house as a kid," a voice says from the kitchen table, the tapping paused, "she says I was nothing but crying and diarrhea. Worst orphan ever."

"Salamat for the share, Iggy," Jun says.

"Anytime, Kuya."

The doorbell rings. Jun picks up two plastic-wrapped packs of the graham-cracker crumb cookies he made, and goes outside. He returns with a handful of coins.

"Always hustling," Iggy says.

Jun crouches near me. "Ate Nene wants to call the healer," he says. "You want healing?"

"Sexual healiiiing!" Iggy sings, and Jun shushes her.

I text Bea.

> Yo. Im way sick

The reply comes quick.

> Oh no cuz, again? Did you do more drugs? Seems like you should go straight-edge.

> No jus sick, Mayb food

> Maybe stress too. Manipulative relationships are a lot to recover from. Try to rest.

The Nokia keypad feels too small for a response to that. I rest instead, like she says I should.

The doorbell rings again, waking me from another sleep. Ate Nene goes out to the gate. I sit up, feeling my brain slosh back and forth in my skull.

Now there's an altar in the middle of the living room. It's a little like my parents', with fresh loops of flowers set around a different bust of Jesus's head, and three Our Lady of Guadalupe candles and a couple of rosaries. The tablecloth is a dark red T-shirt: *Jesus Nazareno* in yellow script under an illustration of Jesus looking skyward, the crown of thorns cruel around his head.

Jun's sandals slap down the stairs. He looks at the altar and shrugs. "The healer," he says. "She's here every so often, mostly for the neighbors."

"The healer?"

Images come to me: an old, wizened man with long gray hair and a loincloth and a leather sack full of herbs. Before I can ask, Ate Nene opens the door. Behind her is a young woman with a smooth, unlined face, her hair in a ponytail, her eyes sparking with laughter, like she's always ready with a prank. She's wearing blue jeans and a black Nirvana T-shirt from the nineties. She and Ate Nene are snickering with each other, speaking Tagalog too rapid for me to catch. Ate Nene holds the door open with a chair, letting a breeze in. The young woman sets her bag down, crouches, and looks down at me. I wonder what she sees. The last time I looked at myself in the bathroom mirror, even my hair looked ill, wilted, thin. Deep pockets of shadow under my eyes.

"Napaano ka, ading? LBM?" What's with you, little sister? Diarrhea? She stares hard at me, then her laughter erupts.

She opens her canvas bag, taking out small plastic bottles labeled with worn blue crosses and setting them before the altar. She crosses herself, lights the three Mary candles, and sets a plastic chair in front of the altar. "Upo ka," she tells me.

I look at Kuya Jun. He's decided to sit on the stairs to watch. He shrugs, leaving it up to me. I wobble up and sit in the chair. The doorbell rings. Ate Nene opens the screen door and tells an elderly couple to sit outside to wait. Other people arrive: an older man with his teenage son, a young couple with their baby.

220

"Are you a doctor?" I ask. "Er, doktor ka?"

The young lady grins. "I just try to help," she says in Tagalog. "It's good you can speak! So many FilAms cannot."

She lifts the back of my shirt and rubs me with something from one of the bottles. I flinch. It feels like oil, smells sharp. Eucalyptus, maybe, or another plant I don't know. She frowns. "Wow, hah," she says. "What happened with you?"

She sets her hands on my shoulders, holds her hands close to my ears. She sprinkles water on me. I realize no one's told me her name.

I hear the snap of a cell phone camera. "Hoy!" the young woman calls. "Bawal yan!" Ate Nene goes outside; the teenage boy waiting had tried to take a picture of the altar through the window. Ate Nene takes his phone, presses a couple of buttons to delete the image, scolds him as she puts the phone back into his hands.

"What's the diagnosis, Dr. Ate?" Jun drawls from the stairs.

"Know-it-all UP student," the young woman mutters. "Go back to your books!"

She hums to herself, hovering her hands around me. I recognized the Black Eyed Peas song "I Gotta Feeling."

I think of my parents' faith—do Catholics allow this?

But then I remember. Whenever one of us dropped a utensil, my mom would say a visitor was coming; a girl if it was a spoon, a guy if it was a fork. I always rolled my eyes, since my dad's crew and Tita Baby were always coming over anyway. They told me to finish all my rice, since every grain meant another year in purgatory. I figured they just didn't want me to waste food.

When she speaks to me, she says it loud enough for both Ate Nene and Jun to hear.

"Ah, the wound of the father. It wounds you, too! Your heart, no? Drowning. Painful."

I frown at Jun. But he looks at me wide-eyed. He looks at Ate Nene. She shakes her head; she didn't tell the healer.

"You had a spirit in you also," the healer goes on. "It was a strong spirit. Greedy. Selfish. It took your energy, took up too much space everywhere inside you. You had to feed it, always. It was hungry. But recently the spirit left you, and now you're weak. It was holding you up. Now you have to hold yourself up. Your body must learn again, to live without it."

My eyes fill with tears and my throat burns. My sorrow happens too fast for me to hide it from Jun and Ate Nene. I want to replace all this new feeling with skepticism, with denial, but I can't.

"Good! Good that you cry," the healer declares, grinning again. "It's part of the process. It means you're letting go." She unrolls a worn, dark red bamboo mat. "Lie down, little sister," she says. "On your stomach."

I obey her. The bamboo mat smells like kindling, like straw. It reminds me of Papa and his sawdust smell. Tears draw wet tracks on my cheeks.

The healer massages my back through my shirt. She pauses at my shoulders, sprinkles more holy water on my head. I feel the texture of another, different oil, this one with no smell. She massages my shoulders, rubs my neck.

"There's something else, eh," she says. "You angered an old man. An old woman is sad. You want to make penance. But only to the old woman. Not the old man."

Manang Merlie. I remember her happiness at seeing me, and the mess I made that she had to clean up.

The healer murmurs a prayer in a language I don't know— close to Tagalog, but all the words are different. She tells me to sit up, then holds a bottle out to me.

"When you feel the weakness, the pain," she says, "you rub this on your forehead, only a little. Then you rest."

I nod. "Salamat, Ate," I say.

"Ingat, ading," she says.

My session with the healer is over. Ate Nene tells someone else to come inside. The young couple comes in first, holding their baby. I sit below Jun on the stairs. I wipe my face, brace myself for him to say something sarcastic. He doesn't say anything at all. He texts a bit, staring at his Nokia, then starts to play a digital snakes game.

I watch the healer minister to the guests. The baby has an ear infection, a piece of her past life following her. The mom has something else, too—something in her womb. An elderly man has a decaying knee, something wrong with his karma. Some people get oil, some people get little cloth scapulars. Each of them leave a few coins in an old peanut butter jar on the altar.

I turn to Jun, finally getting it: I should pay something for what the healer's doing. "Does she have, like, a price list?"

Jun sighs. "You pay the albularyo whatever you think her

services are worth," he says, the bitter note returning to his voice. "Whatever your healing tells you to pay."

I take a couple of purple bills out of my pocket, get up and put them in the peanut butter jar.

Then a man comes in, and he looks the sickest of all. His legs are spindly, thinner than my arms, and under a tank top, his chest curves inward. He looks toward Jun and grins. His grin holds two teeth. There's something familiar about him. Jun rises, solemn. "Tito Leroy," he says.

"Junior!" Tito Leroy says, and there's a wheeze in his voice. Jun touches the back of the man's wrinkled hand to his own forehead. Jun looks to me, uncertain, then, after deciding, says, "Kapatid ko. Pamangkin niyo." My sibling. Your niece.

"Anak ni Rommel?" Tito Leroy says. He grins even wider and hugs me. This is my uncle. My dad's brother. I look for some resemblance between them; in their voices, their smiles. I should be happy to meet him for the first time. But I stiffen and try not to pull away. Tito Leroy smells like diesel and sweat gone bad.

Jun looks at Ate Nene. She avoids his gaze.

The healer gets solemn. "Tito Leroy," she says. "Still sick." She murmurs some extra prayers and gives the older man two bottles of holy water. "You take this instead, hah? When you feel the urge."

"Come for dinner," Tito Leroy says to us. And, to me, "I miss my brother. My brad. You know, I taught him everything. Mechanic. Machine. Because of me."

He lingers at the door. He seems to want to stay longer.

He seems to want something more. Jun nods and opens the screen door for him, showing him outside. "Sige, Tito," he says. "Soon, po."

His mouth opens and closes. He blinks hard. Then he leaves.

We're alone now in the house with the healer, who begins to pack her bag. "Ate," Jun says, "how did Tito Leroy know to come here?"

Ate Nene lowers her eyes. "I saw him at the palengke, po. He does not look well."

"He's not," Jun says. "Tanduay is bad medicine."

I don't know what Tanduay is. I'm guessing it's not fantastic, and not really medicine.

"Illness is illness, little brother," the healer singsongs to Jun. "We all deserve healing, even from heavy drinking. We all need help." She stops and stares at his face. "You. Come here."

"Hay naku," Jun says, and I can hear our father's exasperation.

The healer picks up the chair and taps it briefly on the floor. She turns to me. "You, little sister, what do you think your brother needs?"

I look at Jun. "Why not sit? Are you scared?"

Jun frowns at me, mutters to himself, and drops himself into the chair. He crosses his arms. The healer scolds him and uncrosses his arms. She tells him to take off his glasses. He shakes his head, but takes his glasses off, letting them dangle from his right hand. I'm stunned, again, by how much more he looks like our dad without his glasses; the same eyes, the same shape of his forehead. Just his hair longer on top, parted to the side, instead of buzz cut.

The healer puts her palm against his chest, like she's feeling for a heartbeat without a stethoscope. She puts her other palm against his back. He straightens, waiting. She shakes her head. She's silent for a long time.

"He's worried about you, eh. He's not angry at you, little brother," the healer says. "Not like you are with him. You don't have to carry around all that shame. So heavy."

Jun bursts up and slams out of the house. A few moments later we hear the front gate slam too.

Ate Nene calls out after Jun, but stops at the doorway, letting him go. The healer keeps packing up her altar as if nothing has happened at all. "When he comes back," the healer says to us, "tell him no spicy food, only cooling. Apple, pear. No chili pepper. So his head can cool. His heart, also."

I wake again in the dark, chilled by my own sweat.

I hear the screen door creak, Jun taking off his shoes. I pretend to keep sleeping. Jun sets something down beside my mat and goes up to his room.

When I'm alone downstairs, I turn on a light to see what he left me. It's two books, laminated, with digital tags on them that say UP DILIMAN. One is a history book by Alfred W. McCoy, *Policing America's Empire*. And one is a book of comics, *El Indio*. On its cover, a guy wears a mask and holds a machete. It looks like something from the 1950s, full of intrigue and spies and fights. I bet my dad would like it. I wonder if he already knew it.

A note falls out of the comic book, scrawled on the back of a flyer for some indie rock band night.

Hope these help for your history test. And for fun—Jun
P.S. Don't lose them, too expensive to replace at the UP library.

PENANCE

Ru sure its dis Jollibee, ther r like 1000000

Bea texts back.

You do realize it's 1am in CA. And yes, I told Manang
Merlie the Anonas Jollibee. I did my part of the recon-
naissance. You can call her if you want, you know. I gave
you the number to the house.

Sory to keep u awake. Thx. 1 mor thing, what do i order
4 her

Ask her!!!! But definitely two piece fried chicken with
spaghetti. At least. Plus rice. And don't forget to pay her
jeepney fare.

I stare at the Nokia screen, then put it in my pocket. I was a half
hour early to Jollibee, reading my history handouts and trying and
failing an AP practice quiz at the end of a chapter. I drew some
Jollibees of my own—sad ones, crying. I keep watching the door.

Manang Merlie enters the Jollibee, wearing frayed gray dress pants and an old white blouse instead of her scrubs. She feels like a grandparent again, one I never had in California.

I don't know if I should call Manang Merlie family. She works for Lolo Joe, and raised my mom. I know she's an employee, that he expects her to obey no matter what. But I can't ever imagine commanding her.

I spring up. "I'm so sorry, po. I made such a mess." I take her hand and press it to my forehead.

She nods. "It's okay, ma'am," she says.

She's cautious, meeting me now, not as warm as she was when she first met me. I wonder if she thinks I'll suddenly get angry again. I wonder if she thinks I'm like Lolo Joe. Am I?

I look up at the busy Jollibee lines, the families crowding for their fried chicken and spaghetti burgers. I ask, "What would you like, po?"

"Whatever you like, ma'am. No need for me." I remember Bea's text. I order her a whole bucket of fried chicken and two spaghettis and extra rice. A pie and a little burger for me.

"So much!" she says, as I carry it carefully to our table.

"Maybe you can share with the other maids when you get back," I say.

She nods. She begins to eat, shy. She seems to have relaxed.

"Are you okay here?" she asks. I realize she means the Philippines.

"Opo," I say. "And you, po. Are you okay?"

She smiles a tired smile.

"What story do you want about your mom?" she asks me.

I smile back. "Lahat, po." All of them, ma'am.

She's quiet for a moment. Then she starts slow.

Manang Merlie tells me how Lolo Joe delighted in my mom at first, as a baby. Until her first word: "no." From then on, it was always no.

If Lolo Joe told her to come downstairs, my mom would stay upstairs. If he said to wear patent leather shoes, she would wear sneakers. If he wanted her to ace her classes on manners, she failed those classes and she aced math and gym instead.

The house was full of Lolo Joe's yelling. Any small mistake: my mom's Catholic school uniform out of place, a stray comment from a teacher about my mom being a strong woman, a whisper in church, and Lolo would take away her books, lock her in her room, ban her from the dinner table. Lola Irma sided with her husband no matter what. He was the leader of the household. So Manang Merlie, not my Lola Irma, would bring my mom meals. Then she'd secretly take the plate back to the kitchen and wash it herself. She could have been fired. But it was her small rebellion, caring for my mom.

When Tita Baby was born, she was the peacemaker, the obedient one, the girly, well-mannered one. The one Lolo Joe and Lola Irma preferred.

School was my mom's outlet. If she couldn't please her parents at home, at least she could please her teachers. She was clever, reading ahead of her grade level, doing problems ahead of her math level, memorizing the Catholic rules of the catechism. She was a year younger than everyone else when she went to Ateneo, the Catholic university next door to UP. And she graduated before everyone else.

But she and her father never made peace. No achievement was enough. The more my mom's academics made her independent, the crueler Lolo Joe became.

"Sayang," Manang Merlie said. "Sayang talaga." Really, what a shame.

So when my mom went with the family to California, to attend Tita Baby's wedding to Uncle Dan, she stayed in the airport bathroom while the plane took off with her parents.

In California she could be free, even if she was broke. She started taking on programming jobs, and, without telling our lolo Joe, my mom convinced my aunt to petition the US for her citizenship.

Lolo Joe threatened my mom, sent her letters and phone calls promising to cut her out of her inheritance if she didn't return.

She didn't return. So he did cut her off.

Manang Merlie tells me: Lolo Joe was hoping my mom would take over the family business. Microloans and import-export. He didn't want to die without someone taking over what he'd built for the family. And he knew my mom had the mind for it, not Tita Baby.

I think of my dad; how he showed me regret, happiness, solemnity. How he never went a day without making my mom laugh. How he wanted me to know my brother, even just through the computer.

"Your papa!" Manang Merlie says, like she can see my thoughts of him playing on my face. "Oh, your papa. I never heard your mama so happy. When she met him, oh. So kind, your father. So kind, so loving. But your lolo. Ay. For your mother to marry such a man. Married already. No money. Simple life. For your lolo, no more. He never spoke to your mom again."

I think again of my father leaving his first marriage, the unresolved new pain that keeps returning.

But I think of my mom, happy at our kitchen table. All three of us there, at home.

I wonder if Jun will ever join us. Or if my parents will ever be able to come here to see us, together.

Manang Merlie nods. "It was a lesson for me also," Manang Merlie says. "As a parent. To tell my kids what I think is best, but to let them be. Even though they are far, studying, working. We are close. They want me to stop working. But not yet. I'm still able-bodied."

"I think your lolo suffers a lot, still. Under his anger. He's a good man also. Always pays me on time."

Her eyes cloud. She takes my hand. "I pray for your father. Life is so difficult sometimes, no?"

I nod. Tears prick my eyes. "Me too, po." I squeeze her hand. "The doctors say there's progress. Small progress."

"You never know what will happen, even to a good man. I pray for him to come back to us."

We finish eating, and I pick up our tray of wrappers to throw away. A uniformed Jollibee employee takes it from me instead. Bea says Manang Merlie's weekly break is only for a few hours. She'll have to go home soon to start Lolo Joe's dinner.

I realize, when I sit back down for her last few moments with me, that she's mostly talked about my mom. She hasn't told me much about herself. She has children living far from her. She has her own family, her own history.

"Manang," I start. "What about you?"

She smiles. "What about me, child?"

I don't know what to say. I decide to ask, "What did you want to be? When you were my age?"

She laughs again. She shakes her head. "Dreams are for my children," she says. "For the young. Like you. Not for me. I'm old now."

I look at the sticky surface of the table, swallowing my words. I had wanted to show her that I knew she was more than just a maid, more than just someone who worked for the family. But my question wasn't right. When she was sixteen, she had already been a maid for two years. Maybe my question was even cruel.

We get up. I hand Manang Merlie a blue bill. I think my mom would be okay with that.

Manang protests a little. I say it's from my mom, for her kids. So she takes it, packing it into her small purse.

Manang Merlie points her chin to the door. "That's your brother, no?"

Jun is there, hanging around the door, waiting for me, texting on his Nokia.

"Yes, ma'am," I say.

Manang Merlie says, "He's handsome. Just like you! He is guwapo, you are guwapa." I blush and shake my head. "You'll have many boyfriends. You just choose the one who is kindest, like your mom did."

I fill up with explanations and protests, but I let them go in silence.

"When you see your mom," Manang Merlie says, "tell her I think of her always. I want to see her again one day. If it's God's will."

She reaches to touch my forehead, and traces a cross there, sending me away with her blessing like my parents do.

THE 1890s

On our morning Skype chat, Papa is still. I watch his hands and his eyes, willing them to move. I don't look at Jun, but I think he wants the same.

"There have been good signs," Ma says. "But he's very tired. What is easy for us is exhausting for him."

There's something else she wants to tell us. I can see it in how she's waiting.

"Maybe I should leave you to talk to Corazon, Tita," Jun says, glancing at me.

"Hindi, Jun," Ma says. "I'll tell you also."

He stays sitting next to me.

"Anak, I'll be moving in with your tita Baby for a while, and renting out the house here. Maybe to a family from church. We need the income. Sana we won't have to sell. For now, we rent."

I think of Papa's work shirts ironed and hanging, and the

memorial photos on the fridge, and all the appliances Papa repaired. I swallow.

"It's a hard decision, Ma. But it sounds like we need to."

She looks at me and nods.

"You let us know, po," Jun says, "if we can do more from here."

Ma shakes her head. "Remember. Your job is your studies."

There's a sound from Papa; a small moan. We lean toward the screen.

"Involuntary," Ma says. "Normal. Not a sign of pain."

She takes his hand again.

Later I wake from an afternoon nap, a pile of history handouts near my head. I'd written two sentences of a sample essay question, then slept by accident.

Iggy's on the computer nearby, checking Facebook.

"Yo," Iggy says. "Don't worry, it's my internet load stick, not Jun's. Just doing my weekly spying on relatives in Romania. With Jun's blessing, of course."

I sit up. "Romania? Is that a joke?"

She frowns.

Then she leaves.

I'm surprised. I wonder if she left because she's mad at me.

A screen door slams open and shut. Iggy returns and drops a laminated news article on my mat. She gets back on Jun's computer.

The article is from 1993.

BENGUET, Philippines—Six people, including one foreigner, were killed in a traffic mishap early yesterday morning. The driver of the Full Moon bus from Dau, Mabalacat, lost control of the vehicle around Poroc, Pampanga, on Tuesday morning.

An infant, Ligaya Adrian, was the sole survivor, with only a leg injury when she was thrown to the road. Police called the baby's survival a miracle.

Her mother, Nancy Adrian, a half-Aeta Filipina, was recently married to her father, Kenneth Adrian. Kenneth Adrian is a Romanian citizen.

According to a statement from the Romanian embassy, the infant will be placed in the custody of her aunt in Quezon City.

"Whoa," I say. "Sorry. I didn't mean to—"

"Nah, nah, it's fine," she says. "My aunt keeps that around to explain why she's raising a kid who looks so different from her. An Aeta Filipina Romanian child, instead of just Aeta Filipina like her. Also so that I get more scholarships at my hippie high school, and discounts at the orthopedist."

I don't know what to say. She sounds sarcastic. But her face isn't smiling.

Before the silence goes on too long, I offer, "My cousins are Filipino with a white American dad," I offer.

"Lots more FilAms than FilRoms," she says. She gets up, done with looking at Facebook. "You wanna check your email or something? Aren't you, like, studying for some AP test?"

I shake my head. I haven't wanted to look for anything online since freaking out at the mobile phone shop.

"Guess you're a weirdo millennial who never does?"

She sounds a little harsh now. I wonder if I said something wrong.

"See ya," she says, and goes back next door, walking slow and careful. "Oh, hey, tell your brother we want a word tonight, whether he likes it or not."

She leaves before I can ask who she means by "we."

I set aside my history printouts and open my notebook to a blank page. According to my AP study schedule, I should be taking another multiple-choice practice test.

Instead, I draw.

I doodle-copy images from the Indio comic Jun checked out for me. I can't quite get the style—the masked man looks abstract and innocent in my doodle, not like the brutal avenger he is.

I draw Manang Merlie's gold-rimmed glasses. The crack in one corner.

I try to draw Jun's glasses. Then his fade haircut, his black clothes. I draw captions pointing to him, an asterisk under JUN with his full name: ROMMEL EMMANUEL TAGUBIO JR.

I draw Ate Nene; her short haircut, her basketball shorts. I don't even know her last name. No one told me. Do Papa and Ma even know?

I draw Iggy, her curls, her partially shaved head. I start to draw her ankle, the crisscrossed scars I saw there, but I don't know if that's wrong to do. I cross it out instead.

* * *

The doorbell rings around six in the evening. Ate Nene and Jun look up from our adobo dinner, frowning. "Boyfriend, mo?" Ate Nene asks me. "Girlfriend?" She laughs. I glance at Jun, panicked. He shoves another spoonful of meat and rice into his mouth, ignoring us.

"Hoy, Junior!" Iggy calls. "We're hungry!"

I remember what Iggy said earlier; that she and a mysterious "we" would be visiting. I feel bad for not warning him.

Jun swears. But his tangina sounds oddly affectionate. "I told them not to come," he mutters. He goes out to the gate.

Soon a noisy group around Jun's age crosses the apartment doorway. Iggy carries a bag full of zigzaggy meat on sticks. Two guys grip Jun's hand, half hug him, and hand him bottles in paper bags. A girl with a shaved head carries two Shakey's pizzas. She besos Jun like my tita besos: an air peck on each cheek. She besos me too, and Ate Nene, and they all say, "Welcome home, little sister!" to me in Tagalog. I wonder what Jun told them.

Ate Nene sets out a tin can of peanuts and jerky from the box my mom packed. Soon Jun's friends are gossiping in Tagalog too fast for me to catch, drinking gin they pour into chipped plastic mugs. Jun eats slice after slice of pizza.

I feel like I'm always at the edge of gatherings here, a quiet detective trying to figure out who everyone is to each other. This group of friends slow down and speak enough Taglish for me to figure out: They're a band. They're Jun's band.

Jun goes around and names them for me. There's Pol, a round

guy with a thin beard, long floppy hair, and a rainbow bracelet. "The lovebird," Jun says, "keyboard." Pol curtsies and blows a kiss to Jun. "Nic," Jun says, jutting his chin at a muscly guy in a dark red UP Mountaineers T-shirt, "second guitar. Iggy, drums, obviously." He looks across the room at the girl with a shaved head and a black T-shirt with a skeleton print of a human chest. "Luna," Jun says. "Steady. Bass."

Then the band chats. I let their Tagalog wash over me again, like I do when my parents have friends from church over. The band is talking business and gossip that doesn't have much to do with me. I get the gist; they're arguing about the next playlist, wondering if they should join the UP Fair gig, talking about acquaintances who broke up and got back together.

I watch Iggy and Luna. Iggy keeps her hand on Luna's shoulder, and they pass jokes back and forth with an ease I envy.

At a lull in their talk, Luna asks, "You understand?" I shrug and smile a little. "How is it to meet your brother in person after all these years?" she asks.

Jun rolls his eyes. Luna frowns and throws a peanut shell at him. I see something in the way she looks at him—longing? Annoyance? Affection? All of the above?

"He's . . . he's cool," I say.

"I am," Jun agrees, brushing the shell off his shirt. "I am cool."

"Have you seen his YouTube videos?" Iggy says. "His sullen solos?"

Jun frowns. "I don't know what you're talking about."

"He deleted them," Luna says, and rolls her eyes.

"Hay naku. That's why we're here," Pol says. "Intervention! For the lead singer who won't sing!"

Jun swigs his beer. Now I know why he has the headphones and the four-track upstairs. But the house has been silent of music since I've been here.

Jun's mobile phone buzzes. He reads a text.

"Guys, guys," Jun says, quieting the room. "Ading," he says to me. "It's your mom. She wants to Skype us now."

I get up and join him at the computer. The group whispers behind us, sometimes erupting in their own whisper-giggles. But they still themselves to listen.

My mom appears onscreen. Our dad's bed is elevated; a couple of nurses are talking to each other, another nurse writing something on a clipboard. I feel scared at all the motion. I don't like that I'll have that feeling in front of Jun and his friends.

But Mom seems different, lighter, even though her eyes are tired. "Jun, anak," she says to us. "Your papa is blinking his eyes in response to questions. He's going to the rehabilitation ward. His Glasgow score is a ten. He's leaving the ICU today."

I feel a sudden lightness too. I forgot what it felt like, living with less of a threat.

I hear a lift in Jun's voice when he speaks. He puts his palm on his chest. "Salamat sa Diyos," he says to my mom, formal, grateful. Thank God.

"Can we talk to him?" I ask. "Will he answer?"

My mom's eyes turn sad. I get angry at myself for asking too much.

"He's not yet talking," she says. "He still has the feeding tube. He opens his eyes and closes them. But yes, anak, you can talk to him."

My mom aims the computer camera. She whispers to Papa that it's us. Our father's face is less swollen, though it still seems gray. His eyes open a little. He blinks at the camera.

"'Tay," Jun says.

"Papa," I say.

But a nurse off-screen tells my mom they're ready. "More later, anak," my mom says.

We look at the blank screen. I can sense it without looking at Jun: We want to see more. We want to go with our dad to the other part of the hospital.

"That's good, no?" Luna says from behind us. "He's improving."

Jun goes to the clear bottle of gin and pours a mugful. He swigs it all in one go, sighs, and talks to the ground. "Yes," he says. "That's good."

The bandmates look at each other. It seems like they want to ask Jun something more, but no one speaks. Then Iggy raises her beer. "To Mang Rommel," she says.

Everyone else lifts their cups. "Mang Rommel," they say, like we're in Mass, praying his name together.

Everyone is quiet for a moment, sipping, waiting for Jun's cue. I wonder if they usually do that, since he's the singer. But he sits back down at the computer and doesn't say anything else.

I ask the room, to break the silence, "Uh, what's your band name?"

Luna sits up straight and gazes at me. I feel like I'm in trouble. "He didn't tell you," she says, and glares at Jun. He's the one in trouble.

"We forgot to mention it," Iggy says, helping my brother out. "The 1890s," Iggy says. "Or, more like, the Eighteen Nineties!!!!!" She headbangs and raises the pointer and pinkie fingers on one hand.

The 1890s. I search my memory for any mention of that decade from Ms. Holden.

"Why the 1890s?" I ask them, when I can't remember. "Did something happen?"

The room explodes with laughter so loud, I'm sure it shakes the walls. Jun's smirk returns to his face. "Tangina," he swears, and covers his smirking mouth with his hand. I feel ashamed and curious at the same time. "Oh, ading!" Luna says, wiping her eyes, when she can finally speak through her laughing. "Kawawa ka naman!" You poor thing! "Stuck in America!"

Iggy suppresses her own laughter and helps me out this time. "It's the America tax," she says. "Stealing her knowledge. Let's give her a break."

"Are you, like, punk?" I ask the band, to direct them away from my ignorance. But I'm just showing more ignorance. I don't really know genres.

"You haven't listened!" Pol says.

"It's more post-rock," Luna says. "Not really punk."

"With some indie pop," Nic says. "Think, like, the energy of Phoenix crossed with Godspeed You! Black Emperor."

"Don't be too America-centric with your references," Luna scolds him.

"Godspeed is from Canada," Nic grumbles.

Iggy sits up, and says, sounding like Bea at her most sarcastic beauty queen: "Local Philippine influences: Up Dharma Down's lo-fi feel, with Pedicab's wicked pace!"

I have no idea what any of that means. I grew up with my dad's American pop songs and my mom's classical. Again, Jun doesn't explain. He toys with the computer keyboard. I sense a heaviness in him.

I think I know a little of how he feels. I'm in two places at once. Here in the living room with Jun and his bandmates, but back at the hospital with my mom, waiting, waiting. Bilocation, Mrs. Scott called it: the ability of saints to be in two places at once. But I'm no saint.

"I treated him like an ATM," Jun says.

It's like his voice is coming from a different kind of place. From a dark, suffocating room, not a living room full of friends.

Everyone quiets. Luna gets up to put her hand on his shoulder. He doesn't relax, but he doesn't shake her off, either.

"When he was healthy, I was barely speaking to him," he says. "Sometimes I just lashed out. His last conscious thought of me, his last conversation with me, was me being a sullen dick. His ungrateful eldest, always asking for money."

I straighten up. He's been carrying so much, never talking about any of it. Till now.

"I was angry at him for so many years," he says, and he covers his eyes with his hands. "Baka I'm still angry at him, even now. Tangina."

The whole band gets up to put their hands on his shoulders. I have the sense of a team, or a group blessing. He laughs wetly. "Why are you guys group-hugging me," he says. "Ano ba?"

"It's not your fault," I tell him. I want to comfort him, too. "He sprained his ankle a couple of weeks before the accident. He was working alone. It must have messed with his balance. There's no way any of it was your fault." It reassures me to reassure him.

Jun shakes his head. "I should have asked how he was at least a few times," he says. "I shouldn't have just demanded and demanded."

"You were asking for the right things," Luna says. "It wasn't like you wanted a car. Last time wasn't even for you that you were asking."

"I'm not talking about now," he says, his voice thick with sadness. "I'm not even talking about the day he fell. I'm talking about my whole damn life."

Jun shakes his head. He goes upstairs to his room.

I follow him there. I don't know what to say to take away the sadness that just burst out of him.

I poke his door open. He curls up on his bed like a boy in his stifling room, not bothering to turn on a fan or a light.

"Kuya Jun," I say.

I want to tell him Papa wouldn't want him to be in this much pain. Wouldn't want him to feel guilty. But I feel useless.

I feel a hand on my shoulder. It's Luna. "Ako na lang," she says.

She enters his room, turns on the fan, then closes the door behind her.

There's not much left to say, after I come back downstairs. Pol says, "We'll go ahead." Nic follows his lead. I half hug the guys as they go, asking them to come back. It's something I've seen my mom do with guests to our townhome, sometimes just to be polite. But I do hope they come back, even if Jun might not want them to.

Iggy stays behind, cross-legged on the living room floor. I'm not sure why. Maybe because it's like a second home to her, living next door. She sits silently for a while, thinking to herself. Then she gathers up peanut shells to take to the trash, and dishes to take to the sink.

Ate Nene stops her. "Ako na diyan," she says, and neatens the room herself.

"How's your eyes, Ate?" Iggy asks.

Ate Nene raises her eyebrows and nods. Iggy nods too. She looks at me.

"I'm just next door, you know?" She pats my shoulder. Then she goes home. Luna and Jun stay upstairs.

HISTORY LESSONS

The band keeps visiting at night. Sometimes Pol has to work at Jollibee; sometimes Nic is on some hike, and the rest of the band teases them with relentless affection in their absence. Luna and Iggy never miss a visit.

There's a rotation of snacks and drinks: chicharron, McDonald's fries, more barbecue on sticks, fried quail eggs. Always a Shakey's cheese pizza for Jun, purchased by Luna. After the first night, he only eats three slices, then shares the rest with Ate Nene.

Jun starts to laugh more, though his face always returns to its solemn frown, until someone throws a bottle cap at him or teases him too.

The nights end the same way: late, with Luna and Jun going upstairs, and Iggy and Ate Nene and me staying downstairs, watching TV.

One night, I insist on washing dishes instead of Ate Nene. Iggy joins me, putting away open packages of snacks.

Then Ate Nene takes a dish from me. She says to me in Tagalog, looking at the floor, "Last time. With your father. It was for me, Jun was asking."

It takes me a moment to understand. Jun was asking Papa for money for her.

"It was what you needed, Ate," Iggy says.

She shakes her head. "I told him, don't trouble your father."

I wait. I remember my dad slamming shut his bedroom door, Jun arguing with him, texting him.

"What was it, Ate Nene? What did you need?"

"Eye surgery," she says, looking down. "I was having a hard time, with my eyes. Even just cooking. I needed a procedure, for cataracts, infection."

I remember Papa that last day at the breakfast table. His hard silence, his sudden anger at me.

I remember more, too. That we had been eating canned meats and frozen veggies at home, because they were cheaper. That my mom and dad had both lost clients over the past few months.

And Jun. Both his parents had new families. Did he feel abandoned every day, all these years? Except by Ate Nene? Did he feel betrayed, when Papa said no?

I want to fix this. I have no idea how.

"Let me ask my mom," I say.

"Never mind," Ate Nene says. "The procedure is done already, healed already."

"He sold his guitar," Iggy says. "That's how he paid for it."

I think of what Papa chose, to save money for me and Ma.

How he took on dangerous jobs by himself. How he said no to Ate Nene's eye surgery.

I think of what I want to do for Jun.

Ate Nene smiles crooked at me. It's a smile with no happiness in it. She excuses herself and goes upstairs to her own room.

I can't sleep, though, and Iggy still doesn't leave. She watches me.

I go back to the living room, turn the TV on, and keep the volume low. ABS-CBN plays a scene from a seventies movie. Two women gaze at each other in a garden. The camera keeps moving between their faces. One tries to speak. The other urges her on with her face. But for three long minutes they stay silent. Their faces barely move. Their eyes say everything. Piano music swells. One woman leaves. The movie ends.

"You're cool," Iggy says. "You know that?"

She's solemn and certain, looking at me, direct. Her certainty makes me blush and shake my head in denial.

"Why are you denying your coolness?" she asks.

"I'm a mess," I say.

"Me too," she says.

I shake my head. "I haven't had to go through anything like you went through," I say.

She shrugs. "I'm not gonna lie. It sucks a lot of the time. There's a lot I'd like to ask them, you know? Just their opinions. I just have to guess. The guessing never ends." She sits up, carefully rearranges her left leg. "I still have family, though. My tita. My relatives in Sibiu. They help me guess. They tell me the parts of me that are like my parents. Tita Ana says I frown like my mom.

My cousins say I play drums like my dad.

"And anyway, neither of them was Filipino Romanian. Maybe I would have just confused them. It is what it is. And what it is, is a little different each day, I guess."

I'm quiet, listening to Iggy's history. How she seems to hold the sad parts and the happy parts so close to each other. How steady she still seems to be, how open she is to the different possibilities of her past, even after everything. I'm caught between admiring her and feeling embarrassed at myself. What she went through feels so much bigger than what I'm going through.

"Anyway, it's my story," Iggy says. She sounds older now, more tired. "It's still going. Just like yours."

The ghost of Ms. Holden returns to me then. Telling me everyone has a history. Asking me to tell her some of mine.

I clench my hands, then open them. They're shaking.

"What does your aunt think about you dating girls?" I ask.

She laughs. "Eh. She knows and we don't talk about it. Ever? Like good Asians. I dunno what my parents would think. Maybe they'd freak out. Maybe they're freaking out now." She looks up at the ceiling. "Sorry." She raises her beer and takes a drink.

"My mom . . ."

"Yeah?"

". . . she made me come here," I say. My voice sounds like someone else's.

Iggy waits. She puts her beer down on the table.

I think of when I talked to the Mary statue, asking her for

things, apologizing to her. It seems like so long ago, when I prayed, when I admitted my sins, and asked for help.

My words come in a rush.

I didn't realize how tired I was, hanging on to the words, until they left me.

"I fell in love with my history teacher," I say. "And my mom saw me with—with her. And she freaked out."

I sit frozen, exposed. I listen to the dark outside. I hear a diesel engine and a rooster. But it's the quietest the neighborhood ever is. It'll be morning light soon.

I don't look at Iggy. I wait for her wordless horror, like my mom's. I wait for her to judge and define what I went through, like Bea did. I wait for her to ignore it but keep it in her mind, cautious and distant, like Tita Baby.

I fight with myself, wondering whether to go on.

I look at Iggy. Her face is open, her dark eyes watching me. "Tell me," she says.

A wild animal rises in my throat. I swallow it down.

A door opens upstairs. Luna pauses on the stairs, looking at her phone.

"Parents are texting me ultimatums," she says. "Guess they finally realized I'd been missing from Katipunan for a few evenings now. . . ."

She looks up at our faces. "Oh my," she says. "Anyare?"

Iggy waves her hand at her to come downstairs, without taking her gaze off me. "I think this one needs listeners," she says.

"Is my brother okay?" I ask.

Luna sits, leaning her shoulder on Iggy's shoulder. I look between them.

"Never mind him, he just needs to be alone with his feelings like a boy does sometimes," she says. "Now you, ading."

I think of taking the truth back, saying never mind, I was joking, I'm drunk.

Instead I talk.

I talk about history class. About tutoring. What I knew about myself in secret. Then my dad's accident. The surfing lesson. The house where my dad fell. The parking lot. My mom, pulling me out of the car. Flying here. Talking to my cousin. Finding out on Facebook.

I go quiet and tired, emptying out of words.

I've been keeping my eyes to the floor. My shoulders have turned stiff, my hands pressed to my mat. I finally look at them. They're both gazing at me. Iggy looks at Luna.

"She colonized you," Luna says.

Iggy shoves her shoulder. "Don't bring your UP postcolonial thinking into Cory's confession!" she protests, laughing. "She needs support, not theory!"

Luna shakes her head. "I'm not joking. She took you over. You were vulnerable. You had something she wanted and she took it."

"People keep saying that," I say, remembering what Bea said, "but . . . she was also . . ."

"Good? She also gave you good things?" Luna says. "People say that about colonizers, too. Sure, we wrecked your lands and left you destroyed, but look at the sanitation system and all the

English dictionaries we brought!"

Iggy grins and shakes her head. But I don't like that Luna guessed what I was about to say. It makes me feel weak and predictable.

"Let me guess more," Luna says. "You blame yourself. You think if you did something different, it would have been different."

Her words catch in my heart, like something sharp cutting into something soft in me. I sniff. Iggy reaches out and holds my shoulder.

"It happens here too," Luna says. "Teachers using their power, feeding off the attention of students in the wrong way. But that's not what a teacher should do. A teacher should teach."

"Oh man," I say, my voice thick. "Did you guys make out with your history teachers too?"

Luna and Iggy laugh. I try out the feeling: being able to joke about it. The truth still feels too heavy to treat lightly.

"I've made out with a few guys," Luna says. "People think I give parang a gay vibe. Shaved head, confidence, et cetera. But no. Ally lang."

"A guy and a few girls," Iggy says, raising her hand. "Guilty."

"Was the teacher your only MOMOL experience?" Luna asks.

"MOMOL?"

"Make out make out lang!" Iggy says. "Acronym."

"Oh," I say. "Uh. Yeah. That's the only person I've ever kissed or anything."

"My gaaaaahd!" Luna exclaims. She springs forward and gives me a hug. "What a year you've had, ading! Your papa, and the colonization of your heart! And your grouchy brother!"

"Super intense, dude," Iggy says. "But I can be your HOHOL friend. Hang out hang out lang."

"Iggy naman!" Luna exclaims. Iggy laughs.

I haven't had many friends, ever. I like how they're claiming me, all of a sudden, as part of them.

She lets me go. "How are you now?" Luna asks. "About it all? Have you told him?"

I shake my head. I don't know what to say.

"Take your time," Luna says. "Don't tell anyone you're not comfortable telling."

"And, hey. It's always brave to love," Iggy says.

"What movie is that from?" Luna asks.

"Sis, I'm trying to make her feel better!" Iggy says. "Anyway, that's what they said about my parents. Romanian factory worker meets a half-Aeta Filipina? Only that kind of powerful love could make this," she says, framing her own face with her hands.

"It is beautiful, sis," Luna says. "The love story. And your face."

I think of my mom's cruel dad in his fancy house, and my own dad growing up in a neighborhood of shanties. "My parents too, I think," I say. "Even though . . ."

I think of Jun, and his mother—my father's leaving them still new to me. The fact of my existence depended on my dad's cheating.

Luna thinks through what Iggy said. She watches me think.

"Yes," she decides. "It was brave of you to love. And it was wrong of her to use you. Both can be true."

254

"Both are true," Iggy says. "No?"

What they say rearranges me. Puts me back together in a way I didn't know I needed.

The shame and dread and silence my heart was drowning in recede a little.

Both can be true.

"It was so real," I say. "But it, it wasn't. . . ."

I stop. I can't say yet what it was or what it wasn't. I wonder when I'll be able to.

"In due time," Luna says. "Give it time. It will be clearer."

The pain in me recedes a little more. It makes me wonder what else my recent history could mean. How else I could tell it.

We hear more roosters.

"I should get home," Luna says, "before my parents freak. Your tita will be looking for you soon, sis," she says to Iggy.

They stand. I stand too, to walk them to the door. I wish they would stay, sleeping near me.

Luna hugs me and goes out, leaving me and Iggy alone.

"I'm just nearby," Iggy says. "You're not solo with this anymore. Yeah?"

Then she hugs me too, for longer. Her arms feel strong. Her back feels strong. She smells like coconut oil and suntan lotion. She's as warm as her smile was.

We part a little, and she squeezes both my shoulders. Like she wants to leave part of the hug with me. Then she goes home, next door.

* * *

The next day, Jun and I watch our dad angled up in his new hospital bed. He has a roommate now, a pale, elderly man with a broken leg.

We watch nurses wipe down our dad's bare arms and legs, like a gentle baptism. My mom asks him to move the fingers of his right hand. He does, one by one. She kisses his forehead and laughs at how strong he is. He blinks and blinks, like he wants to joke back at her, I think. I can imagine his voice, though not what he would say. That belongs to him.

Jun just nods at each of these movements. I don't know if his nods are relief or apology or both. After a while he goes upstairs, like he usually does, to give my mom a few moments alone with me.

I don't know what comes over me then. Maybe it was the rush and relief of telling Iggy and Luna.

I say to the screen, "When I got here a few weeks ago, and we visited the house, I broke Lolo Joe's dishes. And wasted food. I got mad when he said something mean about Papa."

I cringe, waiting for my mom to slap me with her voice from California.

But she laughs. It's the first time I've heard her laugh in weeks. It's a quiet laugh, and maybe a little bitter. But it's still a laugh.

"Alam ko yan, anak," she says.

"You know?" I say. "Did Tita Baby—"

"Your pinsan," she says. "Bea. She told me. I asked her how your visit was."

I shake my head. Bea, the living news feed.

"Manang Merlie says you took her to Jollibee," my mom says. She looks at me, warm. I realize the look is pride.

"Now you know a little more," my mom says, "of why I chose to move away. My tatay is the opposite of your papa."

"I'm glad," I say. "You decided what you did. When you were younger. Maybe . . . maybe I'll—"

I pause. I still don't know how to talk about having a relationship someday.

"One day, anak," my mom says.

I look down at the computer keyboard. "Ano?" my mom asks.

I look up. "I'll type it," I say.

I open the chat box in Skype. I type a request. I explain what I'm thinking, how I know it's a hard thing to ask.

I finish and look up at my mom. She scans the words again and again.

"I'll see what we can do, anak."

HOW IT IS

Each day I find myself listening for Iggy coming and going. I start to recognize her careful shuffle outside the door, in her sneakers or sandals, her aunt's quiet voice asking her to carry something for her, her own voice humming to herself, calling out hi to us.

At each sign of Luna and Iggy I feel relief, like she's keeping something safe for me. Especially Iggy. Like what she's keeping safe is me.

I figure out a way to talk to Jun, though it isn't quite talking to him. I decide to try it one night.

"Can you sing for me?" I ask.

He swings around to look at me from his computer chair. He furrows his eyebrows and adjusts his glasses like he's seeing me for the first time. I think he's wondering if I'm making fun of him. "I'm serious," I say.

He stares a little longer. Then he clears his throat. "Happy birthday to you," he sings. "Happy birthday to you . . ."

"My birthday's in January."

He shrugs and turns back around to the computer. "We'll have spaghetti," he says. "For long life."

"I mean it," I say. "I wanna hear your stuff. You deleted it from YouTube."

"I knew I shouldn't have let the 1890s into the house," he sighs.

"Papa sings," I say. "He sings to my mom all the time."

"I'm sure he does," Jun says, his voice low.

I wince. That was the wrong thing to say.

This isn't going how I want it to.

"Whenever you're ready," I manage, "I want to hear one of your songs."

He stands and stretches, ending the conversation, then sits back down.

He clicks on a YouTube tutorial. He grips his own hair and takes notes while a guy with an Indian accent explains control systems in engineering. Then he goes out to tutor someone— another elementary school student—in math.

I finally open the history book Jun borrowed for me. I've never read anything like it—none of our history classes at Saint Agatha's talked about America's war in the Philippines.

I finally get it, why the band laughed so hard. The 1890s. The Philippine Revolution fought Spain. Then the US took possession of the Philippines, and Filipinos resisted again. I wonder why our high school history lessons didn't cover this. I wonder if I can use what I'm reading for the essay part of the AP test.

I draft an answer to a document-based essay question in my AP handouts.

I start doodling the soldier saluting on the cover of *Policing America's Empire* instead.

I fall asleep after the first couple of sections, my face pressed into a chapter titled "Colonial Coercion."

In my dreaming I hear jingling. It sounds like keys, or little instruments on my dad's tool belt.

I open my eyes in the dark, at my usual place on my sleeping mat, under the barred windows. The curtains rustle above me. I hear the jingling again.

It's the front door. The chain is moving. Maybe it's the wind.

I hear a scraping in the lock, like Jun using his key.

I groan, "What time is it? Are you tutoring this late on a Tuesday?"

I get up to help Jun in. But something stops me. His silence.

I wait for Jun to say something wry, or to ask me to unlock the chain. He doesn't.

Then I see a hand. It's pockmarked and wrinkled with small, round scars.

The hand reaches through the window screen.

The screen has a new, huge gash in it.

The hand gropes around for the door chain, trying to open it.

I back away, then stumble up the stairs. "Ate Nene," I whisper. I don't know why I'm whispering; should I be yelling?

"Kuya Jun," I say. I slap Jun's door with my palm. Ate Nene opens her own door, in her blue-and-white housedress and bare feet. "May—meron—" I try. But I forget all my Tagalog. "Someone's trying to come in," I say.

Ate Nene opens Jun's door. He's dressed in just plaid boxers, mouth open, drooling in his sleep like a kid. "Junior," Ate Nene says. His head rises. He squints at us. "Akyat bahay," she says, another phrase I don't know.

Jun bursts up. He slips a metal bar from his dumbbells, letting the metal weights slap to the floor. He throws on a black jacket and stomps down in his bare feet. We follow.

The hand has torn open more of the screen. Fingers grip the chain lock.

"Fuck!" Jun yells. He slams the metal bar down on the hand. "Aray!" someone yelps.

Jun rips open the front door and the screen door. He uses his own body as a battering ram, slamming someone to the ground. Ate Nene turns on the light. "Jun!" she warns.

But Jun shoves the someone again. It's a skinny guy. His face looks old and wrinkled, and his mouth is caved in, like he's missing teeth. He keeps trying to stand, but Jun won't let him. There's a small, dull utensil in the guy's hand. A butter knife. His other hand is floppy, useless now after Jun hit it.

Jun drops the metal rod and grabs the guy by the front of his too-big, green T-shirt. Then he lets him go, shocked.

"Tito Leroy," he says.

Our father's brother. The one who came to see the healer,

the one Jun was so careful around.

Tito Leroy sinks to his knees and begins to cry. "Forgive me," he says in Tagalog. "I'm sick, nephew. Forgive me."

Then his face curls in on itself. Like he's getting angry at his own groveling.

"Rich niece from California," he snarls, "and you give nothing to your uncle. I'm the elder of Rommel! You owe—"

Jun closes his fist and rushes Tito Leroy. Tito makes a high, whining sound.

"Jun, stop!" I cry.

Ate Nene is faster. She takes Jun's arm, strong. "Huwag, anak. Tama na. Awat na." Don't, child. It's over. It's over.

Jun shakes Ate Nene off and yells at her in Tagalog, "What did I tell you? What did I tell you about him?"

Ate Nene lowers her eyes, ashamed. I remember Manang Merlie picking up shards of my mess. "Pasensya na, po," Ate Nene says. I'm sorry, sir. Like she's just now remembering she's Jun's servant, not his parent.

Shame breaks across Jun's face, tightening his mouth. He swears again and turns away.

Lights come on in the other apartments. Neighbors look out their windows. A round woman, also in a housedress, opens the curtain of the window next door. Iggy stands next to her, in basketball shorts and a tank top.

"Please don't call the police," Tito Leroy whimpers. "You know what they did to me last time?"

"You deserve everything they did!" Jun yells. He looks at me and stops himself. He forces himself to get calm. "Tita, can Cory wait inside with you and Ligaya?" Jun calls to them.

"Opo, Junior," the woman says. They open the door to me.

"Cory, this is my tita Ana," Iggy says. I nod at the curly-haired woman, and remember to mano her for respect. Tita Ana brushes me away, warm and kind, saying she's not that old. Then she tells me to sit on one of the dark wood chairs. I can't, though. I stand at the window, watching. All three of us do.

"You okay?" Iggy asks. She puts her hand on my shoulder, briefly. I'm not, really, but I nod. She nods too.

Ate Nene leaves and returns with two sleepy guys in green vests. Jun tells them what happened, getting angrier as he speaks. They shake their heads at Tito Leroy on the ground. One of them uses his own Nokia to call someone else.

I don't think Tito Leroy looks anything like my father at all.

I wonder what kind of brother he was. What my father would do if he were here, if he'd get his sledgehammer out and go further than Jun did. Or if he'd be gentle and forgive his kuya.

A police officer in a blue shirt, with a yellow PNP emblem on the sleeve, comes in through the gate a few moments later. He doesn't look much older than Jun, with a military haircut, tall black boots, and a gun at his waistband.

The lights of the other apartments stay on. I can feel the neighborhood watching. I see a plastic wall clock above Iggy's dark wood couch. It says 2:16.

Jun tells the story of the intruder to the officer. I wonder if the police will have me make a statement. I try to remember what I know of investigations from my parents' movies and TV shows. In California my parents never really interacted with police. We didn't have to.

There was the one time, when Rika and I toilet-papered a house. The police just seemed amused, my parents relieved at how relaxed they were. Another time, a highway patrolman stopped Papa for a cracked windshield. Papa was super apologetic, repeating over and over how sorry he was. The patrolman just shrugged and handed him the ticket. Papa paid it by mail.

I remember now that Papa never looked the American police in their faces. Not the way Jun makes demands of the Filipino officer now.

"Hoy, where are you going? Where are you going?" Jun yells in Tagalog.

The officer touches Jun's shoulder, holding him back, and says something I can't hear.

Jun yells again, speaking English now. "No crime? Are you fucking kidding me?"

"Oh, shit," Iggy whispers, and Tita Anna doesn't scold her for swearing.

"Ganyan talaga dito sa Pilipinas," Tita Anna mutters. That's really how it is here in the Philippines.

The officer straightens and puts his hands on his hips. His right hand moves to rest on the gun strapped to his waist. My throat closes. I want to call Jun's name but I can't.

The officer says some calm words in Tagalog. Jun answers in loud Tagalog too, fighting not to swear again. "He tried to break into our home. That's a crime."

"He did not succeed in entering, sir," the officer answers in English. "And he's your uncle, he's family. How can you do that to your uncle?"

"You're lazy," Jun spits in English. "That's why you won't move."

The officer stares at Jun, his hand still resting on his gun.

The memory of Ms. Holden comes back to me yet again. Telling me about her brother dying. How she thought his death was her fault.

This time, the memory is actually useful. It spurs me forward. I don't want my brother hurt, or worse.

I charge out the front door. I ignore Tita Ana scolding me, telling me not to go outside.

"Pasensya na, po," I say to the officer, repeating Ate Nene's phrase.

"Cory, get back inside," Jun says.

But I keep saying it to the officer, ignoring Jun. "Pasensya na, po. Pasensya."

The officer looks at me, his brow wrinkled under his military buzz cut. "American?" he asks Jun, amused. "Visitor? Girlfriend?"

"Hey that's my sister," Jun says in quick, loud Tagalog, warning him. The officer chuckles at his anger.

"We're just very shocked, sir," I say, switching to English. "We were just scared. We know you're doing your job. We know you're working hard."

I don't know how I know to say all that. I feel like I'm

channeling both my parents, how they appeased authority figures when they needed something back in California. At least the officer's arms are crossed now. His hand is off the gun at his waist. He's smiling at me, still amused.

Tito Leroy stays on his knees, his head bowed, whining and pleading. No words. Just noises. I'm angry at him then, too—that he's the one able to walk and talk, while our dad is trapped in a wounded body.

Then the officer's mobile phone rings. It's the sound of a dog barking. We all jump, the ringtone so loud and harsh and repetitive, like it's going to bite us. The officer answers his phone and the barking stops. He turns away from us. He laughs a little, talking quick. He's going to meet friends at a bar on Quezon Avenue.

"Sige, sir," the officer says, grinning. "Miss. I have another call. Another case."

He turns his back to us. I brace myself for Jun to chase him.

But Jun doesn't. He watches the officer go, letting the gate slam shut behind him.

Then it's just Ate Nene and Jun and me outside. The lights of the other apartments turn off.

Tita Ana comes outside, Iggy behind her. "Junior? Corazon? Are you all right?"

"We're fine, Tita Ana," Jun says, formal, speaking to the ground. "Thank you, po, for checking on us."

"If you need anything," Tita Ana says, "you just knock here."

"Salamat, po," Jun says. Thank you, ma'am.

I stand there, feeling useless. Iggy looks in my eyes. She looks like she wants to stay outside with us. But Tita Ana tugs the sleeve of her pajama shirt, pulling her back inside.

"Call him a tricycle," Jun orders Ate Nene.

She obeys. She taps Tito Leroy's shoulder. He gets up and follows her like a child.

Jun paces in front of our open door. He picks up the metal rod, grips it in both hands.

I take the metal rod from him. He lets me. It's heavy. I put it down in the soil of the box garden.

A tricycle pulls up, then buzzes away. Ate Nene returns and goes inside without a word.

I wonder if Jun's going to walk off by himself for a while, like he usually does. I wonder where he'll go at two a.m., in his boxers and black jacket, shirtless, barefoot, without his glasses.

I want to say something perfect. Something to comfort him and me. But nothing comes to me.

"You shouldn't have gotten involved," Jun says. "It's not safe. It's never safe, with pulis."

I'm about to apologize. But he talks first, interrupting me.

"You know, it's funny," Jun says. "When I was younger, Tito Leroy was a really great guy. When he was sober. He could be sober for months at a time. He taught Papa all his handyman shit. He's the one who taught me guitar, you know? Then he'd disappear. Come home falling-down drunk. I asked Papa to help him. But there's no proper treatment here; proper rehab's only for people richer than us, in other countries. And now . . ."

I sit still, listening.

"Don't tell your mom about this. I don't want to worry her about Tito Leroy. She has enough to worry about, no? And don't—don't tell—"

His voice goes silent, suspended. When he finishes his sentence, his voice is broken.

"Papa," he says.

His shoulders shake. Tears track down his cheeks.

He whispers it again. "Papa."

I see it, the huge thing his anger and his silence are trying so hard to tamp down. His lifelong grief.

I think of something to tell him. How Papa would be proud of him, how nothing was his fault, how he's a good brother and a good son. How I know how he feels.

But I don't know how Jun feels, even though we both miss Papa.

Instead I inch my arm around one of Jun's arms. I hold his hand. I feel him shudder as he breathes. I remember what Iggy told me the other night.

"You're not alone with this anymore," I say. "I'm family too."

Ate Nene turns on the lights inside, then leaves us alone together. We stay out there until Jun is calm again. He sniffs. He takes back his hand and crosses his arms.

"Maybe you'll catch cold," he says, even though it's not cold.

We go back inside together to wait for dawn.

AFTER THAT NIGHT

Without asking me or telling me, Ate Nene moves my things upstairs to her room. She sleeps downstairs on the mat instead.

I keep waiting for another police officer to come to the door, to say it was all a mistake, and they'll be making an arrest. At least citing Tito Leroy, giving him a ticket.

I wonder if Jun will make a complaint. But he doesn't. And no one comes.

Jun buys layers of mesh window screens and repairs it himself. He tells me our dad used to instruct him over the phone, and computer, on household repairs.

He figures out the window repair by himself this time, from memory.

Jun buys two new deadbolts too, and screws them tightly onto the doorframe.

*　*　*

We're all quiet over the next few days. We watch our dad and my mom on the computer screen at the hospital. His facial bruises are faded. His eyes follow us on the screen, before he gets tired and closes them.

Dr. Chiu tells us about another kind of scale, the Level of Cognitive Functioning Scale. The best score is an eight. Papa's at level five. Simple commands followed consistently. New information not yet retained.

We don't tell my mom what happened.

Ate Nene cooks for us, and we eat without chatting. She goes outside, using two chairs to play solitaire instead of lingering with us at the table. She and Jun don't talk, except about small chores and grocery lists and buyers for his cookies, students scheduled for his tutorials.

Outside of meals we spend less time in the house. Jun takes me on errands he used to do alone. We go to campus, where he makes photocopies at the little shopping center. We eat more fish balls. We ride the open-air jeepney, where we're packed in, shoulder to shoulder, with other UP students.

Iggy comes along with us for walks down Maginhawa Street, and for walks around a circular road inside the UP campus. We share roadside fruit shakes and sticks of barbecue and plates of garlic rice and sweet banana fritters. Then we all walk home together.

My mom texts my Nokia.

It's there na.

I go next door and knock on Iggy's door.

"Ready to go?" I say.

She smiles and puts her slippers on. She leads us to Kalayaan Avenue, where we hop on a jeep. We stop at a money remittance stall. Then I follow Iggy through the crowds of shoppers and commuters to some secondhand stores in Cubao.

LIGHT

That night, Jun goes upstairs and opens his door. I get up and stand at the foot of the stairs. I wait for him to say something when he finds it.

He doesn't say a thing. He closes his door.

I wonder what happened, if Iggy and I got the wrong one.

Then it starts.

It starts as a repetitive chord. Something simple, low. I wonder if someone next door is playing a radio.

The chord stops, then starts again.

Then I hear a voice. It's mournful and strong, moving through the air toward me.

I open the door to Ate Nene's room. Jun's door is closed. His voice gets stronger. He's singing a phrase. I recognize the words in Tagalog.

Nasaan ka?

Nasaan ka?

Where are you? Where are you?

He sings the phrase again and again. But each time it sounds deeper, stronger, new.

The guitar chords get harder, but stay slow. The music travels upward somehow.

Jun pauses. Maybe he's making notes.

Then he begins again.

Ikaw ang liwanag

Ngunit na wala ka

Nasaan ka? Nasaan ka?

You are light. But you are gone. Where? Where?

The words and the chords are so simple. But my heart goes into my throat.

I've never heard something like this before. There was nothing like this in my mom's or Ms. Holden's classical music, or in the pop songs on my dad's radio.

Jun doesn't sound like our dad, or anything from the radio at all. He sounds like himself.

No, he sounds like more than himself. He sounds like he's channeling everything we're going through, all the sorrow and the uncertainty. All in a few notes, a few lyrics.

"Ganda, no?" Ate Nene says to me. Beautiful, no?

She's sitting at the bottom stairs, listening too. "Bago yan." It's a new song.

I nod. "Opo. Maganda." Yes, ma'am. Beautiful.

We smile. Something relaxes between us. The tension of the

house, the danger we feel, all the lingering not-knowing how our father will be—Jun replaces it all with music.

He comes downstairs.

"You didn't have to do that," he says. "The medical bills are a lot."

"We wanted to," I say. "My mom and me both. I told her it was important. For your future."

I don't tell him we sold some of Papa's tools. Since we don't know when he'll use them again.

Jun nods. "Salamat, kapatid."

THE TEST

I see my notebook open on the kitchen table. It shows my drawings; one of Jun, one of Ate Nene, some doodles of the Indio comic Jun lent me. My ears get hot again. I move to close the notebook.

"You made me look cute-weird," Jun says behind me. "Like drunk anime. Thanks."

I'm annoyed at him. Then I'm worried he's annoyed at me for drawing him.

"Lots of comics artists here in the Philippines," he says. "I didn't know I had one in the household. Sakto. Our gig needs a flyer."

He writes down the details in my notebook: the name of a bar, Mag:net. The date a few days from now, and the time; 8:00 p.m. "We'll need to take it to the copier tonight, and photograph it to share online," he says. "Make it a quarter of the page so we save money."

"But I'm not an arti—" I say.

"No use denying it," he says. "By seven. And your AP test is tomorrow, don't forget. Your mom said I'll take you to Makati. Hope you're ready. Cram after you draw, though."

He goes up to his room. I hadn't forgotten. I'd been studying just that since I'd been here. But the words ring in my head: Artist. Gig.

"You're playing with the 1890s again?" I call up to him, realizing.

"We have to practice for studio time somehow," Jun calls back. "Might as well be in front of an audience."

I sit outside with a thin black marker and a blank piece of computer paper folded into quarters. I think Jun was joking when he said to draw before I cram. But I test out the words in my mind: comics artist.

I make a few doodles, thinking of the buzz-cut hair growing in on Luna's shaved head, Pol's thin beard, Nic's bodybuilder biceps, Iggy's dark eyes and drumsticks. And Jun, of course, all dressed in black. I draw them in a row, and then a thought bubble from each head with the gig details.

Iggy comes outside, carrying a chewed-up pair of drumsticks. The happiness I feel when I see her is new and light, so different from what I've been carrying around for months.

"Whoa," she says. "This is seriously good."

She looks more closely. She reminds me of Luna's skeleton shirt and Pol's bracelet. I pull out another blank square of paper. I realize I'm glad to draw the flyer over again.

"And your brother always wears these sneakers when he performs. They're—" She looks at the entryway to our house, then reaches just inside to the bottom of our shoe shelf. She pulls out a pair of once-checkered slip-on sneakers. They look like they were run over by a car a few times, then put through a shredder. "He says they help 'get him in the mood.' Whatever that means."

Jun comes downstairs with his guitar—the secondhand blue electric guitar Iggy helped me choose at a music store in Cubao. "Ready?" he asks Iggy.

"God, so ready," she says, and they go to practice together.

The next day, the test is in an office building in Makati, the neighborhood where Bea had her modeling gig. We take a tricycle, a jeep, and a bus to get there. I'm ready to fall asleep again, by the time we arrive. Jun gives me some printouts my mom emailed him, and a code that says I'm registered to take the test. "Good luck pleasing the hegemony," he yawns, and goes downstairs to get coffee at McDonald's. I scowl at his back.

A young woman wearing a College Board T-shirt sits me down at a cubicle in an empty office, and hands me a multiple-choice packet and an essay booklet.

I get through the multiple-choice packet. Some of it is familiar. Some of it isn't. If I don't know a question, I just pick B.

Old memories come back to me. Things she told me with a wink, that made me feel like a special audience. "Standardized tests aren't an ideal way to measure what kind of scholar or thinker you'll be. They just test your memory, your conventional understanding of well-known events. How you study and interpret what isn't talked about, that's what makes you a thinker, a scholar."

I think about getting up and leaving the test unfinished. I want the feelings to go away.

I think of my mom renting out our house and sitting next to my dad in the hospital. I gulp, shake my head to myself, and keep going. I think of Mary. I pray that I'll pass.

I get to the essays. I outline something quick for the first one, a document interpretation exercise. Intro, supporting paragraphs, conclusion.

Then I get to the last page. It's the final part, where I get to choose to answer one essay question out of three.

My gaze falls on the middle one.

Analyze various ways in which the Thirty Years' War (1618–1648) represented a turning point in European history.

I remember her calling on me. Telling me she set the curve. How fast my mind worked, answering her. I think of the themes we talked about, between the two of us. Religion. Conflict. Family. Phases. Unrest. Nonconformists. Pressure.

"Five minutes, po," the young woman calls to me. I scribble a paragraph without really knowing what I'm writing.

On the shuddering bus ride home, I tell Jun.

It's like the test filled me up with ghosts, and I want to exorcise them by telling him.

I tell him the way I told Iggy and Luna. Telling them, I realize, was good practice.

When I'm done, Jun's eyes are wide. He adjusts his glasses, pressing the flat of his forefinger against the center of his frames several times. He frowns. I can't stand his silence, but I force myself to wait for him to speak first. I watch the billboards on EDSA highway: the whitening creams, the canned tuna, the fast food, the pale models. They've changed out Bea's ad; now other models are advertising bathing suits instead.

"If that teacher were a guy, I would beat him up," he says. "It'd be clear, eh. So . . . I guess, since she's a girl, I should imagine retribution with a sense of gender equality."

I don't know what to say to that.

"It's good that it's over," he says, still frowning. "No?"

I still don't know what to say.

"I thought maybe my mom told you," I decide. "Or Luna or Iggy."

"No," he says. "Definitely, no. Your mom just said you might be a little spoiled, since you grew up in America, so I should be patient with you."

Now I feel annoyed at my mom. "I'm not spoiled," I mutter. But maybe I am. Compared to Jun and my dad, anyway.

"Nah," Jun says. "You're okay."

Then he frowns. "You told Iggy and Luna before you told me?"

He seems a little hurt. It makes me feel warm toward him, at his desire to be a brother. "Sorry," I say.

He nods. "It's okay," he says. "Maybe you needed an audience of women first. And I think, you know, Iggy's like you." He colors a bit. "I mean, not that I'm uh, labeling either of you."

"It's cool," I say. "You're cool."

He studies his own hands and adjusts his glasses yet again. "But maybe more, uh, age-appropriate crushes from now on. No? Kahit sino, basta . . ." Whoever it is, as long as . . .

"Maybe no crushes ever again," I mutter.

I'm trying to say it as a joke, but something stings my throat. I don't know how to tell Jun: I'm afraid my crushes are dangerous for me. Maybe my heart will lead me the wrong way, always. Back into something that'll always end bad. Into the wrong waters, where I'll drown.

"Hindi, ading," Jun says. No, little sister. "Love is weird. But it'll find you again. The right kind, next time. Let it be. Give it time."

"Now you sound like Luna," I say. But I feel warm again.

I notice his ears redden a little at the mention of Luna.

"By the way," I say. I pull out the finished flyer from my notebook.

"Galing, oh! Wasak!" He grins wider than he's ever grinned. "Do them all for us from now on, Corazon!"

ENCORE

Jun has enough energy for a stadium. It's the most movement I've ever seen out of him, besides the explosion of his fear and anger at Tito Leroy's attempted break-in.

But there's no anger or bad tension here like there was that night. Now, in his ratty sneakers, wearing a white tank top and ripped jean shorts—finally he's not wearing all black—Jun keeps hopping up on his toes, like a boxer ready for a bout. He took off his glasses as soon as he arrived to play, and I wonder how he can see. Maybe he doesn't need to see?

We're a few miles from the apartment, closer to the UP campus where Jun goes, and the Ateneo campus where my mom went. The room is hallway-size, and it doubles as an art gallery; it's between exhibits, with only blank hooks up on the white walls for now. There's no stage, just the floor.

Two other bands have already played; they sounded poppy and cheery, with keyboards and synthesizers. One of them played all covers of pop songs.

Now, a half dozen students drink San Miguel beers and stand around chatting. The room is mellow. No one really danced for the first two bands. It's a Thursday night, not a Friday, so I worry for Jun that this little audience won't match his energy. But he doesn't look worried at all. Just ready. Hearing some rhythm in his head that makes him keep moving.

I wonder if one of the sounds in his head is our father's voice, newly returned. Papa's new voice keeps ringing in my own head, anyway.

It was just a few hours ago. That light of hope in my mom's eyes— what we saw when she said our dad was leaving the ICU—was back. She didn't explain or prepare us this time. She just aimed the computer camera and spoke to our dad. "Mahal," she said. "Mga anak mo." Love. Your children.

And our father's eyelids fluttered open. There was a sound. A damp whisper. Jun and I both leaned forward, our eyes and ears fighting between the microphone and the screen, straining to take in our father's voice. "Mga anak." He said it over and over. The words sounded mashed together, and he couldn't get louder, even though he seemed to be trying. But the words were his.

Then he said something else I couldn't understand.

"Mahal!" Jun said to me. He understood it first. Having Jun translate it helped me hear it myself, when Papa said it again. "Mahal." Love.

"Tatay!" Jun cried back, into the microphone, loud and strong.

"Mahal kita." I love you.

Jun half rose from his seat, excited, like the computer screen was a door our dad was going to walk through, and Jun needed to get up, to honor our father's presence by standing.

But I held back. I stayed sitting.

Don't get me wrong. I was glad to hear my dad's voice. But I could hear other stuff, too.

He was so tired. Just those three words were so much for him. And he was repeating what my mom said, repeating her words over and over again.

It felt like he wanted to say more, but he couldn't.

The dad I had grown up with was different now. Something in my expectations had to shift, in order to meet this new, altered version of my dad.

I could feel something roiling in me. I had expected either his death, his total departure, or the laughing, gentle, joking, fix-anything dad to totally return, whole and unchanged. Now I knew: I had to learn to expect something else.

Our dad's eyes closed. My mom spoke again.

"Your papa will need speech therapy," she said. "Both for physical and mental practice. But he is responsive. More responsive than before. I can tell him things, ask him, and he answers. It takes him some time. Sometimes he only holds on to my hand. We just have to listen to him a little harder, no? Give him some time."

I felt something else, then, like a tsunami through all of me. I could hardly hear Jun answer my mom, positive, agreeing.

My dad wasn't going to come back the same dad.

But the way my mom loved him.

The way he loved us.

The love was still there.

It hadn't gone anywhere. It was still so steady.

I had grown up around it. When my mom told me the thing that stung—"That wasn't love"—I had hung up on her. I hadn't thought about what love was. I only thought I'd be shut out of love forever.

But my parents showed me all my life, and they were showing me now. This was love.

My mom wasn't just the mom I knew in California. I thought of what I'd learned of Lolo Joe, what Manang Merlie told me. My mom was also someone who'd loved someone she wasn't allowed to love. Love was her steady rebellion—against her parents, against poverty, against, now, my dad's accident.

And my dad still returned that love. They'd built something that would last beyond any way they, or the world, would change.

It's like I'd felt the sun warming me, felt its light every moment. But only then, at the computer, did I look directly at it.

I wondered if I'd ever be there for someone the way my mom was there for my dad. If someone would ever be that kind of presence for me.

I didn't know I was crying until Jun clapped one hand on my shoulder and looked at my face. "This isn't sad, little sister. He's still alive! He's still here! Be calm."

My mom sat in bed next to my dad. "Oo nga, anak. Tama ang kuya mo." Yes, child. Your brother is right.

She stroked the edge of our dad's hair. I remembered when he would come home tired from his landscaping jobs. Sometimes he'd fall asleep on her shoulder, then her lap, while we watched reruns of the movies he liked, and she'd run her hand along his hair in the same way.

Iggy arrives. She sits and pounds the pedal of the bass drum, testing its tension. The 1890s are almost done setting up. Tonight Iggy's tied her curls back, and she's wearing a maroon basketball jersey, leaving her brown arms bare.

I'm surprised by how relieved I am to see her. I'm so looking forward to seeing her play, it makes my own pulse loud in my ears.

I don't say any of that. I say, instead, "Aren't you going to be cold in here? The air-con is so strong."

"Nah," she says. "With the 1890s, get ready to sweat."

She taps her sticks together and grins.

Her super-confident response makes me shy again. I look around the room. There are still barely a dozen people here, including a guard armed with a rifle, dozing off on a stool at the front door, and a gallery-gig employee in a black polo shirt, yawning. The 1890s arrange their instruments. Everyone seems more interested in their own beery conversations, or in sleeping soon, than in whatever's about to happen onstage.

I'm anxious now. What if this is bad? What if the 1890s crash and burn?

The band doesn't look worried. Nic strums some chords before plugging in his keyboard, listening to himself. Jun keeps hopping around, doing high knee kicks now every time Iggy snaps the snare drum. Luna turns the metal keys of her bass. "Hello, ading," she says. "Handa ka na ba?" Are you ready for this?

"I've only ever seen my church band," I say. "Singing, 'I will go, Lord' and 'Halle, halle, halle, lu-u-jah.' Stuff like that. I was never invited to any house parties in California where, like, real bands played."

"Well," Luna says. "You're home now. You have an invite for life."

I feel held, included. I breathe easy.

Jun's near the mic—not singing yet, just standing with his guitar strap slung around his shoulder. He lets loose one loud shred of his guitar, and now he's running his hand along the vibrating strings, letting the feedback reverberate through the nearby speakers. It seems like just noise, noise that swallows up our conversations. But he waits a movement in all that sound, then runs his fingers along the strings again, and presses a pedal with the heel of his right sneaker.

People keep talking above the noise, but they look toward Jun and the band. A few new audience members join me, facing the band in what I guess would be the front row, if there were any seats.

Iggy nods and grins at me from behind the drums—a just-you-wait grin.

Luna adds steady, low notes from her bass, like a secret heartbeat under everything.

It goes on like that—just Jun and Luna at first, layering noise into something their own. The small audience presses forward, and people start nodding along. I wonder if they're musicians too, or if they just understand what's happening better than I do.

More new people come in from outside, curious. The security guard wakes up, keeping an eye on the door in between gazing at Jun and Luna. Tricycle drivers and passersby and shoppers and students linger outside the windows, watching and listening too, curious at what the band is building together. Nic and Pol and Iggy keep their heads down and their hands still, for now, nodding and nodding.

Then, after we've lost track of time, immersed in the layers of sound, Jun presses the pedal twice again, and the feedback washes away into distant shushing, like waves dragging along sand. He finally opens his mouth at the mic, breaking the quiet that follows. He sings a single word. Bakit? Why? He stretches the two syllables, singing and singing, so that the single word—Bakit? Bakit?—goes on forever, making room for whatever listeners might bring to it. The rest of the band is still for a moment, even Luna, taking his lead.

Then he sings the rest of the verse in Tagalog: *Why does your leaving stay with me?*—and the band crashes together, frantic drumbeats, galloping baseline, the two guitars writing a fierce melody. In the audience we're all shoulder to shoulder now, the small room feeling smaller and louder. Iggy was right—it's hot now, sweaty with everyone aiming forward, wanting to be a part of what the band is making.

Iggy told me it was only going to be a short, five-song set, but by the end of the first song, Jun is soaked in sweat. Every transition between songs sees a member of the band keep playing, bridging and looping one moment to the next—Pol ringing out one keening note on his guitar, Iggy teasing out a golden beat on her cymbals, Luna climbing the muscly highs and lows of her bass.

Jun's back turns from the audience, and some sweaty, stinky guys dance too hard, knocking into me. I stumble, and they're about to knock into me again—

Iggy drops her drumsticks, letting the band continue, and pulls me to the other side of them. She juts her chin at the guys and says some friendly words to them that I can't hear; they smile, say sorry, and hop in place, taking care not to swing around. "You okay?" Iggy yells toward me, above the music; I nod. She grips the top of my arm for a moment, making sure I'm extra steady, then flashes her smile. The band all checks in with me too, then Iggy sits back down behind the drums and finds the beat again.

For the last two songs I stay still, awash in the band's music. Then, for the first time ever, I think, I dance, hopping up and down like Jun does, like the drunk guys do. The room is full of good sounds, of bodies in motion, taking it all in, and the world is only as big as the warm, sweaty room.

Then, after the last crash of the last song, Jun presses a pedal twice more, making the sound loop again. "Thank you, everyone, we're the 1890s," he says, short and cool. A roar comes up from the crowd, the kind of cheer from an audience that knows it's experienced something surprising and special. I whoop too this time, the sounds in my throat free, and I clap. One by one, the band members stop playing as Jun announces them. "Iggy Adrian on drums." Iggy twirls her sticks and bows. "Pol Sanchez on keyboards." Pol puts down his guitar, then kisses Jun on one sweaty cheek. The crowd cheers again. "Nic Osorios on second guitar." Nic shakes Jun's hand. "Luna Herrera on bass."

Luna puts down her bass, takes Jun's face in both hands, then kisses him on the mouth for a full minute. I feel myself blush, watching my brother make out with someone, but I'm sure the crowd's roar is going to shatter the windows. "Init, no?" Jun jokes when Luna lets him go, and he tugs on the collar of his tank top like he's letting off steam. "I'm Rommel Tagubio Junior, good night!"

But the crowd isn't done with the 1890s. They clap together, and then Iggy's standing next to me, shoulder pressed to my shoulder, and she and I are joining in: "Isa pa! Isa pa!" One more! One more! Luna pushes Jun forward. He puts his guitar strap back over his head and exhales into the mic.

"You're too kind," he says. He looks out over the crowd, then sees me and Iggy and grins. "I wanna introduce you to my sister, Corazon, from America. Everyone say hi to Corazon." The crowd says in unison, like we're in Mass, "Hi, Corazon!" I feel my own face flush again. Iggy drapes her long arm around my shoulders and ruffles my hair. Jun keeps talking idly into the mic. "We were OFS," he says. "Overseas Filipino Siblings. Now we're IPS. In the Philippines Siblings." Someone whoops randomly. "Yes," Jun intones. "Woo, indeed." The audience laughs. He turns two of his guitar keys. "This song is dedicated to our OFW father, Rommel Tagubio Senior."

Then Jun sings a song I recognize. The one Ate Nene and I heard from the bottom of the stairs, from behind his closed bedroom door. It's stronger now, steadier, rougher on the amplified guitar.

> *Nasaan ka?*
> *Nasaan ka?*
> *Ikaw ang liwanag*
> *Nandito ka*
> *Nandiyan ka*
> *Lapit na, lapit na,*
> *Ikaw ang liwanag*
> *Ikaw ang aking liwanag*

He's changed some of the lyrics. It's not "You are gone" anymore. It's "Where are you? You are here, you are there, closer now, closer now. You are light. You are my light."

I wish I could show this to our father. I wish he could take this in like we do. I sense it again, what I sensed when I first heard Jun play the song at home.

With music, my brother isn't the reluctant, sullen engineering student. He isn't the kid left behind by his parents, full of secret anger and pain. He isn't the self-blaming eldest child. He is himself. He is fully Rommel Tagubio Junior.

It makes me wonder what I'll find, eventually—what I'll do

that will make me most me. If I ever will find that thing.

When Iggy drops her hand from my shoulder, my own hand moves ahead of any other thought, any other feeling.

I close my fingers around her wrist. I swear I can feel her pulse there, or maybe it's just Jun's guitar.

Iggy looks at me, questions in her face, and for one panicked moment, I think I've made a horrible mistake, one that makes me a disgusting intruder. I drop my fingers from her wrist, ready to make our contact a joke, an accident, and I face the stage instead.

But I feel Iggy take my hand. She smiles and nods and pulls me closer to her.

Jun's song, rough, unfinished, simple, ends. Another roar comes up from all of us. It's beautiful. Iggy and I keep holding on to each other's hands.

We all spill out into the night, to the side of the no-sidewalk roadway where the little gallery space sits. The band members are whooping, loud, chattering, the energy of the gig not yet dissipating. Everyone's hopping around and affectionate, hugging and singing other songs, pouring bottles of water over each other's hair, and it's Nic who suggests it first: "Hoy, I have the Avanza, my brother's out of town, let's go to the beach!"

We all pause, struck by the craziness of the plan, but Luna calculates it for us: If we go now, we'll be there by sunrise, and we can spend all Friday on the beach, coming back early Saturday morning to avoid traffic. Pol says we could get a couple of hammocks at a hostel, and Jun says he can pick up old towels for us, and Iggy and I can grab swimsuits. Nic decides to call out sick from work; Pol makes some excuse to his family too; Luna shrugs and says she disappears for days at a time and her family's used to it, even if they get mad.

Then we're picking up Pol's cute boyfriend, Mac, from the Jollibee near the house, and he's presenting us with a sack of leftover burgers. Jun reminds Nic we'll need a place near the beach with Wi-Fi so he and I can check in with my mom and our dad; Luna says we can borrow her smartphone.

We stop by the house for the towels, and so we can beg Tita Ana for Iggy to come along. Tita Ana frowns at us, ever the skeptical aunt ready to say no, but Luna puts on her best older sister, says "po" a million times, and promises Iggy won't sleep anywhere near the boys. Tita Ana looks at Jun. She likes Jun, considers him a responsible older brother, and anyway we'll only be gone a day, and it's still summer, so Iggy won't be missing schoolwork, and Tita Ana looks at us and says, "Keep an eye on her, no?" We promise we will, and she tells Nic to drive slowly and safely, and Nic promises he will too. Tita Ana presses a cross into Iggy's forehead with her thumb.

When Jun's done packing, and the band's unloaded all their gear into the living room, he presses a roll of money into Ate Nene's hand, his share of the door donations from the gig. "Bonus day off, Ate," he says. "Massage. Pedicure, manicure. Gerry's Grill."

She frowns at him, a frown full of affection. They're both wordless, looking at each other. I can see this is a sort of apology from Jun, for being so harsh and then silent with her. I wonder how many times they've had this scene, while Jun grew up so far from me.

Finally, Ate Nene traces a cross on his forehead, and mine, blessing us both, and tells us to be careful.

LA UNION

We're in Nic's Avanza, a fat van, Iggy and me in the back where the band equipment was, and we're zooming out of Quezon City, passing rice fields and toll booths and rest stops in the dark. The band sings along to cheesy pop songs on the radio. But eventually I can't stay awake. Iggy puts her arm around me, making a nest of her shoulder for my head. "Sleep," she says. And I do.

I wake against Iggy's shoulder. The light is gentle now. It's dawn, and strips of ocean blue rush past us along a two-lane highway road. Only Nic seems alert, humming along with the radio to himself and letting the wind rush through his open window. Jun is asleep against Luna, his mouth open with snores; Pol and Mac are cuddling too, eyes shut. I spot a red-and-yellow sign arched over the two-lane highway: La Union.

Iggy's head shifts, gently leaning her curls against the top of my head. I like that she can rest on me, too. She wakes when we pull into the driveway of a hostel.

We pile out, squinting in the early morning. I can hear waves landing on the sand somewhere nearby. Luna collects fifty pesos from each of us, then reserves three hammocks for the day at the front desk. "We can nap in shifts before we go back to Manila," she says. "Anyway, there's a whole beach to lounge on."

Jun asks for the hostel's Wi-Fi password. He checks his email on Luna's phone first, then hands it to me. "Your mom said you should check your email," he says. "The AP test results will go to you, not her."

I don't want to break away from this beach scene. But I log in. I scan, then find the College Board email. I got a five. The highest score.

It's over, I think.

Then I see an email name I've never seen before: nichtsprechen. The title is "(no subject)."

I'm about to delete the message as spam. But then I remember the German phrase she used.

Wovon man nicht sprechen kann, darüber muss man schweigen. She translated it for me weeks later, after I bugged her about it. Whereof one cannot speak, thereof one must be silent.

All my insides freeze. I stare at the screen.

"What?" Jun asks, frowning. "Oh no. Did you fail?"

I shake my head. "I got a five," I say. "It's the highest score."

"Galing, ading!" he says. He holds out his hand for a high five. I leave it empty.

"She wrote me," I say.

"She? Oh!" Jun says. He drops his hand and clears his throat, not sure what to say next.

Pol interjects. "The creepy teacher wrote you?! Sis!" He calls Luna over from the front desk.

"Your colonizer wrote you?" Luna asks. She leans over the phone. "The teacher?"

I widen my eyes at Jun. He looks truly mortified. "We talked about it as a band," he mumbles. "During practice. Sorry."

"He was just concerned," Luna says, ruffling Jun's hair, making him blush again. "He wanted band guidance, to make sure he was being a good older brother."

His frown gets deeper. "Isn't that kind of fucked up? That she's contacting you again? After she already made you feel so bad?"

I don't know what to say.

Iggy hangs back, watching. She looks older and tired now. I recognize the look. I think I've had the look myself. She's steeling herself.

"Are you going to open it?" Nic asks. "Or just delete it into oblivion, like I do with my ex's messages?"

"Open the email for us, at least!" Pol says, and his boyfriend Mac hits him in the chest, lightly, to stop him.

I swallow. I feel the old anxiety, the old need, coming up like tendrils to drag me down, drown me.

Then I feel it fall away.

I realize I don't mind that everyone here knows. It's a new feeling, not being so alone with the situation. I feel them waiting, accompanying me, waiting to hear the new message from that old story.

I repeat it silently to myself, so I believe it. I'm not alone.

Then I open the email.

. . .

I scroll and scroll.

But that's it. An ellipsis. Three periods. No words.

"Yun lang?!" Luna exclaims. That's it?! She clicks her tongue, disapproving, and mutters to herself in Tagalog. "They always do that," she says. "These kinds. They sense from afar you're moving on. So they try to keep you close to them. Selfish nga, truly."

The 1890s chatter with each other. They wonder if it's an accidental send of an old draft, judge the email address, close-read the punctuation for hidden meaning.

Somewhere, as I'm searching to name just what my feelings are, I notice that Iggy's quiet waiting. Jun goes quiet too.

"Pagod na ako," he says.

He takes up a hammock and closes his eyes. Soon he's snoring and swaying. The rest of the band looks at Jun. I can tell they want to gossip more, or stay to see if I'll write back. But, again, the band takes Jun's lead.

Pol and Mac walk toward the beach. Luna climbs into the big hammock next to Jun, settles her head onto his chest, and falls asleep too. Nic tosses off his shirt, does a few push-ups, and

297

then goes for a barefoot jog down the sand.

Now it's just me and Iggy.

"Want to talk about it?" she asks. "Need a sounding board?"

I pause, thinking. Just a few weeks ago I'd write thousands of words back, maybe. Asking things. Apologizing. I'd be so full of need, so frantic, wanting the calm that could only come from her.

I get angry at Grace Holden then. And sad for myself.

I'm sad that so much of me kept going in her direction.

I'm angry that she left me feeling chaotic. Sad. Hungry. Self-doubting. Abandoned.

I lower the phone.

I shouldn't feel like that with someone, I think. I shouldn't feel so off-balance. Love doesn't feel like that.

Real love would feed me. It would shore me up. It would keep me from dark waters.

I look around. I see Luna's bag, resting under her and Jun in the hammock.

I tuck the phone into a side pocket, then walk back over to Iggy.

"I've never seen the beach in the Philippines," I say.

Iggy nods. She seems guarded, still. "You almost forget you're on an island when you're in Quezon City, no? All the roads and traffic. Yeah, there are trees. House gardens growing wherever. But over there, the ocean feels like it's nowhere."

I stay still, waiting. She seems to be waiting too. Something softens between us. We smile and walk together.

* * *

A concrete path, and then the beach: a wide stretch of white sand. Only a few fishermen and surfers are out, and some little kids wearing wet, oversize shirts, splashing each other in the waves.

This beach is bigger than the beaches I grew up near in California. We see surfers along a break, closer to the horizon line than to the shore, riding lazy lines in the water toward us.

"Did you ever surf in California?" Iggy asks.

I keep my face still. Silence fills my throat. Iggy considers my nonresponse. She looks toward a rack of dented boards, then back at me.

"I limp," she says. "I got that Iggy shuffle. So I—I have my own rhythm, on land. And on surfboards."

I'm about to say something, but I just keep listening. "I'm just saying. I like swimming. And drumming. Water's like music. It's a different element. There, I flow."

I look at her face, more and more golden as the sun gets stronger. I watch her grin again, the widest smile I've ever seen, full of something new. Something I want.

The ocean looks good to me. Like it'll wash away whatever bad feeling's left lingering in me.

"Yeah," I say, my voice coming back to me. I smile at her. "Let's swim."

The earliest memories I have: My parents and me at the beach, a half hour away from our townhome. My dad would drive us along Malibu canyon, tell me to hold my breath in the tunnels and make a wish. My mom would have the windows open, playing classical music. And we would park at Leo Carrillo, the quietest, rockiest beach, where I'd pick through tide pools and look at pretty rocks and poke shy sea anemones, watching them close at my touch. My parents would have a picnic; fried chicken and pan de sal.

Every time, before we left, my dad would hold me up to the Pacific. "There," my dad would say. "Wave home! Wave to the Philippines! Wave to your brother, Jun!" And the three of us would wave. As if the country where my parents were born was just across the street, my brother someone I could see from another window. I'd always wave, not really understanding who or what I was waving at.

Now I face the waves, following behind Iggy, moving my arms in the surf. When she says it's time, I turn my back on the ocean, and I let the water push me back toward the shoreline my parents always aimed me toward when I was little.

We don't speak. We don't have to translate the joy moving between us. She's in board shorts, probably from the fifty-peso ukay-ukay store near the house, and a bikini top. She's warm in the light and water, the sun getting higher and shining on both of us.

Soon we're tired and hungry in the best way, ready for breakfast. We let the waves push us all the way back to the sand. I try to stand, then a wave knocks me down hard, and I laugh. Iggy laughs too, and grabs my hand, but then another wave knocks her down also. We struggle together toward a calm part of the shorebreak, then we both sit to rest, panting and happy. We can't seem to stop laughing at something.

Then finally, when we're calm, we look at each other. I don't know what to say. She squints in the sunlight, flashes her smile again, and speaks for me. "Yeah," she says. "Yeah."

She leans toward me. I lean toward her. I taste the salt of the ocean, and the shy salt of her. I feel a little scared then; like maybe she'll pull away, deciding what an error this is, that I'm an experiment gone wrong.

But her hand finds my wrist, like she did at the gig. She holds me there, steady, warm. I lean my forehead against her forehead. Without opening my eyes, I feel her smile. We kiss again, our smiles smiling against each other.

I feel my heart underwater here. It's strong and steady now, not drowning. I'm held. I'm afloat. I'm home.

We're like that, halfway underwater together, kissing in between the gentle striking of the salt water, until we hear our names. It's Luna, grinning at us from farther down the sand. "Young ladies," she says. "Sorry to interrupt. Breakfast na."

I feel scared again—like this is the moment when Iggy will decide how gross I am, that she's done with me. But she takes my hand and pulls me toward the hostel. She doesn't mind that someone saw.

"I hope they have tapsilog," she says.

They do have tapsilog; it's one of Jun's favorites too. We devour flat, vinegary steak, fried eggs, and garlic fried rice. Luna slices a mango for us to share. I look at her, wondering if she'll say something to Jun, but she winks at me. When she passes a slice to me, she whispers, "I approve. And I know Jun will too."

Jun doesn't hear her, and doesn't notice me blush. He asks Nic to hold Luna's phone with the camera aimed at us, since Nic has the longest arm, and we call my mom together.

"Hi, Tita!" Jun calls, when Ma and Pa appear on the other side of the phone. Then the whole table answers. "Hi, Tita!" I call out my hi too.

"Wow, fiesta!" we hear. "Ro, look, oh, your children are having a fiesta."

Jun and I turn to look at the screen on the other side of the camera. Our dad is sitting up now, an oxygen tube still in his nose. He smiles a half smile. "Fiesta," Papa whisper-calls to us. Jun holds his ear to the phone in Nic's hand. "Yes, Tatay," he calls. "Breakfast fiesta."

Our dad's half smile gets bigger. Nic turns the camera to face the two of us, then we look at the screen again. We see our father's mouth work, then we hear, just a little louder than a whisper: "Junior."

My brother's eyes fill with tears. "Opo, Tatay!" he says, grinning.

Papa's mouth clicks. But he can't quite say it, though I know he's trying. "Opo, Papa," I say. "I'm here too."

"Corazon is there too," my mom says to my dad. And kisses his forehead. "Magkasama sila." They're together. He nods, still half smiling.

The band gets up, waving goodbye to my mom. Iggy goes last, setting a hand on both my shoulder and Jun's shoulder, then walking back toward the sand.

"Was that Jun's neighbor?" my mom asks Jun. "The one raised by her aunt?"

"Ligaya, yes, Tita," Jun answers.

"But her nickname is Iggy," I say.

"Iggy. I always thought she was very kind, no? She and her tita. Good neighbors."

We look at the screen again. My mom seems to be thinking to herself. She watches me. She strokes the hair out of our dad's eyes. I feel scared again. I wonder what she sees.

Then my mom smiles. First at our dad, then at the screen. We wait for her to speak.

"Make sure you are as happy as often as you can be," she finally says. "Both of you. You both look happy there. Before, your eyes were so worried. Try not to worry so much, no?"

"Jun's, like, an awesome musician!" I blurt at the phone. He rolls his eyes at me and interrupts. "We'll study hard, Tita," he says. "And thank you again, po, for the guitar. I'll save and earn to pay you back."

"Don't you dare, Jun. You just do the work you're meant to do."

He nods. His eyes shine. Then he claps an arm around my shoulder and speaks into the phone mic.

"Tita, Cory got a five on her test," he says. "The highest score."

"Ang galing!" Ma says. I love the sound of her happiness. We watch the screen again. Papa's eyes are open. "Rom, your daughter scored so high on an important test. Galing, Corazon."

"Galing," Pa whispers, repeating after her.

Then he says it. I put my ear close to the speaker to listen.

"Corazon. Corazon." Again and again.

We look at the screen. Ma is kissing his forehead again. "Yes, mahal. Corazon."

I smile and cry. Jun keeps his arm around my shoulder.

"Go swim before you return to Manila, all of you," Ma says. "To celebrate. It looks like Cory and Iggy were already swimming. Don't sit in your salty bathing suit, Cory! Shower!"

"I'll make sure she showers, Tita; sometimes she forgets," Jun says, unsmiling. I wipe my face and shove him a little.

The hours stretch on, a peaceful time outside of time.

I obey my mom and shower under the hostel's cold, outdoor faucet. Jun swims with Luna. The guys go out somewhere else along the beach.

Iggy starts to doze off in the hammock. "Hey," she says. She opens her arm in her half sleep.

I climb in carefully next to her, feeling the strong netting hold us. She shifts a little, making room for me to nestle against her shoulder. I do. I can hear her heartbeat again, along with the waves, and the wind shuffling leaves of palm trees nearby. The sounds lull me to sleep.

I wake at dusk. Iggy's still asleep. I hear the guys and Luna laughing somewhere nearby. Maybe they're watching the sunset over the waves.

I get up alone, restless and thirsty. I walk out of the hostel, go a little ways down the road, and buy a bottled water from a sari-sari store.

On my walk back, I stop mid-sip and stare at something sitting on the side of the road.

It's a shrine of Mary. Her statue is set inside a handmade concrete pillar, just about my height.

It looks a little bit like the statue at St. Agatha's, but smaller and older. Her blue garments have long been washed by salt winds; now there are streaks where the stone shows. People leave flowers for this Mary statue like my parents leave flowers for their Jesus statue. There are fresh sampaguita strands and dried ones.

But really, what stops me is that this statue is like none I've ever seen before. Someone has pressed plastic toy googly eyes onto Mary's face.

I hold my water bottle and stare. I'm searching for how to name my feelings again. I remember the fear I felt, looking at the Mary statue back in California.

I think this Mary statue should make me laugh. But it doesn't make me laugh. Somehow, it doesn't feel sacrilegious, the googly eyes. It feels like whoever put them there was earnest, wanting to show us that Mary is watching over us from every direction.

It doesn't feel funny. Somehow, it just feels right.

So I look at the Mary statue, at her googly eyes going everywhere. I think of her gaze looking toward me too.

I think of the old words I thought to myself so long ago, back at St. Agatha's.

Mary, I think of you. I think of you.

And I think of my father. I think of him upright, finding his voice again. I think of my mother beside him, keeping her ability to laugh, her generosity in telling me and Jun to have fun.

I think of my brother singing, pointing me out as his sister in a crowd. I think of Ate Nene and Manang Merlie, how hard they work to care for us, and for their own families—the ones they live away from.

I think of my cousin Bea, trying to help me. I think of Tita Baby and how hard she tries.

I think of Ms. Holden. The wrongness of it all.

And then I let the thought of her go.

I think of the band's laughter and music together, how they're waiting for me. I think of Iggy's steady heartbeat, and my heart underwater with hers.

I wonder what Iggy and I are now, and what we'll be later.

The dusk gets darker, and then I sense my brother near me. "Okay ka lang?" he asks, padding down the road in his old sneakers.

"I'm okay, Kuya," I say.

He spots the Mary statue. He presses his glasses against his face, takes in Mary's googly eyes, and accepts them. He makes the sign of the cross and kisses his thumb. It's a gesture just like our father's, the sign of the cross I saw growing up, and it comforts me.

"Ready to go home?" he asks.

I think of my home in California, my parents in the hospital. I think of the home waiting for me in Quezon City. I see Iggy watching me too, smiling my way. The rest of the band spills into the empty road, watching for us and waiting, the sun almost done setting.

"Yeah," I say. "I'm ready."

Acknowledgments

Writing can be lonely, but authors never finish books alone. For years, *My Heart Underwater* has had supportive guides. I attempt to honor some of them here:

My deep gratitude to Andrea Morrison, whose years-ago and ongoing faith in this story—before she became an agent and before it was a book—helped it be. Andrea, with your diligence, your compassion, and your patience, you take excellent care of your writers; Cory and I could have no better literary ninang. Thank you, too, to Geri Thoma Lemert for her early, generous attention to my voice and for bringing me into Writers House.

Thank you to the team at Quill Tree Books and HarperCollins who offered their trust and investment in this story. Editor Alexandra Cooper gave the narrative the essential questions, changes, precision, and insights it needed; salamat, Alexandra, for guiding the book into its final form. Salamat po, Rosemary Brosnan, for your belief in the depth and range of emotion Cory's journey would evoke. Thank you to Allison Weintraub for your essential and diligent support. And with their cover and design, David Curtis, Amy Ryan, and Renz Hendrix brought Cory to brilliant, vivid life. Ang ganda!

Thank you to all the mentors and early readers who cheered

my drafts along, often when I felt too nervous and unworthy to continue them. Robin Hemley, Michael Martone, and Thaddeus Rutkowski held supportive, generative workshops where Cory first arrived. My RMIT University faculty and colleagues in the Practice Research Symposium were challengers and cheerleaders; thank you to my advisors Francesca-Rendle Short and Michelle Aung Thim. The communities at the University of Iowa, Ateneo de Manila, Yale-NUS College, and the University of Hawai'i at Mānoa carried me forward; thank you especially to Alexander Chee, Carissa Foo, Pramodini Parayitam, Chinelo Okparanta, Yuly Restrepo, Inara Verzemnieks, Sarah Viren, Martin Villanueva, Shawna Yang Ryan, and Lawrence Ypil.

Thank you to Dr. Michael Theobald and RN Lyn Frisch for your close medical reading and advice, and for your constant support. You helped me see what a slow and steady recovery might be for Mang Rommel.

Weng Cahiles and Petra Magno gave me essential insights into the Filipino language, Katipunan and Teachers Village hangouts, politics, and relationships in the Philippines of 2009. Salamat, mga kapatid ko, for your language help, your revisions, and your frank and deep reading of Cory's story.

Some time ago, the writers Elaine Castillo and Yael Villafranca shared their own online reflections on the subtle nature of abuse: how individuals who mistreat and take advantage of us, can be beloved by us, and how migration, class, and colonialism feed situations of abuse, making abuse hard to recognize and name. In its literal form here, Cory's story is not my own;

I never had the troubling experience with a teacher that Cory did. But Castillo's and Villafranca's insights haunted me, helped me understand contexts of my own difficult emotional history, and spurred me toward a major vein of this book's body, one I first feared approaching. Maraming salamat, mga mananulat, for leading the way.

The Astraea Lesbian Foundation for Justice provided encouragement and support for this story at a critical moment. For their writer prize, and for the work they do on behalf of LGBTQI communities around the world, I am deeply grateful. The Hedgebrook writing residency offered me peace and fellowship in the early stages of the book; I thank their hardworking, welcoming staff and my fellow residents.

Thank you to my pamilya, whose migration, survival, and hard work allowed their descendant to be an author.

My chosen pamilya in Metro Manila, in the rest of the Philippines, and in the vast diaspora, always offer me the best bonds, food, wisdom, and laughter, shoring me up in perilous times. Padayon! Aurora Almendral, Hossannah Asuncion, Gina Apostol, Ate Gayia Beyer, Karina Bolasco, Tammy David, Direk Lav Diaz, Ate Maxine Tanya Hamada, Ate Ged Hidalgo, Carmel Laurino, Hazel Orencio, Hannah Reyes Morales, Julia Nebrija, Ate Susan Quimpo, Andrea Pasion-Flores, Erwin Romulo, Howie Severino, Kia Sison, Lara Stapleton, Grace Talusan, Tessa Winkelmann, and every other inspiring friend who teaches me to thrive. Thank you for helping make Metro Manila one of my homes, for introducing me to Teachers Village and Katipunan all those years ago, and for your constant care and community.

My wife, Katherine, buoys my heart each day like no one else. Tats, your presence gives me gratitude for all the journeys that brought me, finally, to you. Mahal na mahal kita.

And my thanks to you, reader, for giving your attention to this story. If after reading this, you find yourself needing guidance on healthy relationships, and resources for recovery, two good places to start are here: www.rainn.org and www.loveisrespect .org. They've helped me, too.

I wish your heart well in all your journeys. Ingat po kayo lagi.